Kate Kingsley has lived on both sides of the Atlantic, spending time in New York, London, Paris and Rome – so she's more than qualified to chronicle the jet-set lives of the *Young, Loaded and Fabulous* girls.

Kate has also written for magazines such as *GQ* in New York and *The Sunday Times Magazine* in London, where her assignments included interviewing fashion designers, fellow writers, and actors. She currently lives in London.

By Kate Kingsley

Young, Loaded and Fabulous
Secrets and Liars
Kiss and Break Up
Too Cruel for School
Dissing You Already

DISSING YOU ALREADY

KATE KINGSLEY

headline

First published in Great Britain in 2012 by
HEADLINE PUBLISHING GROUP

1

Cataloguing in Publication Data is available from the British Library

ISBN 978 0 7553 5985 1

Typeset in New Baskerville by Palimpsest Book Production Limited,
Falkirk, Stirlingshire

Printed in Great Britain by
Clays Ltd, St Ives plc

Headline's policy is to use papers that are natural, renewable and recyclable
products and made from wood grown in sustainable forests. The logging and
manufacturing processes are expected to conform to the environmental
regulations of the country of origin.

HEADLINE PUBLISHING GROUP
An Hachette UK Company
338 Euston Road
London NW1 3BH

www.headline.co.uk
www.hachette.co.uk

DISSING You ALREADY

Chapter 1

The grandfather clock chimed two p.m. and echoed down the Rochesters' dim, silent hallway, past a row of antique oil paintings. In her bedroom, Alice Rochester yawned and sprawled across the rumpled sheets.

'This is all your fault,' she grinned, nudging Tom Randall-Stubbs with her big toe. 'I never stayed in bed this late before you seduced me. See what a bad influence you are?'

'Yeah, right, *I'm* the bad influence,' Rando laughed. He shook a wave of dark brown hair off his forehead. 'That's why every time I try to get up and do something constructive with my day, you trap me in the duvet.'

'I do not.' Alice giggled.

'Do too.'

'Do not!' Alice threw back the sheets. 'See? No one's trapping you. You can leave if you're so desperate. Go on, go ahead. Go do something *constructive.*'

Rando poked her in the ribs, his sea-blue eyes sparkling. 'You always have to win an argument, don't you? Such a spoiled little brat. But at least,' he added, inching closer, 'you're a gorgeous spoiled brat.'

Alice smiled as Rando kissed her. He'd hardly stopped kissing her for the past five days. Kissing and stroking and nibbling . . . Her eyelids fluttered shut at the touch of his fingers under the covers, and she buried her nose in his neck, breathing in the warm, sleepy smell of his skin. She couldn't believe it was only ten days ago that the two of them had first made love. They'd done it in secret, in a snowy Alpine cabin under the moonlight, while the rest of their friends were partying away the New Year. From the moment Rando's hands had caressed her naked body, Alice had finally understood what everyone was going on about when they raved about sex. Breathless, blood-pounding, spine-quivering sex.

And the romance had continued from there – despite the fact that both she and Rando were betraying people by carrying it on. But Alice didn't want to think about that now.

'This has been a good start to the year, hasn't it?' she whispered, her lips touching his.

'Mmm.' He grinned, propped on his elbows above her. 'And I can't think of a better way to end the holidays – your family being in Paris and leaving us the house to ourselves.'

'Although it might mean we're spending a bit too much time in bed . . .'

'Of course we're not. We can never spend too much time in bed. In fact, I vote we stay here all day and night until tomorrow.'

'Hmmm. Tempting. What'll that make it? Thirty-six hours straight?'

'Thirty-seven.'

'Oh, yes. Very precise.'

'Let's settle in for the afternoon. We can open a bottle of red wine and watch crap TV under the duvet and let the sun sink outside your window.'

'Or . . .' Alice wheedled, 'we could go get something to eat.'

'Eat?' Rando pulled a face of mock dismay. 'How can you think about food when I'm trying to be all romantic?'

'Because I'm starving. We haven't had anything since that smoked salmon last night. Can you believe that was the only thing my parents left in the fridge?'

'Made a pretty delicious dinner though.'

'Yeah, and now it's lunchtime. I need sustenance. We've been burning a lot of calories, you know.'

'True,' Rando grinned, sitting up. 'Let me think . . . Do you like hamburgers?'

'Love them.'

'Good. I know this great little place near Sloane Square that we can walk to. And then when we come back to bed, we can feel all virtuous that we made it outside at all.'

Throwing on some clothes, they strolled into the afternoon. Alice swung Rando's hand as they meandered through Kensington, along street after street of London's most elegant houses. The weak January sun filtered through the trees, casting spidery shadows on the pavement, and the cold air blazed through Alice's lungs. A smile played on her lips. She hadn't realised it was possible to feel this happy. Being with Rando made her feel free.

It made her feel buoyant – like a ship on a sunny sea. Like a balloon on a breezy day. Everything seemed to sparkle. Everything – even a simple walk like this – was the most fun she could remember having in years. She gave Rando's fingers a squeeze.

'Hey, look,' he said, returning the pressure. He was slowing down in front of a display window. 'I never knew there was a guitar shop here. Looks like a cool place.'

'Mm. Hungry,' Alice reminded him.

'Ooh, hang on.' Rando was peering inside. 'That's a Martin Dreadnought! The same guitar that Johnny Cash played. And look at that one. I've been wanting a new guitar for ages.'

'Starving!' Alice wailed.

Rando draped an arm around her. 'I know, I know! But do you mind if we just pop in? Really quickly? Go on . . .'

Alice smiled as he nuzzled her neck. 'How can I say no? But you'd better remember this favour later on.'

The shop door jangled as they stepped in out of the cold. Rando wandered towards the back, disappearing behind a shelf of sheet music. Alice followed. She watched as he picked out a melody on a shiny new guitar.

'You're getting really good, you know. I like that tune.'

'Thanks. I wrote it the other day. I've been hoping I can play it during a Paper Bandits gig. If Tristan . . .'

Rando fell silent. Alice looked at the floor. The sound of her boyfriend's name – and the name of her boyfriend's band – came between them like a knife. Alice and Tristan Murray-Middleton had been friends since they were toddlers. In the autumn they'd started dating, and from the moment of their first kiss, Alice had assumed they'd be together for ever. Then, out of the blue, she'd fallen for Rando. At first, nothing had happened, but when Alice and Tristan had argued during their crew's ski trip in the Alps, the cheating had begun.

A frown clouded her face. If Tristan had been the only obstacle to her relationship with Rando, it would have been bad enough. But he wasn't. There was Tally Abbott, too. Tally was Alice's best friend in the world – and she was also Rando's ex. Just before Christmas, when Rando had dumped Tally, he'd broken her heart. So painfully that Tally had refused to come on the New Year ski trip. Instead, she'd disappeared, leaving only a cryptic text message in her wake. No one had seen a trace of her in ten days, and everyone was worried. Every time Alice's phone rang, she lunged for it, hoping and fearing that her BFF would be on the other end.

Alice sighed. She couldn't think about this now. She had to push it out of her head. Term was starting in a few days and she'd be forced to think about it then. But for now, all she wanted was for her and Rando to enjoy their last few days of peace.

'Play me another song?' she asked, stroking his arm.

He gave her a smile. 'What would you like?'

'Don't know. Have you written anything else?'

'Well . . . sort of. I could play you this thing I've been working on . . .'

'Go on.'

'But it's kind of embarrassing.'

'Come on, just play it!'

'OK, but it's just a fragment. I'm still tweaking it.' Rando strummed and sang softly, his gaze fixed on Alice's.

> *I always knew somehow*
> *We'd end up here.*
> *Now that I have you,*
> *I'll keep you near.*
>
> *I'd rather be kissing you*
> *Than anyone else.*
> *This is the happiest*
> *I've ever felt.*
>
> *I'd rather be kissing you,*
> *Your smile of sunbeams.*
> *I kiss you every night*
> *In my dreams.*
>
> *I'd rather be kissing you,*
> *Your smile of sunbeams.*
> *I kiss you all night long*
> *In my dreams.*

Alice's eyes were glistening. 'It's wonderful,' she whispered.

'You like it?'

'I love it.' *I love you*, she wanted to say, but she stopped herself. Instead, she leaned in to kiss him. As they pressed into each other, the doorbell jingled again. Alice glanced up through a gap in the shelves of sheet music. Suddenly, her heart stopped. She leapt back from Rando.

'Hide!' she gasped, shrinking into the corner. 'Shit. Keep quiet. Oh my god, we're dead.'

'Why? What do you mean?'

'It's him,' she mouthed. 'Tristan.'

Rando squinted through the music books. His face whitened. 'And not just T. He's with my cousin, too.'

It was true. Behind Tristan, Jasper von Holstadt had come into the shop, his haughty, handsome face still tanned after their week of skiing. Along with Seb Ogilvy, Jasper was Tristan's closest friend.

'Mate, what are we doing in here?' Jasper's voice floated back to them, as Tristan sauntered along the racks of guitars.

'Just looking. I won't be long.'

'Whatever. By the way, you didn't answer my question.'

Tristan lifted a guitar off the wall, played a few chords, and put it back.

'What question?' he said. He wandered towards the rear of the shop, approaching the book-case that was hiding Alice and Rando from view.

Alice held her breath. She watched through the gaps between the shelves. *Stop*, she willed him. *Stop. Please.* T was now so close, she could see the flecks in his hazel eyes. He was wearing his favourite cashmere scarf. His chestnut hair was sticking up in its usual quiff. Alice bit her lip.

Only a few months ago, she'd thought T's hair was the sexiest thing in the world. Now, it just made her sad.

'What do you mean, what question?' Jasper was saying. 'I asked if you'd made things up with Alice yet.'

Tristan stopped in his tracks.

Thank god, Alice muttered to herself. *Stay there. Don't come any closer.* Still as a stone, she waited for Tristan's reply.

Slowly, he turned back towards Jasper. 'Why do you ask?'

'Because that was a pretty serious fight you two had on the ski trip. Do you think you'll be able to patch things up?'

'Of course. I just haven't seen her yet. We got off the plane back from the Alps and went our separate ways. I think we've both been stewing.'

'But are you going to see her soon?'

'Yeah man, don't worry, it's all under control.' Tristan smirked. 'And by the way, since when do you care so much about my relationship?'

'I don't. I'm just curious. I mean, it's you and Alice. The golden couple. If there's drama, I want to be the first to know.'

'How sweet of you. Well, there's no drama, OK?' T shoved his hands in his pockets. Through the shelves, Alice stared. Maybe she was wrong, but a glimmer of doubt seemed to flicker across T's face. 'We're meeting up tomorrow and we'll sort it out. We love each other, we've known each other forever and we totally understand each other. It'll be fine.'

'If you say so.' Jasper yawned. 'Whatever. Come on, man – I'm bored of guitars. Let's go back to yours and play on the Xbox and smoke some weed.'

'Can't argue with that plan.' Tristan grinned. He turned on his heel, away from the bookshelf. A moment later, he and Jasper were out the door.

Alice's shoulders drooped in relief. For the first time in five minutes, she felt like she could breathe.

'Fuck,' Rando murmured. 'I thought we were done for.'

'Yeah. Thank god they're gone.' Alice sank her head on to his shoulder. 'We have to be more careful. We can't let Tristan find out. Or Tally. Or anyone. No one can ever find out.'

For a moment, Rando said nothing. Then he nodded. But as he stroked Alice's hair, there was a troubled look in his eyes.

Chapter 2

Bluebird, on the King's Road, was noisy, packed and hot. Dylan Taylor folded her arms over her beige cashmere coat and sighed. It was the Friday before term started, and she should be out shopping and seeing friends like every other normal sixteen-year-old in London. But she'd promised her mother she'd come to this family lunch, instead. And, at half past two, they were still waiting for their table.

'Pardon me,' simpered a voice.

Dylan glanced to her left. Victor Dalgleish, her mother's fiancé, was waving the manager over, one eye contorted into a conspiratorial wink. As she watched, Victor (or Vic, as he insisted that everyone call him) slipped a fifty-pound note into the man's hand and flashed him a bleached white grin. Dylan had to stop herself being sick at the sight of it. Not only was *Vic* unbelievably vulgar, but he actually thought he had class. Which he didn't. He looked like a used-car salesman. The ratty sideburns. The pointy shoes. The gold rings on his chubby fingers, which were right now resting on her mom's bum. Dylan couldn't believe their wedding was in less than four months. With the speed they were arranging it, you'd have thought they were two randy teenagers.

'I hope everyone's hungry,' said Dylan's mother, Piper, as she settled into the maroon leather banquette.

'I'm starving!' Dylan announced. 'Yum, that steak looks awesome.'

Piper shot her an appreciative smile. A few weeks ago, Dylan would never have answered without being hostile. In fact, she probably wouldn't have answered at all. She and her mother had been at each other's throats since September, when Piper had suddenly transplanted her two daughters to London from New York, so she could be with the new love of her life. Dylan absolutely hated Victor. But, over the Christmas holidays, she'd promised her mother that she'd try her best to get on with him. After all, he was about to join their family.

'I think the organic sea trout sounds good,' Piper mused, holding up the giant menu.

'Oh, no, absolutely not,' Victor interrupted. Victor was incapable of hearing a conversation without interrupting. 'I forbid you to have something so boring. You have to try the fish and chips, baby. It's a classic here. Classic.'

'But sweetheart,' Piper objected, 'the wedding. I have to watch my figure.'

'Ah yes,' Victor purred, 'well I suppose I'll allow that. But only if *I* can watch it, too. Mmm, and what a nice figure it is.' He slid his hand round Piper's waist, practically groping her boob. 'We have to keep you nice and svelte, don't we, baby? For all our public appearances.'

Dylan almost gagged on her sourdough roll. Victor was a B-list TV personality, adored by housewives and old ladies, and he was always taking their mother to what he described as 'jet-setting media ragers'. Recently, Piper had travelled round Europe with him on a book tour for his new memoir.

Now he was stroking her thigh. 'Just look at your mother. Isn't she a stunner, kids?'

I'm not a kid, Dylan wanted to snap. But she forced herself to smile. 'Oh, yeah. She's great.'

Dylan's fourteen-year-old sister, Lauren, said nothing. She was hunched in the neighbouring seat, and her lower lip was trembling.

'Now,' Victor went on, patting the menu magnanimously, 'I want you kids to order yourselves a nice big meal. Don't hold back. Don't tell me you're on any of these bloody stupid New Year diets. You're both growing girls, heh heh, and God knows what rubbish they feed you at that posh boarding school. Fried fish sticks and tinned spaghetti – that's what it was in my day. Ah, I remember it well.' He sniffed, and crossed one denim-clad leg over the other. Victor was one of those middle-aged losers who wore his tapered jeans just that little bit too short. 'The sight of the tough old dinner ladies. The sound of homesick little boys crying for their mummies. The swish of the masters whacking you with—'

Suddenly, Lauren slammed her menu on to the polished tabletop. Her blue eyes were flooded with tears. 'Mom, please!' she cried. 'Don't make me go back. *Please!*'

Dylan squeezed her sister's shoulders. The couple at the next table glanced in their direction.

'Darling, shush,' Piper murmured. 'We'll discuss this at home.'

'But Mom . . . I hate that school. I *hate* it!' Lauren burst into tears.

The neighbouring couple fixated on their plates of asparagus. Dylan could tell they were hanging on every word. That was so English. To pretend you were politely ignoring a ruckus when you were eavesdropping within an inch of your life.

'Darling—' Piper began.

'Now, now, Lauren.' Victor cut her off. 'Chin up. You only started at St Cecilia's a month ago – you haven't given it a chance. It's one of the most prestigious schools in England, and lots of little girls would give their right arm to go there. So pull yourself together, and don't upset your mum.'

'I'm not a little girl,' Lauren snarled. 'And why should I listen to you? You're not my dad, so butt out.'

'Lauren!' Piper cried.

'It's none of his business, Mom! You can't make me go back to that place. Everyone in my class – they're so mean and horrible. They all know my secrets – they've read my diary! Even the boys at Hasted House.' Tears were streaming down Lauren's usually rosy cheeks.

'Come, come!' Victor chuckled. 'Don't be ridiculous. Of course the boys haven't read your diary. How could they possibly have got hold of it?'

'Dear,' said Piper, laying her hand on his lap, 'don't you remember? I told you what happened. One of Lauren's roommates, what's her name . . .'

'Georgina,' hiccuped Lauren. 'Fortescue.'

'Right. Fortescue. She stole Lauren's diary and published it on Facebook. Everyone *did* read it. Don't you remember how upset Lauren was at the end of term?'

Victor shrugged. 'I'm a busy man. I can't remember every little teenage drama that unfolds in our house.'

Piper patted his hand. 'Lauren, darling, listen. The school has assured me that they've suspended Georgina for the first week of term. So she won't be bullying you again in a hurry.'

'The first week?' Lauren shrieked. The asparagus couple flinched. 'She should be expelled! She ruined my life. Why didn't they kick her out?'

Dylan opened her mouth to remark that Georgie's family was far too rich for the school to dare. But before she could get a word out, Victor slapped his hand on the banquette.

'Bloody hell!' he guffawed. 'Stop making such a stink. You were probably desperate for the boys to read your diary – all you young people post your private lives online these days. You're all exhibitionists. And anyway, this little incident is nothing. You should be thankful you're not a celebrity, such as myself – then you'd have to learn to cope with invasions of privacy. All publicity is good publicity, that's what I say.'

Dylan shot him a death-stare across the table. For

Lauren, having the entire school read that she'd never even kissed a boy – never mind the fact that she had a massive crush on Alice Rochester's younger brother, Hugo – definitely wasn't good publicity. Dylan shuddered. She knew all about how horrific the St Cecilia's girls could be, first hand.

'Victor has no idea what he's talking about, Mom,' she said. 'You should let Lauren go back to day school in London. You don't know what it's like.'

'Please, please please!' Lauren begged. 'I can't go back to St Cecilia's. I can't.'

But Piper only shook her head. 'I'm sorry, but it's impossible. Vic and I are planning to travel a lot, and you can't stay home alone. St Cecilia's is a wonderful school. Besides, it's good for you to face your fears.'

Before Dylan could argue, her phone beeped. She sneaked a look in her lap.

OMG! read Alice's text. *Massive close call this afternoon. Was with Rando and almost bumped smack into T.*

Dylan gasped.

'What's wrong?' her mother asked.

'Oh . . . uh, nothing. Just some homework I forgot about.' Dylan's fingers raced over the keypad. These days, she was Alice Rochester's only confidante, the only person who knew about Alice and Rando. The two girls had been arch-enemies when Dylan first started at St Cecilia's last September, but Alice, the queen of the school, had slowly learned to trust and respect her.

Shit! she wrote. *Did he see you??*

15

No. But almost. He was with Jasper. Phew.

Dylan's eyebrows creased as she read her boyfriend's name. *Jasper? He was out and about? R U sure??*

Yeah. Why?

No way! He was supposed to come to lunch with me & my family 2day but he bailed. Claimed to be sick. Liar.

Dickhead! Alice replied. *He was definitely not sick. He and T were off to play Xbox and get stoned.*

Dylan felt a surge of rage. *Deep breath,* she told herself. *Deep breath.* She shut her eyes, trying as hard as she could not to leap up and throw a fit. Dylan had a dangerous temper, which, thanks to a recent stunt by her vile room-mate Sonia Khan, had become famous throughout St Cecilia's and Hasted House. She'd been trying to get it under control, but it wasn't easy – especially at moments like this. Frowning, she weighed her phone in her palm. Maybe she should send Jasper a text. A cold, calm, caustic text just to let him know she was on to him. Because she wasn't going to let him get away with this. No way.

But right now, the waitress was coming to take their order. And Lauren was crying again. And Victor was snogging her mother so disgustingly that it looked like he was about to swallow her face. Dylan would have to deal with her love life later.

Chapter 3

Seb Ogilvy gazed out the window of his father's Bentley as it pulled up at Trafalgar Square. Outside, the fountains sparkled under the black sky, while the huge hulk of the National Gallery glowed under columns of white light. Droves of people in cocktail dress were already drifting inside through the gallery's grand portico, even though it was only six o'clock.

The chauffeur held open the door.

'Thank you, Tobias,' said Sir Preston Ogilvy, sliding one perfectly polished evening shoe on to the pavement. Before disengaging the rest of his long, thin body from the car, he raked his eyes over his son. 'Straighten your tie.'

Seb glanced down. His skinny-knit tie looked perfectly straight to him, but he tweaked it anyway, and clambered out after his father. Now that Seb was seventeen, he looked more like his dad than ever. He'd inherited the tall, skinny Ogilvy frame, the chalk-white skin, and the blond hair, which flopped haystack-style over his blue eyes. Sometimes it seemed to him that as he grew up, every trace of his mother was being slowly but surely rubbed out of his appearance – along with his memories of her, which were fading too.

Seb's mum had run off when he was still a baby, and since then, it had been just him and his dad.

Sir Preston paused near the entrance.

'Remember,' he said, once his son had caught up, 'Professor Johann Smythe is the most important person here tonight. When I introduce you, try to be pleasant.'

'I'm always pleasant, Dad.'

'Yes. Of course.' Sir Preston buttoned his jacket and stroked the carnation in his lapel with long, smooth fingers. 'Now, as you know, Professor Smythe has just been appointed the new Gallery Director, and he has plenty of visions for the future. It'd be useful if you were on good terms.'

Seb gave a nod. *Idiot*, he told himself; he shouldn't be so disappointed. He'd known all along that his dad hadn't brought him to this benefit so they could enjoy some quality time together. That would be a first. No, this evening was all about networking. Sir Preston was Chairman of the Ogilvy Trust, which he'd recently set up to sponsor the arts, and he wanted Seb around to make him look like a good family man. Which he wasn't. He was hardly ever home, he ignored his son, he had a mistress in practically every European capital and the whole of London knew it.

'Sir Preston!' gushed a man as they strode into the museum. The man was wearing a bright purple suit with an orange shirt. 'Just the character I wanted to see. And *who*,' he grinned, looking Seb up and down, 'is this charming creature?'

'Ah! Barry.' Sir Preston gave a tight-lipped smile. 'How

nice to see you. Allow me to introduce my son. Sebastian Ogilvy, Barry Fitzgibbon.'

'Well, hel-*lo*.' The man took Seb's hand and flashed him a wink. 'Now, now, Sir Preston, where have you been hiding this little treasure?'

Seb felt his mouth go dry. He turned to his dad – but Sir Preston had somehow managed to vanish. And this Barry Fitzgibbon character was beaming in his face.

'That naughty father of yours – always the socialite, always the hobnobber. How about you stay with me and have a drink? These events tend to be rather intimidating, don't they?' Barry gestured round the main hall, which was packed with braying, tippling movers-and-shakers of the art world, all of them at least ten years older than Seb.

'Yeah, they do. I suppose,' Seb said.

A pudgy hand settled on his shoulder. Seb inched his fingers into his pocket and touched the silver whisky flask that he carried with him everywhere. He had no clue what to do – how to act. This Barry Fitzgibbon character seemed to have sussed out his biggest secret: that he was gay. Seb had never told anyone in the world. In fact, he'd only recently admitted it to himself. Sweat collected on the palms of his hands. He fancied Barry about as much as he'd fancy his grandad. Besides, he'd only ever flirted with a guy once – a beautiful actor called Will who he'd met at Sir Lucian Scott's Christmas party last month. Seb sighed. He'd stupidly lost Will's number; he didn't even know his last name. And that had been the end of that. Right now, the only thing he could do was escape from this man.

Unfortunately, Barry seemed to have a different idea. Grinning, he skimmed two champagne cocktails off a tray.

'Cheers, darling. Now, tell me all about yourself. Starting with how you got so delicious.'

Seb choked as the bubbles fizzed up his nose.

'Careful there! All right now?' chuckled Barry, patting him on the back.

Seb nodded, still sputtering.

'Not used to the strong stuff, I suppose. You must be still at school, yes?'

'Yes,' Seb gasped. 'Hasted House.'

'GCSEs, or A levels?'

'A levels. I'm in the Lower Sixth.'

'Charming, charming. How's your love life? Single, are you?'

'Not at all,' Seb said, finally catching his breath. 'I have a girlfriend.'

'You don't say.' Barry sipped his cocktail.

'Oh yes. We're extremely serious.'

'Ah.' Barry's gaze fluttered off to the side.

'Yeah.' Seb swallowed the rest of his drink, keeping one eye on his companion. 'We're thinking of getting engaged. She should be turning up here any minute, actually. I think I'll get a refill.' He paused. 'Can I get you anything?'

'No, dear, no, that's all right.'

'OK, well, nice talking to you.'

'Yes, yes . . . Yoohoo, Lord Philpott!' Barry waved, already not listening.

Breathing a sigh of relief, Seb retreated to the bar and

checked his phone. He still hadn't heard from Jasper and Tristan. They were probably stoned out of their minds already, deep into an Xbox session. And he was stuck here. Great. He reached for a glass of champagne, and felt something poke into his chest – something inside his jacket. Rummaging in the hidden pocket, he pulled out a card.

WILL LARKIN. ACTOR.

Seb gasped. Of course! He hadn't worn this suit since the Scotts' Christmas party – the housekeeper had sent it to the dry-cleaner. He stared at the bit of paper, his heart pounding. There was a phone number on it. Should he text Will? Was it too late, more than two weeks on? No, surely Will had given him the card for a reason – he *wanted* Seb to get in touch. And he couldn't chicken out now, not after this stroke of luck.

Hey. It's Seb, he typed. He bit his lip. His fingers were shaking, so he downed the rest of his drink. *From Lucian Scott's party . . . Don't know if you remember me?*

Squeezing his eyes shut, he sent it.

The seconds ticked by.

Finally, after what seemed like centuries, his phone pinged back.

Hey! Course I remember you. The cute blond who was too busy to come clubbing with me & my mates. What u up to?

Seb grinned.

At a benefit with my dad. Ugh.

Oh gawd. Hate those things. ☺ So . . . Wanna meet up sometime?

Seb blinked at the screen. A date – was this a date? No way. Will was probably just being friendly. He probably just didn't want to be rude. But then again . . .

Sure, Seb typed. *Next week? I can sneak out of school for the evening?*

He held his breath. Then he took the plunge.

Chapter 4

'Stop hogging the crisps,' Alice giggled, leaning across Rando and snatching the bag of Kettle Chips off the duvet. It was Saturday morning, and the two of them were in bed, dozing and snacking and watching *The Hangover* on her computer.

'Want one?' she said. She snaked a sea-salt-flavoured crisp towards Rando's mouth. 'Yummm. Open wide . . .'

Rando dodged. 'No thanks. I'm fine.'

'Whatever. All the more for me.' Alice flicked her hair. They watched the film for a moment in silence. Then she leaned in and nuzzled Rando's cheek.

His eyelashes fluttered, but the rest of his profile was impassive. 'Hey, stop, I'm trying to concentrate. I like this part.'

'Hmmm?' Alice whispered into his ear. 'You like which part?'

'Al! Stop it.'

'Humph. Fine.' She hugged her knees to her chest. 'Ugh. I wish I didn't have to get up. I want to stay in bed with you all day, not go see T.'

Rando stared at the screen. His jaw was tight. After a

moment, he cleared his throat. 'So are you going to break up with him?'

'I thought you wanted to watch the film.'

Suddenly, Rando shut the computer. He turned to Alice, his eyes fiery. 'Answer the question! Are you going to break up with him?'

'Hey, calm down. Why are you looking at me like that?'

'Because . . . because! Shit, I'm sorry.' Rando rubbed his forehead. 'I just feel so bad. What we're doing, it's . . . it's . . .'

'I know.' Alice rubbed his knee. 'It sucks. I've been trying not to think about it.'

'Me too. But when we bumped into Tristan yesterday, it all hit home. We can't keep doing this. You have to break up with him. And then we have to come clean.'

'Come clean?'

'It's the only way. Don't worry,' Rando added, seeing the look on Alice's face, 'I'm not saying we have to tell everyone we were cheating. That would be stupid. After you break up with Tristan we can wait a few weeks, and then we can be together. Out in the open.'

'Out in the open?' Alice echoed again. 'Hang on, are you serious?'

'Of course.'

'But we can't date out in the open. It'd never work!'

'What do you mean?'

'Be real, Rando! No one's gonna welcome us with open arms if we suddenly come out as a couple. They'll all hate us. They'll destroy us!'

Rando laughed. 'Bit dramatic, don't you think? I mean, yeah, it'll be hard. Tristan and Tally will be upset. But they'll get over it.'

'No they won't!' Alice's face was contorted. '*I'd* never get over it if Tally did it to me. And everyone'll take her side.'

'You don't know that.'

'And I have no intention of committing social suicide!' Alice ploughed on, her voice sounding desperate. 'Don't tell me you want to either – everyone turning away when you walk down the halls, no one sitting next to you at meals. The silent treatment. I refuse to make that my life.'

'So what's your idea, then?' Rando cried, flinging up his arms. 'That we keep seeing each other in secret?'

'Yes!'

'No. No way.'

Alice's jaw dropped.

'Excuse me if I'm wrong, but we've *got* something here. Come on, Al!' Rando grabbed her wrists. 'You and me – this is real. It's special. And I refuse to let us drag it through the mud by sneaking around and lying.'

'But . . . but you're looking at it the wrong way! I don't want to lose all my friends, and neither do you. Neither of us would be happy that way. We'd just be two miserable, unpopular losers trying to cheer each other up.'

'I can't believe what you're saying!' Rando pulled at his hair. 'Can't you be a bit brave? Can't you weather a few weeks of whispering and dirty looks, for the sake of *us*?'

'No!' Alice bellowed. 'I can't! I won't!'

Rando sank back in disbelief. Alice watched with a mixture of fear and fury as he threw back the sheets. 'Fuck this. I thought you were better than that.'

'And I thought you were smarter!'

'Al, please . . .' Rando stood naked in the middle of the Persian rug. He looked like he was in pain. 'Say you didn't mean that. Stop being so fucking stupid.'

'Don't you dare call me stupid.'

'Then don't *be* stupid.' His eyes were blazing. 'This isn't one of those silly arguments to get all proud about – you can afford to lose this one. Don't ruin everything because of some lame, vain popularity contest. Come on, one last chance. All or nothing: we do this in the open, or not at all.'

'Fine! Not at all!' Alice hurled back, trying to ignore the stabbing in her chest. Her voice was drowned by the ringing of the doorbell and she marched into the hallway, yanking the intercom off its roost. 'What?'

'Hi babes!'

Alice's blood seemed to drain out through her feet. That silvery voice. The shimmering laugh. She hadn't heard them in almost two weeks.

'Baaabes? Hellooo?' the voice repeated.

'H-Hi!' Alice stammered, hoping the hesitation in her voice would be lost as it travelled down the wires. 'It's *Tally*,' she mouthed to Rando, wringing her hands.

His usually rosy cheeks turned pale.

'*Quick! Get dressed.*'

The bell buzzed again, four times. 'Hey!' came Tally's voice. 'Al. Do you expect me to wait out here all day?'

Alice glanced back into the bedroom, where Rando was struggling into his jeans. She shut her eyes. She had no choice.

Chapter 5

'Surprise!' Tally cried, as Alice flung open the front door.

Tally looked good. She always looked good, but today, as she stood on the threshold in her peach-coloured winter coat, there was something different. Alice blinked. Maybe it was the flush in her porcelain cheeks. Or the strange light in her sea-grey eyes. Or the slight hunch of her narrow shoulders. But before Alice could decide, a pair of arms landed round her neck.

'Babes!' Tally giggled. 'You look shocked.'

'Duh. Of course I do.' Alice disentangled herself and straightened her dress, which she'd thrown on in a panic. 'Wasn't *shock* what you were going for? I mean, you just disappeared! Where the hell have you been?'

But Tally didn't answer. She'd already shoved past into the foyer.

'OMG, babe, it is so good to see your house again. Feels like home,' she trilled, shedding her layers as she went. Her handbag hit the antique French oak floor. Scarf. Coat. Tally was like a tornado, always leaving havoc in her wake. 'Did you miss me? You'd better have missed me. Even if it did take you, like, two hours to open the door. What were you doing up there? Staring at yourself in the mirror? Oh!' She stopped short at the foot of the staircase and made a small, surprised sound, like a confused chick. 'H-hi.'

Alice's heart plummeted. Rando was standing at the top of the stairs – fully dressed, thank god. But she'd told him to hide. What was he doing out in the open? What if Tally guessed?

'Hey.' He stuck up his hand, traffic warden style. 'How's it going?'

Tally darted her eyes to Alice.

'What's happening?' she whispered. She raised her voice as Rando came down the stairs. 'I didn't know you guys were such good friends. What are you doing here?'

Alice watched as Rando cleared his throat. It looked like he was about to say something. *Confess* something. 'We—'

'We . . . we were just looking for you!' she yelped, leaping forward. 'Trying to find a trace of where the hell you'd gone. Facebook stalking. Googling. Seeing if you've been mentioned on any blogs. Right, Rando?'

There was a silence. Then he nodded. 'Yeah. Right.'

'Wow,' Tally said. 'That's mega-sweet of you guys. I mean, seriously. I'm touched.'

'Sure.' Rando pursed his lips. 'Anyway . . . I have to go.'

It was only then that Alice registered he was wearing his coat. Her stomach wrenched. She balled her fists. 'Oh. Right. Fine.'

He stood there looking at her, so she flicked her gaze away. 'Well, see you. Thanks for coming round.'

Rando's look darkened. 'Yeah. You're welcome. Glad you're back safe, Tally. Bye.'

A second later, the door slammed behind his back. It sounded like a coffin lid landing in place. For a moment, Alice couldn't move. A great sob rose in her chest but she stuffed it back down. She could handle this. She could play the role. Cool and indifferent – that was her speciality. It was the secret of her success.

'Oh. My. God.' Tally spun round. 'How awkward was *that?* I mean, did you see how weird he was acting around me? It's kind of amazing he came round here to help you look for me, though. I didn't know he cared about me that much.'

'Oh, yeah.' Alice's voice was hoarse. She cleared her throat. 'Of course he cares about you. As a friend.'

'Yeah. As a *friend.*' Tally bit her lip, and her hand moved to her neck, where Alice caught a glimpse of a thin, gold chain. 'Whatever. Did he hook up with any random slappers in Val d'Isère?'

Alice swallowed. 'I don't think so. But I wasn't watching him every second.'

'Not that I care, anyway. I am so over him. He is so last year.' Tally started up the stairs.

'Wait! Where are you going?'

'To your bedroom. Duh. Where do you think? To hang out in the linen cupboard?'

'But . . . but . . .' Alice fought back the panic. If Tally

saw the state of the bed, she was done for. Not to mention the discarded condom packets. Or the empty bottle of wine on the floor. 'Let's go to the kitchen! Don't you want a snack?'

'No. Why? Do I look hungry?'

'No, but . . .' *Quick*, Alice cursed herself. *Think of something. Think of a lie.*

At the door to her bedroom, she stopped short. She blinked. Her room was pristine; the bed made, the rug straightened, the curtains back. Rando must have tidied it all before he went downstairs. Alice knew she should feel relieved, but all she felt was empty. As empty as the pillow where his head had been lying only ten minutes before. There wasn't even a dent in it to hold his memory.

'Hey, look, crisps,' Tally exclaimed. Throwing herself across Alice's bed, she helped herself to a handful. 'And we didn't even have to go to the kitchen. Yum, sea salt – this is Rando's favourite flavour. He used to eat them all the time when we were dating. Oh, babe, I am so glad to be back. You have no idea.'

'That's right.' Alice folded her arms. 'I *don't* have any idea. So why don't you tell me where you went?'

Tally said nothing. Her fingers strayed again to her neck.

'What is that thing?' Alice demanded. She took hold of the chain. A small gold disc was dangling from it, engraved with strange-looking symbols that glinted in the steely afternoon light. She squinted. 'Where the hell did you get this? It's weird. Where's it from?'

Tally sighed. 'Nowhere.' Whisking the necklace away, she tucked it into her jumper.

Alice frowned. 'Fine. Be secretive, then. But if you don't tell me where you've been, you can find yourself a new best friend.'

Tally's eyes widened. 'Al, what's wrong with you? You're being way cold. And weird. Aren't you even happy to see me?'

'Yes.' Alice bit her lip. 'Of course I am, babe. It's just . . . I'm just . . . You caught me by surprise. So are you going to tell me, or not?'

'Sure.' Tally laughed. 'It's no secret. Spain.'

'Spain?'

'Yeah. I was staying with my aunt. My mum's half-sister. Don't tell me you forgot she lives there.'

'Huh? But you never even talk about her. Why would you run away to her?'

Tally shrugged and looked out the window. 'Change of scene. Oooh, hello!' Grinning, she reached behind the curtain and plucked out a lacy black bra with pink bows on the straps. 'Sexy lingerie you've been modelling for a certain someone?'

The blood rushed to Alice's face.

'Come on now.' Tally tittered. 'No need to be embarrassed. I take it Tristan was a fan?'

'Tristan? Oh. Totally,' Alice said, forcing her face into a smile. 'He loved it. Ha, ha.' Suddenly, she felt exhausted. Once you started lying, you had to be constantly vigilant. Scrutinising your sentences for flaws, turning them inside out for holes, magnifying them for frays. She stared at the bra. Yesterday afternoon, she and Rando had come back here, giggling and flushed with the wine they'd drunk at lunch. He'd flung off her clothing in the middle of the room, kissing her all over her body and finally carrying her to bed. She blinked. She couldn't quite believe he was gone. Surely tonight he'd be coming back, ready to laugh with her and hold her and bury his face in her hair.

'Hey, space cadet!' Tally called. 'Stop thinking about hot sex with T! Come on, let's go to the Prince of Wales and catch up over some gin and tonics. I want to hear all about your holiday!'

'Oh . . . I'd love to, but I can't. I'm supposed to be meeting Tristan.' Alice felt a jolt as she said her boyfriend's name. 'Shit, I'm late actually, I should be there already. How about we go shopping tomorrow instead? We'll hit the King's Road.'

'Sorry sweetie, no can do. Shopping's out for me.'

'Shopping's out? You can't be serious. I've never heard you say those words in your life!'

'Yeah, that's 'cause my stupid dad's never cut off my credit card in my life. I mean, can you believe it? He was so pissed off when I got home this morning. *How dare you go away like that and not tell me where! You are so irresponsible!*' Tally rolled her eyes. 'As if he cares. He was probably thrilled to have me out of the house.'

'I doubt it, babe. Think how worried he must have been.'

Shrugging, Tally went back to staring out the window.

Alice watched her friend's beautiful profile silhouetted against the light. Tally's story about Spain made sense. All the details were there. But now that Alice thought about it, she couldn't shake the doubt tugging at her mind. Something just didn't feel right.

Chapter 6

'No, no, no, these are totally wrong,' whined Sonia Khan. 'I said I wanted *glamorous*, not chav-tastic.' She shoved the pile of sample invitations back to Penny de Claire, London's most exclusive party planner, and rolled her eyes towards the chandelier on the ceiling. 'My seventeenth birthday party has to be perfect. It has to be the most amazing event these suckers have ever *imagined*!'

'Riiight . . .' Penny cleared her throat and slid the invitations back into her snakeskin portfolio. 'We can do that. You'll have to be a bit more specific, though.'

Sonia frowned. 'Specific? *You're* supposed to be the brilliant party planner. Isn't that specific enough?'

Penny pressed her fingertips together and took a controlled breath. 'No, dear, unfortunately it's not. Just tell me exactly what you're picturing in your head, OK? That way, we can create something especially for you.'

'Especially for me. Hmph, that's more like it.' Sonia drummed her perfectly manicured fingers on her parents' ebony side table, and turned to Bella Scott, her new BFF as of the past week, who was perched on the sofa by her side. 'Bellsy, darling, you can help me – you've always been so creative and amazing at stuff like this.'

'I have?' Bella said, taking a biscuit from the silver tray on the coffee table.

'Of course you have! Remember the way your dad decorated your house for his Christmas party this year? I just know you had something to do with that.'

'I didn't, actually. Daddy got special set designers to do it all for him. His film industry contacts like to do him favours, you know.'

'Of course they do.' Sonia smiled smugly. Bella's father was Sir Lucian Scott, the world-famous director, and Bella was his favourite child. Being best friends with her meant that Sonia would have access to everyone who was anyone – and that would do wonders for her future career as a Hollywood tycoon.

'Never mind, darling, I have plenty of ideas.' She turned back to Penny de Claire. 'Right, I'm envisioning an Arabian Nights theme. The stuff of Arabian legends! Every room in the house has to have its own individual motif. A troupe of belly dancers in the ballroom. A harem in my parents' bedroom – they won't mind. An Aladdin-style cave of wonders in the dining room, where people can rub magic lamps and lie on lush carpets and gorge themselves on balaclava!'

Penny de Claire's forehead furrowed. 'Er, do you mean baklava?'

'Yeah, that's what I said. Duh.' Sonia rolled her eyes in Bella's direction. 'Oh, and I want lanterns hanging everywhere, and velvet ottomans, and— OMG!' Her eyes bulged with excitement. 'I just had the most incredible idea! I want video cameras! I want video cameras everywhere, filming the party and projecting the footage on to massive screens in every room! Then I'll edit it and convince Channel 4 to give me a reality TV show, because I'm London's most fabulous socialista. Amaaazing!' she squealed.

'Mmmhmm, mmhmm,' Penny was muttering, jotting everything down in her red Smythson notepad. 'Right, excellent, that gives me plenty of material to work with. And as for your budget . . .'

Sonia waved her hand. 'Just send the bill to Daddy.'

'Very good, then. I'll email you some sample images, and if you're happy, we'll go from there.' Standing up, Penny held out her hand. 'Until next time, then.'

'Yeah, thanks.' Sonia gave her a limp handshake and yawned. 'The maid will show you out.' Once the door had shut, she lolled her head on Bella's shoulder. 'Moron. Penny de Crap. She thinks she's so clever, but I hope you noticed that every single one of those ideas was *mine*.'

'Yeah, I guess so,' Bella said. 'But you did reject every single one of hers. Why are you hiring her if you think she's so bad?'

'Because, sweetie, Penny does *everyone's* party. Everyone who counts, that is. But she's never done one quite like this. Eee! Aren't you glad you're my co-organiser?'

Bella nodded 'But I still don't understand why you didn't ask Alice Rochester to help—'

'Oooh!' Sonia interrupted, seizing Bella's wrist. 'I just adore this bracelet you're wearing. Adore!' She twisted Bella's bangle, which was embedded with massive fake gems. 'Don't tell me – someone famous give it to you, didn't they? Didn't they?'

'Well . . .' Bella shrugged. 'Drew Barrymore sends our family a Christmas stocking every year. She put this in it for me.'

'I knew it! OMG, Bella, you are. So. Cool! I can't believe we've never really hung out before.'

Bella smiled. 'Well, you were always preoccupied with Alice and Tally Abbott and Mimah Calthorpe de Vyle-Hanswicke. You lot don't exactly have time for anyone else.'

'Well I do now.' Sonia squeezed her new BFF's shoulders. 'Come on, help me draw up the guest list. We'll need loads of cute boys. I'm counting on you, sweetie – maybe we can even invite some famous people! Do you think Drew would come?'

'Ummm . . .' Bella pulled a sheet of paper towards her on the coffee table. 'I guess we should start with Alice Rochester.'

'No!' Sonia snapped. She fluttered her eyelids and adopted a honeyed tone. 'Thing is, I'm not inviting Alice. It's like I told you earlier, Alice Rochester is on the way out.'

Bella blinked. 'Oh. I thought you were joking. Alice is like, your best mate. You *worship* her.'

'Do not,' Sonia practically shouted. 'Why does everyone think I worship Alice Rochester? Just because I'm a faithful, loyal friend. God! Doesn't anyone know what friendship is?' She took a deep breath. 'Look, Alice used to be cool – but that was a long time ago. Like, back when we were fourteen. It's about time someone told the truth: Alice Rochester is a total bitch. No one actually likes her – everyone's just terrified of her.' Sonia clenched her fists, remembering how, on the New Year's ski trip, Alice had repeatedly sided with Dylan Taylor against her, and had ended up insulting her in front of their entire crew. That just showed how grateful Alice was for years of dedicated, slavish friendship. Sonia was determined to get her own back. And not inviting Alice to her fabulous birthday party was only part one of her plan.

'Think about it,' she continued. 'Can you honestly say you like Alice Rochester? What has she ever done for you? Except make you feel inferior.'

Bella bit her lip. 'I suppose. I mean, I never really thought about it. Alice has always been . . . Alice. The coolest girl in school.'

'Exactly. And it's time to challenge that. A new regime is on its way in.' Sonia tossed her hair. If she had anything to do with it, that new regime was going to be *her*. 'Right, we're not inviting Dylan Taylor, either. Dylan is just horrendous, don't you think? I mean, it's embarrassing even having her in our class, never mind as my roommate. Ugh. How do these tragic things happen to me? At least I have you, lovely Bella.' Sonia planted a kiss on Bella's cheek, then seized a pen and started scribbling on the guest list. 'Hmm, yes, we'll invite Tally Abbott. She's a sweet girl, even if she is Alice's BFF – and she'll be able to help legitimise our new crew.'

Bella squinted. 'Legitimise?'

'You know, like, make it legit.'

'I know what it means. I just have no idea what you're on about.'

Sonia sighed. 'Keep up, darling. We have to win over some of the old regime if we're going to form a new one. Haven't you ever studied history? When you overthrow the king or queen, you always need some of their old advisers to make you look legitimate.'

'Oh . . . Right. Yeah.'

'Good. I'm glad we're on the same page.' Stretching, Sonia looked down at her pristine bubblegum-pink blouse. 'Ugh, I detest this old rag. I need a new winter wardrobe if I'm going to be the most popular girl in school. Let's hit Portobello. And then we can go watch films at your place! I just know Sir Lucian has an amazing DVD collection.'

'Sone?' Bella looked doubtful.

'Yes, darling?'

'Are you sure this plan of yours is going to work? I mean, I don't want Alice Rochester turning against me if she's still got, you know, *power.*'

'Of course it's going to work!' Sonia set her jaw. 'Just stick with me, and you'll see – this term, St Cecilia's is going to be a totally new school. Alice Rochester and Dylan Taylor are going down.'

Chapter 7

Tristan Murray-Middleton slumped back in his seat at Tom's Delicatessen on Westbourne Grove and scowled at his watch. Again. Alice was late. An entire half-hour late, in fact. And she wasn't answering her phone. He glared at the bunch of roses on his lap. What a waste – they'd be wilted and dead by the time she showed up, which wasn't exactly a good omen. He'd had the whole day planned out. First, an apologetic coffee, followed by a romantic dinner, followed by an entire night of passion. But now he was in a foul mood. Alice was never late – she'd better have a good excuse.

'Sorry,' said a breathless voice. 'Couldn't find a cab.'

Tristan glanced up. His annoyance immediately evaporated. Alice was wearing one of those teeny-tiny dresses that showed off her gorgeous long legs. Her angular cheeks were slightly flushed and her shiny brown hair was piled in a bun on top of her head, just like a beautiful, breathless ballerina.

'It's fine.' He smiled, practically vaulting out of his chair. 'I was late, too. Just arrived, actually. Here, Squidge – these are for you.'

'Oh! Thanks.'

Alice ducked to smell the roses, pretending not to notice that T had been leaning in to kiss her – or that he'd used her special pet name, the one he'd been calling her since they were four. She swallowed. Being face to face with him was harder than she'd expected. He was wearing her favourite jumper – the blue one that made his chestnut eyes sparkle, its soft wool skimming the muscles of his arms. Her mind flew back to an afternoon last spring, when they were still just friends. T had been wearing it as they lay out in the late sun on the Murray-Middletons' country estate, dozing and talking nonsense in the length-ening shadows. Alice had closed her eyes and rested her head on his chest, breathing in his soapy, boyish smell, while all around them an evening breeze had ruffled the trees. She looked up at him, now. He was twisting his napkin in his hands.

'Um, have a seat.'

'Thanks.'

'It's good to see you. Guess we've both been busy, this past week. What have you been up to? Since skiing, I mean.'

'Not too much.' Alice kept her coat buttoned up. 'Gosh, it's freezing out. I'm chilled to the bone.'

'Do you want to borrow my scarf?'

'No. Thanks.'

'OK.' Tristan cleared his throat. 'Look, before we order anything, I wanted to say, I'm really—'

'Hello, excuse me?' Alice interrupted, flagging down

the waitress. 'A pot of Earl Grey, please. Thanks. Oh, and do you have any of those biscuit things? The chocolate ones? Great. I'm so hungry,' she said to Tristan. 'I've hardly eaten anything all day. I haven't been to this place in ages, by the way. It's always packed.'

'Yeah. Anyway, as I was saying . . . Hey!' Tristan frowned. Alice had shuffled round in her seat and was unravelling her bun. 'Can you listen, please?'

'I am listening!'

'No you're not. You're playing with your bloody hair.'

'Fine.' Alice dropped her arms. Her brown mane tumbled round her shoulders. 'Have it your way. I'm all ears.'

'Sorry, I didn't mean to snap. I just think we should clear the air.'

'Fine. Go on then.'

Tristan took a deep breath. 'OK, well, I wanted to say I'm sorry for the way things worked out in Val d'Isere. I wasn't at my best. But it was just so rubbish not being able to ski while you all had so much fun. I couldn't help getting into a strop.' He glanced at his arm, which he'd injured in a rugby accident nearly two months before. 'At least it's nearly healed now. I can do normal things again. But anyway. Sorry.'

Alice stared at the tabletop.

'Well?' Tristan said.

'Well what?'

'Don't you have anything to say?'

'Um, I don't think so. Am I meant to?'

'Of course!' T said. 'What are you talking about? I've apologised. Don't you think *you* should?'

Alice shrugged. It felt like her chest was in a vice. She knew she was being awful. She had so much to say sorry for: more than Tristan could possibly know. More than she could possibly say.

'Not really.' She blinked. 'What for?'

'Oh, let me think!' Tristan cried, throwing up his hands. 'Maybe for being really insensitive to my situation? Maybe for making zero effort to see me over the past week? Or . . . oh, wait, maybe you could start with saying sorry for being half an hour late!'

'I said I was sorry as soon as I saw you!'

'Oh, right, you were *so* apologetic.'

'You want me to get down on my knees?'

'Maybe!' Tristan clenched his teeth. '*God*,' he snarled, 'that's so not the point. Why can't you just back down and admit you were wrong? This is a *relationship* – we need to meet each other halfway. I can't be the only one who compromises.'

'So don't be.'

'Well one of us has to! What are we supposed to do – argue for ever?'

Alice looked at him. A muscle twitched near her eye; the rest of her face was perfectly still.

'*Hello?* Are you in there?'

The seconds ticked by.

'Say something!'

But Alice couldn't. She felt like T was suddenly

thousands of miles away – like she was gazing down on him from outer space.

He dragged a hand through his artfully mussed chestnut-brown hair – the hair Alice had ruffled countless times. 'What? What is it? Are you pissed off at me? Are you . . . are you trying to break up with me?' His voice cracked on the word *up*. 'Just say something.'

'I . . .' Alice kneaded her fingers. 'I . . .'

'Just say it! If you want to dump me, then fucking dump me.'

'I-I don't know *what* I want.'

'Fuck that.' Tristan shoved at his mug. It was only half drunk, and his eyes were rimmed with red. 'You obviously know exactly what you want. You've known it from the moment you walked in. But you can't say it. And you know why? Because you're a *coward*.'

Alice was shaking now. Tears brimmed and ran down her face. 'I'm sorry. I didn't mean to . . . I never wanted to hurt you.'

'Yeah, right,' Tristan choked, swiping furiously at his eyes. 'Why are you doing this? Is there . . . is there someone else?'

'No! Of course not.'

'Then why?'

Alice shook her head. Her voice was barely a whisper. 'I'm sorry.'

'Fuck "sorry"! You're too much of a coward to dump me, and you're too much of a coward to tell me why. Just stay away from me from now on, OK? Stay out of my life!'

Throwing down a twenty-pound note on the table, Tristan grabbed his coat and stumbled towards the door. *Failure.* The word rang in his head with each step he took. *Failure. Failure. Failure.* He couldn't make anything work. He couldn't even make it work with his best friend. Who else would even want him? His love life was over before it had even begun.

Chapter 8

'How's it going in there, sweetie babes?' Sonia trilled. She was loitering outside the dressing room at Sandro, her new favourite French boutique on Westbourne Grove, fiddling with the tassels of her purple pashmina. She and Bella had been shopping for hours, ignoring the January sales racks, of course, and harvesting the picks of the new spring collections.

Bella poked her head through the curtain. 'Not bad. I've found loads of stuff I like.'

'See? I told you you'd love this shop. Not to brag or anything, but people are always complimenting me on my eye for fashion.'

'Great. In that case, can you give me a second opinion on this outfit?'

'Of course, darling, but I'm sure I'll love it.' Sonia flung back the rest of the curtain. 'You always look absolutely fabu— Ugh!' she screeched, shoving Bella back into the dressing room. 'Quick! Hide yourself.'

'What?' Bella glanced down at the pink and beige harem trousers she was modelling. 'Don't you like them?'

'*Like* them?' Sonia screeched. 'I *loathe* them.'

'But harem pants are so in,' Bella protested, twisting in front of the mirror. 'And I thought I could double up and wear them to your party. Loads of film stars were wearing them when I went to LA with Daddy. We had drinks with Blake Lively, and she was rocking a pair.'

'TV stars. Exactly,' Sonia snorted. 'Just because Blake can pull them off doesn't mean you can. You look like you're wearing an overstuffed nappy. You look like a giant baby who's pooed its pants. You look like—'

'*OK*, shut up!' Bella whipped round. 'So you don't like them. You don't have to be such a bitch about it.'

'Sweetie!' Sonia pouted. 'I'm not being a bitch. I'm only trying to protect you, I promise. You don't want to look like a fashion failure. Do you?'

Bella folded her arms.

'It's just, you're so gorgeous, I hate to see you wearing something that doesn't suit you. Especially at my mega-awesome birthday party. And this place has so much cool stuff.' Drawing Bella out of the dressing room, Sonia plucked a tiny leather miniskirt off the rack. 'Now, which would you prefer: to make your bum look like a nappy, or to make your legs look like a million dollars?'

Bella examined the skirt. 'Hmmm . . . I guess . . . I mean, I never wear miniskirts . . . But Alice Rochester's always wearing them, and she looks amazing.'

Sonia gritted her teeth. *Alice, Alice, Alice.* The entire planet was like one big broken record. 'Hmph. You think Alice Rochester has good taste in clothes? Wrong. It's all down to *my* guidance. I'm the one who got her into miniskirts. I styled her for years. As I said, I'm not the kind of person who likes to brag, but I've been told that I'm the best fashion guru at St C's. Alice once said she thought the school should let me design our uniforms – I'd make them *so* much sexier than they are.' Sonia stared into the distance for a moment. 'But anyway – how many times do I have to tell you: Alice. Rochester. Is. *Over*. Hey!' Pointing, she grabbed Bella's arm. 'Is that Tristan Murray-Middleton?'

'What? Where?'

Bella swivelled. Outside in the wintry night, a tall boy with messy chestnut hair was wandering past the window. He was wearing a soft-looking striped scarf wound several times round his neck. His hands were buried in his pockets, and his eyes were fixed on the ground.

'Oh my god, it is.' Bella clasped her hands. 'Swoon. T is ridiculously fit – trust Alice Rochester to have the hottest boyfriend in school. She knows all the cutest Hasted House guys.'

Sonia suppressed the urge to throw a fit. '*Excuse* me, darling, but you seem to think that Alice Rochester is the only person with an in at Hasted House. I am super-good friends with Tristan. He adores me. T!' she shrieked, waving frantically.

Tristan kept walking.

'Tristan! Tristaaan! Teee!'

'Stop!' Bella grabbed her arm. 'He can't hear you.'

'Hmph. The windows must be double-glazed.' Smiling sweetly, Sonia looked her new BFF up and down. 'I have a good idea – why don't you change out of your nappy, while I go catch him? Tristaaan!' Banging open the shop door, she bolted through the evening as fast as she could on her four-inch heels. 'Wait up!'

The tall figure, which was now halfway down the street, stopped.

'Darling! It's me.'

'Oh.' Tristan gave a forced smile. 'Hiya, Sone. This is a surprise.'

'Isn't it, though?' She kissed him on the cheek. 'How on earth are you, darling? I haven't seen you since the ski trip.'

'Fine. Great.' Tristan paused. He'd been moping round Notting Hill, replaying and analysing and mourning his relationship with Alice for the past few hours, and the last thing he wanted to do was make small talk. But he was too well brought up to show it. 'And how are you?'

'Oh, I'm fabulous! You're so sweet to ask. Bella Scott and I have been shopping till we drop – we're having such a blast. It's incredible! I haven't had this much fun in decades.' Sonia grinned smugly. Hopefully Tristan would pass on her little speech to Alice, and then Alice would know how brilliantly Sonia was coping without her. And then she'd be sorry. 'Bells! There you are!' she added, as Bella swung out of Sandro, hunching into her coat. She flung her arms round her new BFF. 'I was just telling T what an amazing day we're having. Heehee!'

'Hi, T,' Bella said softly.

'Now, darling, tell me you bought that sexy miniskirt like I advised you.'

'Uh, no, I didn't have time to try it on.'

'Silly thing!' Sonia swatted her playfully. 'We'll have to go back and buy it tomorrow. Maybe I'll even treat you to it. I just adore treating my friends. Oh, T, speaking of treats, Bella and I were about to go spoil ourselves rotten with cocktails at Tiny Robot. Weren't we, darls?'

'I don't—'

'Join us!' Sonia interrupted.

'Um, well, I . . .' Tristan paused. He was on the verge of refusing. But suddenly, he shivered. For the past few hours, throughout his dark wanderings, his brooding thoughts had kept him numb to the cold – but now he felt the January chill seep into his bones. He hugged his coat closer. 'Sure, why not? Lead the way.'

Sonia was still chattering five minutes later when she pushed open the door to Tiny Robot, one of Notting Hill's hippest hangouts. As usual, the minuscule bar was packed to the brim. Trendy west Londoners crowded round the small wooden tables, sipping drinks, munching burgers and complaining about the bitter-cold winter. Sonia, Bella and Tristan squeezed round a table meant for two, and ordered drinks.

'So, darling, what's going on in the world of Tristan Murray-Middleton?' Sonia spoke as casually as she could, smoothing her already sleek hair. 'Who have you been hanging out with? What parties have you been to? Any good gossip?' She waited, holding her breath. Surely T would say something about Alice. She hadn't heard news of Alice, or anyone in her ex-crew, for days. Even Facebook stalking had failed to yield intelligence.

But Tristan only shrugged. He gulped back half his beer as soon as the waiter set it down. 'Not much. I sort of want to get back to school, actually. I've had enough of London.'

'Why?' Sonia prodded. 'You mean you haven't been having fun? Are you getting bored of hanging out with the same old people all the time? Are you just so tired of the same old gossip and the same old parties? Because if you are, I *totally* know what you mean.' She took a sip of her mojito, her eyes still fixed on him.

'By the way,' Bella cut in, 'how's Alice? Ow!' she yelped, as Sonia jabbed a spike heel into her shin under the table.

Tristan didn't seem to notice. He was staring into his beer. 'Dunno.'

'What do you mean?' Sonia's eyes darted to his face. 'How can you not know? You see Alice all the time.'

T didn't reply.

'Don't you?'

'No. Not any more.'

Sonia gripped her mojito, waiting. After a few seconds, she couldn't stand it any more. '*What do you mean?* Tell us!'

'I mean . . . Alice . . . She bro— I mean, it's over.'

'OMG!' Sonia gasped, trying as hard as she could to keep the grin off her face. 'Did you dump her? You did, didn't you? That is such major gossip! I can't believe it!'

Biting her lip, Bella turned her blue eyes sympathetically on T.

'Poor you. I always thought you and Alice were the best couple in the world. Are you OK?'

'What happened?' Sonia practically howled.

'I don't really want to talk about it.' Tristan's voice was flat.

'But . . . but . . .'

'It's OK,' Bella soothed. 'You don't have to talk about it. Sometimes if you're feeling sad, it's good just to be with friends.' Tentatively she put out her hand. For a second, it hovered over T's – then she rested it on the table, a centimetre from his.

Sonia fought the instinct to let her jaw drop on its hinge. Bella was gazing at T with sappy puppy-dog eyes. Her big blues were fixed on his lips as he took a sip of his beer. She probably wouldn't notice if Sonia stripped to her thong and tap-danced on the table.

'Ahem!' Sonia declared, scraping back her chair. 'Excuse me. I'm just going to the loo.'

In the toilets, she stood in front of the mirror, her black eyes gleaming back at her in the glass. It was so obvious – how could she not have thought of this before? One way of getting revenge on Alice was right within her grasp.

Chapter 9

The first day of term at St Cecilia's was always chaos, but today, the icy pelting rain had turned the school into an obstacle course from hell, making streams of pathways, lakes of potholes and swamps of the manicured lawns.

'Quick, under here!' shrieked Jemimah Calthorpe de Vyle-Hanswicke. She ducked under an archway, pulling her fourteen-year-old sister Charlie with her, and pushed her damp black fringe out of her eyes. 'Lovely, isn't it?' she chuckled.

'Oh, yeah,' Charlie snorted. 'We're practically in paradise.'

Shivering, the sisters gazed out at Quad, the ivy-covered red-brick courtyard that made up the oldest part of school. Teachers were darting from doorway to doorway, huddled under their raincoats while attempting to tick things off on clipboards. Meanwhile, girls and their parents were hauling trunks and suitcases over the sodden ground, trying their best to fend off the country mud.

'You bloody idiot!' shouted one mother, whose husband had dropped a suitcase into a puddle and splattered her cashmere cape.

Mimah giggled.

Charlie only sighed.

'Hey, what's wrong? Apart from the weather, I mean.'

Charlie shrugged. 'Nothing. But . . . is it weird that I'm kind of glad to be back at school?'

'Yeah, you freak.' Mimah draped her arm round Charlie's waif-like shoulders. 'Come on, what's getting to you?'

'It's just . . . it's such a relief to be out of our house. I know it sounds awful, but being at home with Mummy these days isn't exactly fun.'

'Was it ever?' Mimah laughed. But a shadow crossed her face. Charlie was right. Their mother was in worse shape than ever. For the entire holiday, she'd roved the dark corridors of their Victorian pile, guzzling sleeping pills, popping antidepressants and swigging booze. Mummy had been depressed for almost a year now – ever since their father had been lambasted in the tabloids for sleeping with a prostitute and had abandoned their family for a life in Spain – and Mimah had no idea how to help her. She stared down the wide brick steps in front of them, across the misty expanse of the Great Lawn. Sometimes it swept over her like a gale, how much her life had changed in the past year. Once upon a time, her father had been her hero, but now she hadn't seen him in months; and lately, she'd been taking more care of her mum than her mum took of her. But she did her best not to think about these things – not to let their darkness suck her under. And this, as Charlie said, was a lot easier at school.

Mimah gave her sister a small smile. 'Shall we brave it?' she asked, nodding at the sodden grass.

Charlie drew a deep breath, and mustered a grin. 'I'm ready if you are.'

They ran down the steps, hunching away from the rain. On either side, school buildings loomed in the fog – the Art block, with its disused sloping attics; the shiny new glass-and-steel Tuck In Café; and, in the distance, the boarding houses.

'Ewww!' Mimah cried as mud oozed over her leather boots.

'Watch out for that puddle,' Charlie cackled, giving her a shove.

'Now you've done it!' Mimah locked an arm round Charlie's neck. 'Someone's asking for a mud bath. Or maybe I'll snap a pic of you looking like a drowned rat and send it to Felix! How *is* our darling Felix, anyway?'

Charlie's face turned pink. Felix Hedley-Bunk was her new boyfriend, and her sister hadn't exactly met him under the best of circumstances. Last term, Mimah had caught the two of them with drugs in the woods near school. She'd ended up saying the pills were hers in order to save Charlie's school career, and had come *this* close to being expelled. Only at the last minute had she been punished with community service instead.

'Oh, he's good,' Charlie said, escaping Mimah's stranglehold. 'I think he's turning over a new leaf – you know, not breaking school rules and stuff.' She glanced at her sister, hoping for a sign of approval. 'But how about you – have you heard from that guy you were tutoring at Hasted Community Centre – what's-his-name?'

'Aidan.' Mimah frowned. 'No. Not for two whole weeks.'

'I can't believe it,' Charlie said, gripping her hood against a gust of wind. 'You guys liked each other so much. And those pictures you showed me – he was super-sexy.'

'Don't rub it in,' Mimah sighed. 'God, I wish I hadn't messed everything up. I should never have lied to him.'

She stamped over a clump of wet leaves. Aidan had been her only tutee during her community service, and they'd despised each other on sight. Infuriated at how judgemental he'd been of her posh accent, Mimah had invented a whole new past for herself – one in which she came from Hasted, went to a state school and had been abandoned by her mum when she was a kid. By the time Aidan had found out the truth, his and Mimah's feelings for each other had changed. For a moment, Mimah had even thought she was falling in love. She shut her eyes, remembering that awful moment when they'd bumped into each other at Sir Lucian Scott's Christmas party, him working as a waiter, her swathed in designer clothes and surrounded by her boarding-school friends. *Stay away from me. For ever.* Aidan's hurt, humiliated words had haunted her since that night.

'Why don't you get in touch with him?' Charlie's voice brought her back to earth. 'Just apologise. I'm sure he'll listen.'

'He won't. No way.' Mimah shook her head, her blunt

black fringe swaying like a curtain. 'He never wants to see me again. My only hope is Thursday – we've got tutoring at the community centre. Even if he's requested another teacher, I'll at least get to lay eyes on him.' She stopped. They'd reached Tudor House, home to the Lower Sixth. 'Come up for some tea? You won't be able to unpack till the porters bring your suitcases to your room.'

Charlie nodded. But just as they were starting up the carpeted staircase—

'Jemimah!' snapped a reedy voice. The speaker was a bony, thin-lipped woman whose frizzy hair looked like a tangle of dead worms.

Mimah sighed. Wonderful. Mrs Hoare, aka the Ho – great first person to bump into. She forced herself to smile. 'Happy New Year, Mrs Hoare.'

'And Happy New Year to you, Jemimah,' the housemistress practically sneered. 'Where do you think you're going? I assume you were coming straight to see me to sign in for the new term?'

'Oh, of course, I . . .'

'Because that would have been the sensible thing to do,' the Ho blinked her vulturous eyes, 'considering there's someone here who's been waiting to see you.'

Mimah caught her breath. Who could be coming to see her here? The only person she knew in Hasted was Aidan. Maybe he'd changed his mind. Maybe he wanted to tell her how much he'd missed her and that he'd made a terrible mistake.

The next instant, her stomach sank. Mr Vicks, the Head

of Physics, was emerging from the Ho's office. Of course. How could she be such an idiot?

'Hello, Jemimah. Good holiday?' Mr Vicks said. The Physics teacher was as fierce-looking as the two yappy terriers he was constantly taking for walks around the school grounds, but right now, his eyes were sparkling. He had a soft spot for Jemimah, who he said was one of St Cecilia's most talented science students ever. And he should know, since he'd taught at the school for about a hundred years. It was Mr Vicks who had stopped Mimah being expelled, and who had dreamed up her community service punishment instead.

She gave him a smile. 'Don't worry, I haven't forgotten about tutoring on Thursday. Is it at the same time this term?'

Mr Vicks shook his head. 'Actually, no. I've got some extremely good news. The community centre no longer needs you. It seems your tutee has dropped out.'

'W-what?'

'He informed them last week. He won't be going back.'

'But . . . but why?' Mimah could hear her voice going shrill. 'What reason did he give? Has he found another teacher?'

'I doubt it.' Mr Vicks smiled. 'It's very admirable that you care, Jemimah, but these things happen. I imagine the boy's life got in the way. People fall through the cracks all the time. But the good news is, since you'll have more free time, you and I can start our university tutorials. I'll tutor you for Cambridge every Wednesday lunchtime – I have an idea for a research project we can work on. Does that suit?'

'S-sure.' Mimah somehow managed a smile, even though she felt like her heart had stopped working. 'Thanks, Mr Vicks.'

As soon as the teachers had left, she bolted up the stairs.

'Wait up,' Charlie panted. 'What do you think happened to Aidan?'

'I don't know. But he was so determined to pass his maths GCSE – how can he have dropped out? That exam meant the world to him – he wanted to be an engineer. He was desperate to quit all those odd jobs he was having to work at to make ends meet. Oh god, it's all my fault!' Mimah's eyes filled with tears.

'Sweetie!' Charlie exclaimed in alarm. Mimah hardly ever cried; she was one of the toughest girls Charlie knew. 'It's not your fault. You didn't— What are you doing?'

Mimah was scrabbling for her phone. 'I have to ring him – I have to persuade him to stay. Maybe if I apologise enough he'll realise he's being silly. How can I convince him not to risk his future just because of us?'

She held her mobile to her ear. Then, slowly, she lowered her arm.

'Something's wrong,' she said, her inky eyes wide. 'He's disconnected his phone.'

Chapter 10

'Darling, you'll never believe what fab hols I've just had!' Isabelle Bruin's voice echoed down the corridor of Locke House. 'Mummy and Daddy took me and Prunie to St Barts and we spent ten days stretched out on sunloungers while the locals pumped us full of pina coladas. All I had to do was raise my little finger and a whole gang of massively keen waiters would come running. Paradise!'

Finally, her voice receded. Lauren Taylor crept out of the shadows of the cloakroom, where she'd been crouching among the coats and hats and boots for almost ten whole minutes, and peered into the foyer. Yes, she knew hiding was pathetic – but the prospect of walking out into the brightly lit Year Ten boarding house without a full set of body armour was terrifying. She couldn't delay it for ever, though. Screwing up her nerve, she poked one foot, then the other, into the hall.

Bang! The front door flew open. Charlie Calthorpe de Vyle-Hanswicke burst inside.

'Oh!' Charlie said, and froze, her black eyes fixed on Lauren's blue ones.

'Oh,' Lauren whispered, like some kind of pathetic echo. She shrank back. Charlie Calthorpe de Vyle-Hanswicke was the worst person she could possibly have bumped into. Not only was she one of the coolest girls in Year Ten, but she was Georgie Fortescue's best friend. Lauren's mind flashed back to that moment on the last day of term when she'd discovered that her diary had been posted on Facebook for all her classmates to read. Charlie's face had been right next to Georgie's sneering one, fading in and out of focus as Lauren's knees weakened and she sank to the cold, hard earth.

Lauren shivered at the memory. Out in the hallway, Charlie shifted her umbrella from one hand to the other. She opened her mouth, as if to say something. But the next second—

'Charlotte!' cried a voice. Mrs Gould, the Year Ten housemistress, was bouncing down the corridor. Mrs Gould bounced everywhere – she was one of those teachers who was so cheerful it made your skin crawl. 'Happy New Year, my dear. Lucky to bump into you, I've been wanting— Oh my!' She jumped, spotting Lauren in the shadows. Her hand flew to her chest. 'Lauren, dear girl, you nearly gave me a heart attack. But yes, excellent, I've been wanting to talk to you too.'

Lauren forced a smile, slinking out from between a raincoat and a shaggy faux-fur jacket. She'd been hoping she could slip away while Charlie was distracted by Mrs Gould. Clearly not.

'Now, girls,' said the housemistress, her curly blond hair jiggling up and down, 'here's a piece of luck: it turns out you're going to be sharing a room for the rest of the year. I've swapped Lauren into your dormitory, Charlotte, in order to get her away from Geor— Er, I mean, in order to give her a change of scene.'

Lauren and Charlie glanced at each other. Mrs Gould beamed. 'All right? Everybody happy? Good. Charlotte, why don't you take Lauren upstairs and help her move her things? She's switching into Tabitha Fitzsimmons's old bed.'

The two girls climbed the stairs in silence. There was no way Lauren was going to speak first. She had no idea what Charlie was thinking about this new roommate situation – but probably nothing good. She sneaked a look at her companion. Even though Charlie was Georgie Fortescue's partner in crime, Lauren had always thought she was one of the prettiest girls in their year. She had a delicate, waifish figure, and although her face was thin and pale, when she smiled her features shone as if from an inner light, her black eyes sparkling in her marble-white skin. No wonder she had a boyfriend, when Lauren had never even come close to kissing a guy. She looked like some kind of pixie; a sprite who should be living in the woods. Lauren frowned. If only Charlie *did* live in the woods – then she wouldn't be here, making Lauren's life hell.

'*Loving* the new haircut, Gussie,' came a voice from the

first floor landing. Lauren looked up. Holly Holm and Augusta Chapman were starting down the stairs.

'Thanks,' Augusta replied. 'At first I thought it made me look like a lesbo, but now I'm getting used to it. Oh my gosh, guess who said he liked it at Piers Penfold's party the other day? Hugo Rochester. Hugo is sooo sweet, I— Shit!' Catching sight of Lauren, Augusta clapped a hand over her mouth. She and Holly squeezed past, then burst into giggles as they reached the front hall.

'You idiot,' tittered Holly. 'Mentioning Hugo Rochester around Lauren Taylor? She'll be in therapy for months.'

'Freak,' Augusta whispered loudly. 'Do you think she's still *obsessed* with him?'

'Probably. Her diary was so insane.'

Lauren had turned bright red. This was as bad as all her worst nightmares – everyone was still talking about her. And on top of it all, she'd just remembered: Hugo Rochester was Charlie's boyfriend's best friend.

'By the way,' Charlie burst out, 'I was just wondering . . .'

Lauren swallowed, bracing herself.

'The New Year Social on the weekend – what are you wearing?'

'The . . . the New Year what?' Lauren stammered. She hadn't expected an actual civilised question.

'The Hasted House–St Cecilia's New Year Social?'

'What's that?' This had to be some kind of trick.

'Come on. Don't tell me you've never heard of the Social. It's massive.'

'Um, well considering I only got to this school a couple of months ago, can you really be that surprised?'

Charlie blinked. 'Uh, I guess not. Well, the New Year Social is the major Year Ten party of this term. The school buses us over to Hasted House and they lay on the poshest school ball ever.'

'Hasted House?' Lauren stopped short. They'd reached the threshold of the dorm room, but she didn't even bother to look in. 'W-when is this thing?'

'Friday night.'

'*This* Friday?' A cold hand seemed to grip Lauren's stomach. This couldn't be happening. Not only did she have to deal with the girls in her year; in a few days, she'd have to face all the boys at Hasted House too. Including *him*. Her knees went weak. 'I'm not going.'

'But you have to.'

'No way. I'll stay at school.'

Charlie was shaking her head. 'Listen, Lauren, you don't have a choice – no one does. It's one of those compulsory school things.'

Lauren blinked. For a split second, she thought she detected a hint of sympathy in Charlie's voice. But before she could be sure, Charlie's phone rang. Both girls saw the name on the screen at the same instant: GEORGIE FORTESCUE.

'*Hello?*' Charlie's eyes darted to Lauren's face as she answered. 'Of course I wasn't ignoring your calls! Just got back to school, babe. Yeah, it sucks. He *did?* Really? Oh, and I have news. Uh, hang on, I can't talk in here. Wait one sec.'

Clasping the phone to her chest, she slipped from the room. Lauren sank down on the mattress of her new, bare bed.

Chapter 11

The rain pelted down all afternoon, and before the wintry sun could beat its feeble way through the clouds, the first day of term darkened into night. But inside Tudor House, the Lower Sixth common room was bright and buzzing. Girls were squashed into cushy red armchairs and draped over plump couches, watching TV, listening to music and gossiping.

Sonia marched into the room, a shiny pink thermos dangling from her manicured fingertips, and planted herself on a sofa next to Bella Scott.

'Ugh,' she groaned.

Bella lowered her copy of *Grazia*. 'What's up?'

'I'm exhausted. I wish my masseuse did boarding-school calls. Unpacking my stuff was such an ordeal. Can you believe how long it took us?'

'Um, yes,' Bella retorted, 'considering that you had an entire case just devoted to your mineral-water collection. You literally took an hour lining up all those Evian bottles with the labels facing outwards. Talk about anal.'

Sonia yawned. 'Oh, please, darling. I'd rather be anal than slovenly. Did you see how Dylan Taylor dumped all her clothes into her drawers without even folding them?'

'Yeah.' Bella tossed her magazine on to the coffee table and began plaiting a piece of her layered brown hair. 'It was like she wanted to get away from you as fast as possible.'

'Good. That's just the way it should be.' Sonia took a swig from her thermos. 'Want some no-calorie hot chocolate?'

'Want me to vom everywhere?' Bella retorted. 'Darling, you should honestly stop dieting all the time. You have a fabulous figure. Do you want to turn into skin and bone?'

Sonia tossed her hair. That question didn't even merit a response. She'd always been obsessed with watching her weight – and this term she was stepping it up a notch. If she didn't look uber-svelte at her fabulous birthday bash, she might as well give up on life.

'Now, darling,' she said, slicking on a layer of lip gloss, 'there's no point wasting breath on Dylan Taylor and my delicious diet drinks. We have far better things to discuss. Such as . . . Tristan!'

'Shhh!' Bella reddened. 'Keep it down.'

'I couldn't believe how into you he was,' Sonia went on, just as loudly as before. 'He was practically drooling. I was shocked you two weren't snogging in Tiny Robot by the time I came back from the loo.'

'Don't be ridiculous.' Bella swatted her. 'But . . . but do you really think so?'

'Darls, I don't think so – I know so. Believe me – I've

been mates with T for years, and I've never seen him like that.'

'Really? No. You must have been imagining it. I mean, he only just broke up with—'

'Well, hello, girls,' drawled a voice.

Bella's mouth snapped shut. Two people had flopped on to the neighbouring couch: Alice Rochester and Tally Abbott.

'You've gone very quiet all of a sudden.' Alice shot Sonia a mocking glance. 'What were you talking about?'

'Oh, n-nothing,' Bella stammered. 'Hi, guys. Ali, how was your holid—' She fell silent as Sonia's elbow landed in her ribcage.

'Hello, *Tally*,' Sonia said pointedly, and hid her face behind Bella's *Grazia*.

Giggling, Tally kicked her feet up on the coffee table and swept her white-blond hair into a messy bun. She was wearing grey-and-yellow St Cecilia's trackie bums and an oversized knit jumper – and yet she still managed to look stunning.

'Darling,' she nudged Alice, 'how are you holding up? Have you heard from T?'

'Shhh!' Alice shot a look at Sonia.

'Oops. Sorry. But babe,' Tally whispered, 'everyone's gonna find out sooner or later.'

'I'd have preferred it to be later,' Alice retorted, pulling out a copy of *Julius Caesar* and cracking it open. 'And I don't really want to talk about my love life.'

'OK, grumpy,' Tally chuckled. 'By the way, could you

please stop working? School doesn't officially start till tomorrow morning. Anyway, I thought you'd finished reading that play ages ago.'

'I did. And now I'm rereading it. It would be so like the Ho to give us a start-of-term quiz tomorrow. I refuse to be caught unprepared.' Chewing her lip, Alice jotted a note in the margin.

'Swot,' Tally snickered – even though it wasn't really funny. Alice got her crazy work ethic from her father. Richard Rochester, one of the biggest traders in the City, valued academic achievement above basically anything in the world, and if Alice didn't get top marks, he'd be seriously peeved. Not that he'd yell or anything – yelling wasn't in Richard Rochester's repertoire. He'd simply treat Alice with a sort of disdainful disappointment, which was much, much worse.

Suddenly, as Alice scribbled, a loud snort emanated from behind Sonia's magazine.

Bella jumped. 'What's wrong?'

'Oh, nothing.' Sonia examined her cuticles. 'I was just thinking – isn't it interesting how some people have to work sooo hard to do well, and others are just, you know, naturals?'

Alice's face twitched. '*Loser!*' she coughed.

'And you know what *else* I think?' Sonia went on, her voice becoming shrill. 'I think that really, truly clever people can get good marks without constantly swotting away. What do you think, Bells?'

'Uh . . .' Bella glanced towards Alice. 'I don't know. I

mean, I respect people who work hard. It takes a lot of discipline.'

'Discipline,' Sonia scoffed. 'Exactly. Discipline's the most boring personality trait in the world. I personally wouldn't want to be friends with any dweeb whose major characteristic was *discipline.*'

On the other couch, Alice started gazing around, her face puzzled.

'Do you hear something?' she asked Tally, pretending to strain her ears. 'I think I hear some sort of insect droning over there.'

Tally giggled.

Sonia's eyes narrowed. 'Anyway,' she snapped in a significant voice, 'Bellsy darling, what were we saying before we were so rudely interrupted? Ah, yes! We were talking about *You-Know-Who.*'

Bella shook her head rapidly. 'Oh, no, that's OK, we can talk about that later.'

'Don't be ridiculous, sweetie. Why shouldn't we talk about it now? Free speech is a fundamental human right.' Sonia took a smug sip of her hot chocolate. 'So, we have to arrange for you and You-Know-Who to meet up soon. I have an idea! Why don't I text You-Know-Who in a few days and see when You-Know-Who is free?'

Alice snickered. She nudged Tally. 'Don't you just adore You-Know-Who?'

'You-Know-*Who*?'

'You know, You-Know-Who!'

'Oh! I didn't know you knew You-Know-Who too!'

Both girls cackled. Tally snuggled deeper into her baggy jumper. 'God, it's freezing, isn't it?' she grumbled. 'I hate winter. Do you think anyone would notice if we sneaked off for a holiday somewhere hot?'

'Hmmm.' Alice stroked her chin. 'Where did you have in mind? Hawaii?'

'No way. Flight's too long for a mini-break. I'd settle for somewhere closer. Ugh, if only Daddy hadn't cut off my credit cards, I'd totally take off to Italy. Or Spain. Mmm. I haven't been to Spain in ages.'

Alice laughed. 'Yes you have.'

'No I haven't.'

'Yes, you have!'

Tally rolled her eyes. 'Um, babe, I think I know where I've been.'

'Yeah, and you told me you'd just been to Spain.'

'No I didn't. When?'

'Over New Year! To visit your aunt!'

Tally's eyes widened slightly. 'Oh. Right. I mean, of course. But . . . I meant . . . a different part of Spain. It wasn't very hot there.' She smiled. But Alice was staring at her. And so, from across the coffee table, was Sonia.

In the silence, Tally picked an invisible piece of fluff off her tracksuit bottoms. 'Anyway . . . I've got to catch up on emails. Think I'll go upstairs.'

Perplexity clouded Alice's dark brown eyes as she watched her friend slip through the doorway. Again that feeling nagged at her – that something just didn't add up . . .

Suddenly, Sonia's voice broke in on her reverie. 'This common room feels very crowded, don't you think, Bella darling? I think *some* people have the right idea, leaving. Don't you wish some *other* people would follow their room-mates upstairs?'

Alice rolled her eyes. 'Oh, shut up, Sonia! Can't you just stop being a busybody freak for one second and mind your own fucking business?'

Across the coffee table, Sonia's face went so tense it looked like she might implode. She sat bolt upright, her eyes practically spitting sparks of rage.

'*You* shut up!' she shrieked, grabbing her thermos and unscrewing the lid. 'And take that!' She gave the container a violent shove, sending a thick brown flood across the coffee table. Liquid soaked Alice's jeans and sloshed over her book, obscuring her meticulous notes.

The room fell silent. All eyes flew to their corner.

'Oops,' Sonia smirked. But suddenly, as Alice leaped up, her sneer turned into a gasp.

'How dare you, Sonia Khan!' Alice growled, towering over Sonia's seat. She stuck her thin, angular face right into her ex-friend's. 'You think this is a joke? You think you can take me on and win? Wrong! You'd better watch your fucking back.' Her jeans still dripping, she stormed from the room.

'Bravo,' Sonia called after her, clapping her hands in sardonic one-woman applause.

Suddenly, the Cold War had turned too hot to handle.

Chapter 12

'Rehearsal time, losers!' crowed Jasper von Holstadt, barging into Tristan and Seb's dorm room at Hasted House without bothering to knock. 'Come on, pens down, guitars out.'

Tristan's chestnut eyes remained fixed on his Economics essay. It was only one day into term and he was already swamped with work. Seb, of course, being a genius, had finished his essay, and was lying on his bed, under his posters of the cult 1960s films *Breathless* and *Blow-Up*, staring at his phone.

'Well this place is party town,' Jasper snorted. He shoved a half-unpacked duffel bag off an armchair and replaced it with his bum. 'Sebastian! What's so fascinating over there? You waiting for a spontaneous booty call from some fit bird?'

'Yeah.' Seb rolled his eyes. 'Your mum.'

Actually, Seb was waiting for a reply from Will Larkin, but he wasn't about to tell Jasper that. Sighing, he sent an accusatory glance at his phone. He hadn't heard a word from Will since he'd suggested meeting up this week, and he was starting to panic. Maybe he'd misread the whole situation. Maybe Will had realised he thought this was a date and had run a mile. Maybe Seb was crazy to think someone as cute as Will could ever like him. If only there was someone he could talk to about this. If only, among all his mates, there was someone he could ask for advice.

'Oi, dude,' Jasper said. He was now lounging with one foot up on T's desk, ignoring the fact that Tristan was staring at columns of numbers with his head in his hands. 'I was thinking of taking Dylan for dinner in Hasted on the weekend. What's that little French place you went with Alice's parents? Hey!' He raised his voice. 'Murray-Middleton. I'm talking to you.'

'I know. And I'm trying to block you out.' T massaged his forehead. 'Seriously, why are you here so early? Paper Bandits practice isn't meant to start for another ten minutes.'

Jasper shrugged. 'I was bored.'

'Bored? How can you be bored? I've never been this stressed in my life.'

'Come on, man, it's only homework. You need to chill out.'

'Chilling out is the last thing I need to do. I'm buried under a mountain of work. I haven't even started Jenks's English essay for tomorrow. The Shakespeare one, I mean.'

'Oh. That.' Jasper plucked a rubber band from T's desk and started twanging it between his fingers. 'Piece of piss.'

'What?' Tristan stared at him. 'Don't tell me you've done it.'

'Done and dusted. Printed out and on my desk.'

T shook his head in disbelief. Jasper wasn't even that clever. He wasn't dumb or anything – no Hasted House boys were dumb – but he was nowhere near the brightest in their class. He was usually up half the night when an essay was due, moaning and groaning and downing cases of Red Bull.

There was a knock on the door, and Rando peered in. 'Hey, guys. Ready for band practice?'

'Yep,' Seb said, hauling himself upright. His forehead furrowed as he caught a glimpse of Rando's face. 'Um, dude, are you OK?'

'Yeah. Why?'

'Well . . .' Seb hesitated. The truth was, Rando looked awful. His skin was grey underneath its freckles, his shoulders were slouched and his usually sparkly blue eyes were dull. But there was no way to point this out without sounding rude.

'Er, no reason. You just seem a bit . . . tired.'

Jasper guffawed. 'Thanks for your professional opinion about the state of my cousin's health, Nurse Ogilvy. But can we please start practice? T? This is getting annoying.'

'Fine.' Heaving a sigh as loud as a lawnmower, Tristan shoved his calculator across his desk. 'I can see no one's gonna leave me alone. I'll just have to drink a million coffees and stay up all night finishing this bastard.'

'Aw, poor wittle T,' Jasper mocked. 'He's got too much pwep. Now stop it with the moaning. Are you going to play us your new song, or what?'

'Hold your horses.' Tristan felt a wave of relief as he lifted his guitar from its stand at the foot of his bed. Music was always a welcome retreat when he was upset or stressed. And right now, he was both. Luckily, his new song perfectly reflected his mood.

'It's called "My Harpy Ex".' Tristan ran his fingers over the strings. Long, discordant notes filled the dorm room. He shut his eyes, breathed through his nose and began to sing in a flat, tortured whine.

> *Her fang marks*
> *Pierce my arm*
> *She is poison.*
> *Poisonnn.*

> *Her fist marks*
> *Bruise my face.*
> *She is savage.*
> *Savaaage.*

At this point, the music became frenzied.

> *And when I ask her why*
> *She says, 'Go to hell and die.*
> *I will make myself a crow*
> *And I'll gnaw upon your bones.'*

> *And when I beg and plead*
> *She says, 'Get up off your knees.*

I will build myself a nest
Where I'll feed upon your flesh.'

Her teeth marks
Tear my neck.
She is evil.
Evilll.

Her cruel words
Break my heart.
She is vicious.
Viciousssss.

The shrieking chords died away, and Tristan stared broodingly at the carpet for effect.

Seb coughed.

Rando frowned into the distance.

Slowly, Jasper leaned forward. 'What. The. Fuck?'

Tristan raised his eyes.

'No, seriously, man, what was that? I mean, no offence, but I don't think we have a hit on our hands with that little number. Unless all our fans happen to be S and M sickos.' Jasper chortled. No one else laughed. 'Bloody hell!' He banged T's desk. 'What a miserable crew. Seb mooning over his phone. Rando moping about like an orphaned kitten for no reason whatsoever. And T – don't get me started. I mean, what kind of washout are you?'

'My girlfriend dumped me, OK?' Tristan shouted. 'Ever

heard of sympathy? Ever heard of cutting a mate some slack?'

'Slack is the opposite of what you need,' Jasper shot back. 'You need a kick up the arse. Pining away like a lovestruck virgin, writing freakish melancholy music – yeah, brilliant way to get over a break-up. What you need is a good shag.'

At this, Rando walked to the window and looked on to the dark courtyard below. Tristan rolled his eyes.

'I'm serious!' Jasper insisted. 'The best way to get over Alice is to shag as many girls as possible. She's the only girl you've ever slept with! You need to get the memory of her out of your system. You need to have fun with other fitties. And when you have, you won't be one of those lame gayboys who've only shagged one babe!'

Seb's fingers tightened over his phone.

'Tell you what,' Jasper went on, his tone slightly softer. 'I'll take you out on the weekend and we'll go on the girl-hunt. We'll have you playing the field again in no time.'

'No thanks.' Tristan swallowed and huddled deeper into his chair. 'I know all about your girl-hunting techniques. I reckon I can manage.'

'Oh, obviously you can manage,' Jasper retorted. 'Like you're managing right now. Seb, help me convince him. Seb? Seb?'

But Seb was staring at his phone. A text had just appeared. A text from Will. He could hardly believe it was real, he'd been hoping for it for so long.

Hey! Sorry for the late reply – I'm rehearsing a Shakespeare play at the Globe Theatre and it's busy busy busy. You free a week on Saturday? Don't have a spare minute till then. If you're up for it, it's a date.

Seb shoved his phone back in his pocket before anyone could grab it. He hardly noticed Jasper throw a book to get his attention. He hardly considered the twelve whole days between now and next weekend. Only one thing filled his head, only one word: 'date'.

Chapter 13

Mrs Hoare planted herself next to the cash register of the St Cecilia's Charity Shop in Hasted, her arms folded and her sensibly clad foot tapping the vinyl floor. It was Wednesday, Electives Day at St Cecilia's, when every week girls had the afternoon off lessons to play sport, rehearse plays or pursue supposedly valuable hobbies such as 'Computer Skills' and 'Woodworking'. This week, Alice and Dylan had been assigned Community Service. The Ho had been lecturing them for the past ten minutes and, like some sort of long-life robot, showed no sign of stopping.

'And as I said,' her reedy voice droned on, 'the St Cecilia's Charity Shop is a serious business. It was set up as a way for our pupils to give back to society, by donating and selling their second-hand possessions in aid of good causes, and it is a very important part of our school's sixth-form culture.'

'Yes, Mrs Hoare, of course, we—'

'It is also a very big responsibility,' the Ho interrupted, narrowing her eyes at Alice. 'And not one that I, person-ally, would have entrusted to the two of you.'

Alice gave a saccharine smile. The Ho had had it in for

her ever since she'd caught her hooking up with T during a school social last term, and none of Alice's time-tested teacher-charming methods had been able to get her back on side.

'You can trust us, don't worry,' Dylan jumped in.

'Hmmm,' muttered the Ho, pursing her already narrow lips into a line as thin as string. 'Since it's school policy that every Lower Sixth girl gets a chance to run the shop, I suppose I'll have to.' And with a last suspicious look round the premises, she left.

As soon as the door shut, Alice let out a loud snort. 'At bloody last!' On the sale rack behind her, a Marc Jacobs bag from two seasons ago jiggled on its leather strap. 'I thought that old bat would never shut up. God, she hates me. And what was she rabbiting on about? *Big responsibility* – puhl-ease. It's not like people are lining up to get in here.'

'I know, I'm so shocked.' Dylan giggled. 'I thought the entire population of Hasted would be dying to get their mitts on our designer cast-offs.' She glanced at a pair of scuffed Gucci heels displayed on a shelf. 'By the way, is it just me, or is it kind of wrong, hawking our rejects to the town's inhabitants?'

'Um, it's obviously wrong. I mean, most of them probably don't even know their Prada from their Primark – why should we waste our perfectly good designer pieces on them? But hey, babe . . .' Alice's voice was wheedling. 'I have a really good idea. I'm dying for a coffee. Why don't you run to Starbucks, and I'll man the register?'

'Oh my god, yeah!' Dylan said sarcastically. 'I would just so love to get you a coffee. In fact, why don't I fetch and carry for you all day long? Thanks so much for suggesting it.' She flicked a crumpled old receipt into Alice's glaring face. 'Who do you think I am, the replacement for your lapdog Sonia?'

'Pretty crap replacement, if you are,' Alice huffed. Suddenly, she burst out laughing. No one talked to her like that – Tally was too nonchalant, and the rest of the world was too scared – which was exactly what she'd grown to like about Dylan. 'Fine. If you're too lazy to get the coffees, I suppose I'll have to.'

'Actually, you won't,' Dylan said. 'Because I've got a much better plan. Personalised delivery service.'

'Um, I hate to break it to you, but Starbucks doesn't deliver.'

'Aha.' Dylan grinned. 'But Jasper von Holstadt does. I texted him earlier and told him we'd be here this afternoon. I sent him our coffee order before we even left school.'

'And he obeyed?'

'You bet he obeyed. He's on his best behaviour. He won't be lying again about being ill in a hurry. I've whipped him into shape.'

'Ha! Good thing I spied him in that guitar shop.' No sooner had Alice said this than her smile died on her lips. Why, oh why, had she brought that up? How stupid could she be, reminding herself of Rando, of their last happy day? Pain and longing welled inside her like a wave. She'd been trying so hard not to think about him. Not to think about the sound of his voice. The scent of his skin. The touch of his lips on her neck.

Dylan was staring at her. 'Al? Hello? Are you OK?'

'I . . .' Tears sprang to Alice's eyes. But before she could go on, the shop door flew open. She blinked rapidly and wiped her face.

'Special delivery!' Jasper cried. He was balancing a cardboard tray, piled a mile high with coffee, cakes, pastries, cookies, muffins and chocolates.

'What a feast!' Dylan guffawed. 'Talk about going over the top. Are you trying to murder us with sugar?'

'Nope. Just trying to see how high I can get you. After all, nothing's too sweet for my sweet.'

'Ugh,' Dylan groaned, 'you're killing me.'

'Me too.' Alice put on a strained smile and moved to shut the door. 'Just because you brought us snacks doesn't mean you can torture us with bad—'

She froze in her tracks. Whether the cold that enveloped her had originated in the icy air outside, or in the sight of the person suddenly framed in the doorway, she couldn't tell. All she knew was that her legs were weak.

'Hey, Rando!' Jasper's voice sounded very far away. 'What are you loitering over there for? How about acting like a normal person and coming inside? It's freezing out.'

Rando stepped over the threshold, his wavy hair falling over his face.

'Hey,' he said. His voice rasped like a rusty nail.

Alice couldn't reply. Her throat was too tight.

'Apologies for my antisocial cousin,' Jasper snorted. 'I have no idea why he's being so weird. I bumped into him in Starbucks, and when I said I was bringing you two coffee, I practically had to drag him here by his hair. Anyway.' His lips curved in a slow smile as he slid his arm round Dylan's waist. 'Hello, gorgeous. How about a kiss for the barista?'

Alice studied the floor. It was always awkward, having to watch your friends snog – but right now, awkward was an understatement. Rando was just a few feet away. The heat from his presence was radiating all down her body. Her blood was pounding. Her palms were clammy. It seemed like a bad dream – not being able to touch him. Not being able to fall into his arms.

'I heard about you and Tristan.'

Alice jumped at the sound of his voice. 'You . . . what?' she said stupidly.

'I heard about you and Tristan,' Rando repeated. He frowned and buried his hands in his pockets. 'He seems pretty upset. I'm sorry.'

'You're sorry?' Alice glanced up and, unprepared, met Rando's blue gaze. They both looked away at the same moment. Her heart was hammering in her chest.

Ring ring. Somewhere nearby, a phone went off.

'Oops, that's me,' Jasper said, drawing away from Dylan. 'Sorry, gorgeous. Reckon I'll take this outside.'

'But it's cold out,' Dylan grinned, playing with his lapel. 'Why don't you talk in here? No one's listening.'

'Yeah, right,' Jasper chortled, 'apart from all three of you.'

'We don't count, silly. I'm your girlfriend and they're your friends.'

'And this call's private.'

Dylan's eyes narrowed. 'What do you mean, "private"?'

'Shhh. *Hello? Yeah, hi.*'

'Jasper?' Dylan was pouting. 'Why's it private? What's the big secret?'

Frowning, he stuck his palm up in front of her face.

'Don't do that!' she cried, slapping it away.

'Ow! Why do you have to be so violent? *What? No, not you. Yep. Hang on one second.*' Jasper pushed past her. 'Look, I've got to go, babe. Oh, and by the way, don't worry about the coffee. It's on me.'

'Of course it's on you, you imbecile!' Dylan burst out as the door slammed behind him. 'You think I'm gonna pay for all those stupid doughnuts? You were supposed to be on your best behaviour this week. What happened to *that?*'

Next to Alice, Rando scuffed his shoe on the floor. 'Umm, I better go too. Loads of homework to do. Bye. See you round.'

As the door swung shut for a second time, Dylan flung herself into the chair behind the till.

'Stupid, stupid, stupid! Why do I always have to lose my stupid temper?' Her big blue eyes filled with tears. 'But Jasper was being annoying. Wasn't he being annoying, Ali? Like, why did he have to take that stupid phone call in private? Or am I just going insane?'

'I don't know.' Alice rubbed her forehead. 'At least you

have a boyfriend, that's all I can say. A boyfriend who brings you coffee and cakes and thinks you're beautiful, and is handsome and popular and cool.'

Dylan stared at the scratched wood tabletop. 'Yeah. I guess you're right,' she muttered.

Both girls fell silent, gazing through the shop window at the blank white sky.

Chapter 14

Seb's rusty-orange cashmere scarf flapped about his face as the wind hurtled through the stands. Wrapping his hands tighter around his steaming cup of coffee, he squinted down on to the football field, where a roar had just arisen from the practice session.

'Out of my way!' Tristan yelled. He was zigzagging with the ball, avoiding not only the opposing players but his teammates too. His face was so fierce that it looked like he'd been possessed.

'Over here,' George Demetrios waved. 'I'm open!'

'Mooove!' Tristan bellowed. He switched direction so abruptly that George had to throw himself aside to avoid being mown down.

Seb's eyes widened.

'Teamwork, Tristan, teamwork,' barked Brigadier Jones. The football coach was waving his whistle and hopping up and down. 'Don't hog the ball. Don't—Stop! Careful of the—'

'Scooore!' Tristan screamed. He'd booted the ball straight into the opposing goalkeeper's face, and was now tearing round the pitch, waving his arms. 'Yeah! Go, go, go!' he cried, fist-pumping the empty air.

Seb was frowning now, his coffee cup abandoned on the bench. No one else on the pitch was cheering. George Demetrios was rubbing his arm where T had walloped it. Tom Huntleigh, the goalkeeper, was massaging his cheek, which was bright red from its impact with the ball. And Brigadier Jones was pointing at the sidelines.

'Off!' he yelled. 'Off. The. Field. Now.'

Tristan halted in the middle of his victory lap. 'B-but sir . . . that was a goal. I scored.'

'And almost maimed my entire Lower Sixth team in the process!' The Brigadier, an ex-army officer, was practically spitting with fury. 'This is a practice session, not World War Three. If I've tried to teach you anything, it's good sportsmanship. And that was not it. Clear off and hit the showers. You need to cool down.'

Tristan thrust his jaw out. 'Fine,' he muttered.

As T stomped off the field, Seb jumped up and ran to the bottom of the stands, intercepting him.

'That was quite the show.'

Tristan brushed past him.

'A little too much caffeine this morning? Eh, T, old man?'

'Stupid Brigadier,' Tristan grumbled. 'Isn't the whole point of football to score goals? Idiot. If I have to hear one more arrogant, self-righteous comment from him, I'm gonna punch him in the moustache.'

'Yeah, well, he is a bit macho, I guess. Then again, what do you expect? He was in the army for about a million years.'

'That's no excuse for acting like a military dictator. Next thing you know, he'll be trying to take over the school.'

'Um, right. Listen,' Seb said brightly, 'how about we sneak off for a smoke? Might help you calm down.'

'I'm perfectly calm,' Tristan snapped. But he allowed Seb to divert him from the locker rooms towards a wooded area near the boating lake. They hid themselves among the trees, where the bare winter branches tangled like knotted strings above their heads.

'Right,' Seb said, producing two cigarettes. 'Now you can tell me what's wrong.'

'Wrong?' Tristan exhaled defensively. 'What do you mean? Nothing's wrong.'

Seb rolled his pale blue eyes. 'Come on, man. You just turned into the Terminator during football practice for no reason. Plus you've been in a foul mood all week. Plus you wrote that weird song. Look, I know you must be upset about Alice. We've barely talked about it, but—'

'I'm not,' Tristan interrupted. 'I'm over Alice.'

'Uh, OK. You sure about that?'

'Yeah.' T glared at his muddy football boots. He was clenching one fist so hard that the knuckles shone white. 'She can do what she wants. It's just . . .'

'What?'

'Well what the fuck is wrong with me? Why am I such a failure with girls?'

Seb guffawed. Smoke puffed out his nose.

'What's so funny?'

'S-sorry,' Seb coughed. 'But what the hell are you on

about? If *you're* a failure with girls, where does that leave everyone else?'

Tristan heaved a sigh. 'OK, so girls fancy me. Whatever. I'm not talking about that – I'm talking about *relationships*. Three months, Seb. Three months.' He jiggled three fingers in Seb's face. 'That's how long I went out with Alice, and that's my all-time record. Pathetic. What's wrong with me?'

'Dude, I reckon three months is quite impressive. My longest relationship is three hours.'

'Yeah, but you don't count,' Tristan scoffed. 'You're practically a monk.'

Seb bit his lip. Great way to turn the spotlight on himself. He usually avoided any mention of his love life; he just waited, resigned, for someone else to bring it up. Which was usually when the awkward questions started.

Tristan was biting his lip. 'Sorry. I didn't mean that.'

'It's fine.'

'No, it's not. I'm an idiot.' Tristan sighed and dragged a hand through his chestnut-brown quiff. 'I should just take Jasper's advice and go on a shagathon. Who needs relationships when you can have fun?'

'Um, yeah, I guess . . . As long as you are actually having fun. And I'm not sure that getting off with loads of random girls just for the sake of it sounds so great.' Seb flicked away his cigarette butt, his white fingers trembling in the cold. 'Not to sound like a prude or anything, but isn't sex better when it means something?'

'I wouldn't know.' Tristan laughed bitterly. 'Alice is the

91

only girl I've ever had sex with, and I failed at that, didn't I? I'm a failure at love. I suck.'

'Hey. Shut up!' Seb held his best friend's hazel eyes. 'Stop calling yourself a failure. First of all it's getting boring, and second of all it's completely not true. Look, I know how hard you tried to sort things out with Alice. But a relationship takes *two* people, not one. You can't make something work all by yourself, no matter how much energy and effort you put in. The other person has to meet you halfway. And Alice just didn't. And that's totally not your fault.'

For a moment, Tristan was silent. He rubbed his arms against the chill January air. 'I don't know. Maybe you're right.'

'I'm always right.'

'How true. How could I forget?' Tristan's grin turned thoughtful. 'You know, I don't get it.'

'What?'

'You. You always seem to have all the answers. You're always helping me with my girl problems. But you never have any of your own. You don't date anyone. You hardly even seem to like anyone. Or at least, if you do, you don't tell me. Why?'

Seb heaved an inward sigh. And here they were, the awkward questions. Digging in his pocket for the pack of cigarettes, he shrugged. 'I dunno. Guess I'm just picky. Is that such a big deal?'

'No. But it does make me feel a bit weird – you know, 'cause I'm always confiding in you, and you never confide in me. I mean, my love life might be a mess, but I'm not so bad at helping with other people's. So if you ever want to chat . . .'

'Yeah. Thanks.' For a long moment, Seb stared into the trees, their outlines spidery and stark. *If you ever want to chat . . .* He allowed himself to think how nice it would be to talk to his best friend about Will. To share the excitement – and the terror – of his first ever real date. Because for all his insistence, all his philosophising, the advice he gave T was only theory. He only intellectualised what he hadn't experienced. Tristan had braved the waters, whereas he himself had only stood on the shore, combing the horizon with his eyes.

'Seb? Are you all right?' Tristan said.

Seb looked up into T's open, expectant face. No. He couldn't bear to change things. He couldn't bear to see the slow hardening of T's expression when he learned the truth. Once people knew you were different, they never treated you the same again.

He grinned. 'Of course. Cold out here, isn't it? Let's go see what's for tea.'

As they trudged back towards the Dining Hall, Seb curled his hand around his phone. He thought of Will's text messages, hiding behind the home screen, swaddled in the darkness of his pocket.

Chapter 15

'There's no such thing as too revealing!' Mimah insisted into her mobile. 'Not when you're fourteen and have a fabulous figure. Totally wear the red dress.'

'But you haven't even seen it!' Charlie groaned on the other end of the line. 'And I can dance better in the black one. I'm worried it's a bit grannyish, though. It comes down almost to my knees. Oh, help! What did you wear to *your* Year Ten Social?'

'How am I supposed to remember?' Mimah rolled her eyes. It was coming up to half past six on Thursday, and she was crossing Hasted Common under the dark sky, the path only intermittently lit by orange bulbs. She'd rung Charlie for reassurance against the vast, dim, windy stretch of footprint-flattened grass, but now she was rethinking her decision. Dispensing fashion advice until her brain rotted wasn't her idea of fun.

'And I can't believe it's tomorrow!' Charlie went on. 'I should have planned my outfit earlier. The Hasted House–St Cecilia's New Year's Social is practically a fashion show.'

'For god's sake, can you please stop freaking?' Mimah

said. 'You'll look fine. You'll look great. What's everyone else wearing?'

'Don't know. Georgie's still suspended. She's not back till next week. Oh, and guess what?' Charlie lowered her voice. 'Lauren Taylor's still massively embarrassed about the whole diary incident. She asked Mrs Gould if she could skip the Social, and Gould said no way. She said that school parties are how we meet eligible boys our own age, and if Lauren didn't come she might end up a spinster. She said it in kind of a teasing voice, but you should have seen Lauren's face. Georgie really shouldn't have put her diary online. I feel sorry for her.'

'So be nice to her, then,' Mimah said. 'She's in your dorm now – you've got plenty of opportunity.'

'Yeah, except that Georgie would kill me if I got all cosy with Lauren Taylor. Georgie hates her.'

'Oh, please! Don't tell me that a sister of mine is afraid of that scrawny bitch Georgina Fortescue. Anyway, I thought you said Georgie wasn't back till next week – how can she kill you if she's in London?'

Charlie sighed. 'That's not the point. She's my friend.'

'Whatever,' Mimah snorted. 'Hey, listen, I have to go.'

'Hang on, is that traffic in the background? Where are you?'

'Town.'

'Where in town?'

Mimah looked up at the building in front of her, hulking darkly at the end of the common. 'The community centre.'

'What on earth are you doing there? You don't have

tutoring any more. Oh no, sis . . .' Charlie's voice went up a pitch. 'Don't tell me you've gone to look for Aidan.'

'Of course not,' Mimah said quickly. 'He won't be here, I know that. But I had to come. If anyone knows anything . . . I have to ask if he's all right.'

'But Mime, just . . . don't upset yourself, OK?'

'Yeah. I've got to go. Bye.'

Mimah took a deep breath. Then she pushed open the heavy glass door. The entrance hall was warm, and smelled of coffee and chlorine and dirty socks. Overhead, neon strips gave off a weak light the colour of dishwater. Bulletin boards lined one wall, crowded with handwritten notices. *Group Music Lessons! Hasted Triathlon Club – Join for Free! Audition for the Easter Play!* Passing these, Mimah turned down the familiar corridor. Classrooms opened off on either side, but her gaze was fixed on the far end of the hallway, where the door to Room 117 stood ajar.

She was halfway there when, suddenly, the door burst open. Agitated voices spilled into the corridor, chasing each other over the linoleum.

'No! I told you, I don't want to stay,' cried a tall, lean boy, striding from the room. He had short dark hair and was gripping a large black file under his arm.

Mimah gasped. Blood roared in her ears and her knees went weak. It was Aidan – all she'd needed was the slightest glance. She darted into the nearest classroom, letting its darkness swallow her from sight, and, her heart pounding, peered through the glass peephole in the door.

'I didn't come back to argue – I came to collect my

96

file!' Aidan's voice echoed down to her. It was angry, stubborn – like the Aidan Mimah had first met, back in November, right there in that room. But why he was yelling, she had no idea.

'No, look, I'm finished with this place,' his voice carried down. 'I thought this whole tutoring crap was optional. So for fuck's sake, stop bothering me!'

The other voice mumbled something.

'I'll swear all I want! I've had enough – everyone poking around in my private life. Bloody community workers. Leave me the hell alone! I can manage by myself.'

Mimah saw Aidan wheel round. She shrank back as he stalked in her direction, and even before she glimpsed his face, she knew there was something seriously wrong. It was in the hunch of his sinewy shoulders, in the disjointed movements of his gait. He drew nearer, and she saw the tension in his mouth and the blaze in his eyes. She pressed her fingers to the porthole as he passed. If only she was brave enough to follow him. If only she could touch him for just one second, maybe she could find out what was wrong. But she didn't move. He'd told her to leave him alone. He'd told her 'for ever' – and it was as if these words cemented her to the spot. Then he was gone, and the hot pulse in Mimah's fingertips beat helplessly against the cold, smooth glass.

Chapter 16

'No way, I can't! I'm not going,' Lauren Taylor cried, folding her arms across her chest and glaring into Dylan's closet. Rows of dresses and skirts stared back at her, while on the opposite wall, Sonia Khan's stockpile of Evian waters loomed like an exhibit in an OCD museum.

Dylan sighed. 'Lau, we've been through this. You have to go. The Social is compulsory. And yes,' she said, holding up her hand before Lauren could interrupt, 'I know it's totally stupid for a party to be compulsory, but that's the way it is.' She squeezed her sister's arm. 'Here's the plan. You go, you look hot, and you hold your head high as if nothing bothers you. Just think how superior you are to all those ugly losers.'

'Oi,' said a voice from Dylan's desk. Alice was ensconced there, poring over a French textbook. 'Ugly losers? That's my brother you're talking about.'

Dylan shot her a look. As if Lauren needed reminding that Hugo Rochester, the crush she'd involuntarily proclaimed to the entire world, would be at the Year Ten Social tonight.

'*Shit, sorry,*' Alice mouthed. Her eyes rested thoughtfully on Lauren for a second before she went back to her work.

Lauren had turned a pale shade of green. 'Oh god, I feel kind of sick. Dylan, what am I supposed to do?' Her voice was panicky. 'I have nothing to wear.'

'What are you talking about? There's plenty of stuff in there. Choose whatever you want.'

'But it won't help! No offence, but we're not the same size.' Lauren pointed at her sister's chest. She usually tried not to mention Dylan's double-D boobs, since Dylan found them so horrifically embarrassing, but today was an exception. Today, she was desperate. She flopped on to Dylan's bed and buried her face in the pillows.

Alice cleared her throat. 'Hey. Lauren.'

Lauren took a deep breath and peeked out from under her hair. Didn't she have enough problems, without Hugo Rochester's sister witnessing this low point in her life?

'Not that I'm eavesdropping or anything, but if you're looking for something to wear, I might have a dress you can borrow . . . What?' Alice snapped, as both sisters swivelled to stare at her in amazement. 'You think I never lend my clothes to people? You think I can't be generous and nice?'

'Um, yes,' Dylan blurted out. 'That's exactly what we think.'

'Dylan!' Lauren whispered. She cast a terrified look at Alice, who chuckled.

'Yeah, Dylan, shut up! Anyway, I obviously didn't mean Lauren could borrow something new. Like, you can forget about the D and G minidress I got for Christmas. But I can probably dig up a few things. If you want.'

'Wow, yeah,' Lauren said gratefully. 'That'd be amazing. Thanks.'

Alice shrugged. 'Wait here.' She sallied across the room, feeling their eyes on her back, and swept into the hallway, nearly tripping over Sonia Khan, who was standing just outside the door.

'Well, well, well,' Sonia sneered. 'Look who it is. How interesting. *Some* people have obviously been in *other* people's dorms. You know what I think? I think *some* people should piss off and stop poking their nose in *other* people's stuff.'

'Sonia Khan, making perfect sense as always.' Alice rolled her eyes. 'And by the way, looks like you've found your ideal career: loitering in doorways. Suits your snake-like personality.' She slammed her bedroom door in Sonia's face, causing Tally, who was sitting at her own desk, to jump.

'God, you gave me a fright,' Tally gasped, quickly shutting her laptop screen.

Alice blinked at her. 'What were you doing?'

'Me? Nothing. Emailing.'

'Who?'

'No one special.' Tally flashed one of her dazzling smiles. 'Why are you being so nosy?'

'Because you're being secretive.'

'I wasn't! I was being sociable. I've hardly seen you all day, darls – it'd be super-rude to keep typing as if you hadn't even come in.' Tally yanked a hairband off her wrist and twisted her hair into a high ponytail. 'So. Hi! What's up?'

Alice cast a final glance at her friend's computer before crossing to her closet. 'Not much. Said I might lend Dylan's little sister something to wear to the Hasted House–St Cecilia's Social tonight.'

'Seriously? Why, what are you gonna do – poison the dress?'

'No!' Alice tossed her hair. 'Why does everyone think I'm such a monster? Don't answer that.'

Tally giggled.

'Anyway, I don't know, I just suddenly felt sorry for the poor girl. That diary thing was horrific. Plus I feel kind of responsible, since the whole crush thing was about my younger brother.'

Tally nodded sagely. 'Yeah, and you're probably identi-fying with her because you're having boy problems of your own at the moment. Brings us girls together. Well, I think it's super-nice of you, hon. And don't worry, you'll get over T sooner than you think. I never thought I'd get over Rando, but over New Year, I really did. I'd go mental if I saw him with anyone else, of course, but I've stopped thinking about him every second of the day, you know?'

'Wow. That's great.' Alice rubbed her nose and stared into her closet. She rifled through a few dresses.

'Hey, speaking of boys,' Tally yawned, 'I was thinking – now that you and I are both single, we should totally go out on the pull. You up for clubbing tomorrow?'

'Um . . .' Alice plucked at the hem of a floaty purple number that she'd bought in New York last year, and bit her lip. *No*, was the answer. But she couldn't exactly say that. 'I don't know. Are you sure *you're* even up for clubbing? I mean, you're yawning in the middle of the afternoon. And you've been up late working every night this week. What on earth have you been doing? I'm sure *I* don't have that much prep.'

'Come on, Al, don't change the subject.' Tally dug her feet into a pair of furry white slippers, which Alice recognised as her own. Tally had never been good at respecting the laws of ownership. 'Dating's like falling off a horse – the sooner you get back on, the sooner you'll feel confident again.'

Alice sighed. The only person she wanted to date was Rando. But that was impossible now. Suddenly she saw him in her mind's eye as he'd been a few days ago at the charity shop in Hasted, staring at his shoes, looking everywhere but at her.

'You're right,' she said, forcing herself to sound enthusiastic. 'A night out would be good. But not Shock Box, please. We'll bump into fifty thousand people we know.'

'Shock Box?' Tally grimaced at the name of Hasted's scummiest club. 'Give me some credit, babe. We'll go out in London. I was thinking more along the lines of LaLa Lounge. That place is like, fittie central.'

'But Tals . . .' Alice paused. 'LaLa's is kind of pricey. Are you sure you'll be able to swing it?'

'Yeah. Course.'

'You mean your dad's given you back your credit cards?'

'Oh. No. But I found some money I'd forgotten about.' Tally beamed reassuringly. 'Don't worry about it, hon – I've got everything under control. And anyway, we deserve a treat.'

Out in the corridor, Sonia Khan snickered to herself as she withdrew her ear from Alice and Tally's door. *Score.* Balancing her phone in the palm of her hand, she tapped out a text to Bella Scott.

Hey babe, how bout clubbing at LaLa Lounge 2moro night? I have a great idea – let's invite Tristan too!! xxS

Yes, she thought, resisting the urge to cackle as she crept away down the hall; it looked like a trip to London was in order for quite an interesting little crew.

Chapter 17

Lauren Taylor clip-clopped down the front steps of St Cecilia's, pursing her lips and concentrating as hard as she could on the tips of her pink suede shoes. Twenty feet away, the coach to Hasted House purred in the driveway. Girls were filing aboard, hanging off each other's arms. The sound of their laughter jangled in the frosty air, mingling with the scent of forty different perfumes. Lauren took a deep breath. She clutched her coat around her body. The pink and brown leopard print minidress she'd borrowed from Alice suddenly felt way too short and way too tight and way too . . . much. Why, oh why, had she chosen to wear something so ostentatious? As if she needed the extra attention.

She was going to vomit. She was definitely going to vomit.

'Hurry up, my dears!' warbled Mrs Gould. 'Come on, we don't want to be late for the boys. I hear they're putting on quite a party. Careful, Miranda!' she shrieked, as Minky Coombes stumbled on the gravel, one of her six-inch spike heels twisting at a crazy angle. 'Try not to break your neck. Your parents would never forgive me. Stop dawdling, Lauren dear, you're the last one.'

Lauren balled her fists. On board the packed coach, she darted her eyes from side to side down the aisle, desperately seeking a seat. The only free ones were piled with coats and scarves and evening bags. No way could she attempt to sit in one of those; the idea of asking someone to move their stuff was enough to give her a seizure. A burn crept slowly up her neck as she realised she was going to have to turn around, walk all the way back to the front of the coach and, under everyone's mocking gaze, sit next to Mrs Gould.

'Hey Lauren,' said a low voice. 'Over here.'

Lauren swivelled. She saw Charlie Calthorpe de Vyle-Hanswicke patting the garish red-and-blue upholstery of the neighbouring seat. She didn't move.

'This one's free. You can sit next to me if you like.'

'Ummm . . . really?'

Charlie laughed. 'Yeah. I'd be pretty unfunny if that was my idea of a joke.'

'Lauren Taylor!' rapped Mrs Gould's voice from the front of the coach. 'Sit down, dear. We're all waiting for you.'

Lauren dropped into the seat, and the bus started to move. She sat rigidly, trying to ignore the whispers of Portia Mehew-Montefiore and Minky Coombes across the aisle. After a minute, her eyes drifted sideways. Charlie was wearing a red leather tube dress with gold-and-crystal earrings, black tights and high gold shoes. Her eye make-up was smoky, and her raven hair tumbled round her pixieish face. She looked cool and alternative and mysterious and sexy. Lauren pulled her coat tighter.

105

Charlie shot her a smile. 'Hey, how come you didn't get ready in our room? Can I see your dress?'

'Um . . . OK.' Lauren inched open her coat. 'It's kind of showy, though. I wish I'd picked something else.'

'Wow!' Charlie exclaimed at the sight of the leopard print. 'No way, you look super-hot. But I've never seen this in your closet – I mean, not that I've been rummaging through your clothes or anything. Did you buy it especially for tonight?'

Lauren shook her head. 'It's not mine. It's Alice Rochester's. I had nothing to wear so she lent it to me for the evening.'

'Oh please,' Charlie scoffed. 'How stupid do I look? Alice Rochester never lends anyone anything. She doesn't even lend my sister stuff, and Mimah's one of her best friends.'

'I promise!' Lauren insisted. 'She offered and every-thing – it was really weird. I'm not as tall as her, so Dylan shortened it. She's really good at art and creative stuff. See?'

'Hmm.' Charlie examined the hem. 'Looks quite profes-sional, actually. I could never do that – I'm awful at sewing.'

'Let's see, let's see!' Minky Coombes was leaning across the aisle. She stroked the dress's soft silk. 'I literally can't believe Alice Rochester lent you that. It's gorgeous.'

'Wow, yeah.' Portia kneeled up on her seat. 'Is it really hers? She is *so* cool.'

'It's definitely hers,' Minky said. 'Don't you remember, she wore it to the Snow Ball in London last year?'

'OMG, yeah, she looked in-*credible*. Isn't that where she snogged Toby van Vooderhof?'

'No! It was where she snogged Henrik Chumley-Porkington.' Minky clasped her hands. 'Alice kisses all the fittest boys. I heard she broke up with Tristan Murray-Middleton. Everyone'll be competing for her now. God, her life is so perfect. I wish I was her.'

'So did you actually see inside her room, Lauren?' Portia cut in breathlessly. 'What's it like? I heard she and Tally Abbott have a couch and a home cinema and a fully stocked bar in the closet!'

'Um, not exactly.' Lauren laughed. She couldn't believe she was actually having a conversation with Portia and Minky. They'd never spoken to her before, except to tell her to hurry up or pass the toothpaste. 'They do have this little nook, though, with fairy lights and big cushions and a sheepskin rug, and an old chest with a secret stash of wine.'

'Wow,' Portia breathed. 'That is. So. Awesome. Eee! Minks, we're here.'

The coach, which had been rolling through town, was now turning in at a pair of high iron gates. It stopped, and Lauren gripped her armrest. Hasted House was even older and grander than St Cecilia's. Its stone buildings loomed above the streets, cutting jagged silhouettes into the sky. Shadowy figures of boys flitted along paths and through archways. She stepped off the coach, the knot in her stomach clenching like a fist.

'This way, girls, this way,' called Mrs Gould, ushering everyone into a small courtyard.

'That's the Founders Hall,' said a low voice at Lauren's side.

Lauren turned, surprised to find Charlie still talking to her. Straight ahead of them, an elegant stone building flickered with torchlight, its entrance draped with a red banner. Coloured lights were flashing in the windows, and dance beats were echoing into the courtyard. 'They hold the New Year's Social there every January.'

Lauren nodded. She was shaking so much her teeth were chattering.

'You probably think it's weird, how excited everyone gets about tonight,' Charlie went on. 'But it's kind of like a rite of passage for us Year Tens.'

'Really? H-how come?'

'For a start, it's the first school social where we're allowed to drink. We're allowed two units of booze each – that's two beers, or two glasses of wine. Not that we rely on those,' Charlie giggled, and opened the flap of her handbag to reveal an innocent-looking water bottle. '*Vodka*,' she mouthed.

Lauren gave a wobbly grin. Her legs felt like jelly.

Charlie stared at her. 'Hey, maybe you should have a shot before we go in.'

'H-huh?'

'You definitely need *something*. You look like you're about to croak. Here.' Charlie thrust the bottle at her as they were ushered into the hall. The room was vast, roaring with music and laughter, and rammed with Hasted House boys. Disco balls twisted on the ceiling. People were hugging and kissing and laughing; everyone seemed to know everyone else. Lauren wrenched the cap off the bottle and tilted her neck back, letting the liquid burn down her gullet. She felt a hand close around her arm. It was Charlie's.

'You're gonna be fine. As soon as you know it, everyone'll be drunk, and no one will even remember the whole . . . you know . . . diary thing.'

'Thanks,' Lauren whispered. As she shrugged out of her coat, questions tumbled through her head. Like, why was Charlie being so nice? And why had Charlie been such a heinous bitch to her in the past? And, most important, when was she going to have to face Hugo Rochester? But before she could voice any of them, a baby-faced brown-haired boy bounded over.

'Charl, hey!' he exclaimed, his eyes practically eating Charlie up. 'Nice dress.'

'Felix.' Charlie brushed the boy's T-shirt, and he cupped his hands around her face, drawing her towards him.

Lauren stared at them as they kissed. She knew it was weird to watch, but she couldn't help it. Charlie seemed to know exactly what she was doing – kissing seemed as natural to her as laughing or holding hands.

'Hey, I almost forgot,' Charlie murmured, drawing away and hanging on Felix's arm. Her face was flushed. 'I want you to meet my friend Lauren. Lauren Taylor, Felix Hedley-Bunk.'

'Pleasure,' Felix said.

Lauren gave a tight smile. She backed up a step. Felix

was the first Hasted House boy she'd ever been introduced to – not to mention Hugo Rochester's best friend. There was no telling what he might do.

He smiled. 'So, how are you enjoying the party?'

'Um, well, it's great. I mean, considering I'm only three feet inside the room and I've been here for five seconds.'

'Fair enough.' Felix grinned. 'I'll check back with you in an hour, then. Assuming we're all still sober enough to have a civilised conversation by then.'

Lauren and Charlie chuckled. At that moment, the music stopped.

'Ladies of St Cecilia's,' a voice burst over the loud-speaker. 'If I could have your attention, please.'

The racket in the room died down. Lauren glanced towards the stage. Suddenly, her heart jumped into her throat. Blood flooded to her head. She'd only seen Hugo Rochester once in real life, across a street, and before that only in pictures. Now he was standing in the DJ booth, leaning over the microphone, a half-bashful, half-cheeky expression on his face. And if possible, he looked even better than she remembered. He had creamy skin, with a haystack of blond hair curling on to his face and around his lustrous, soft, almond-shaped eyes. His lips were full and pouty, his cheekbones high and defined. He was wearing a slim midnight-blue suit with no tie, and the top few buttons of his shirt were undone. Lauren gulped. How could she have even dreamed that a beautiful, popular boy like this might give her the time of day?

'Thank you, ladies and gentlemen.' Hugo beamed. 'And

now, as head of the Hasted House Year Ten Entertainment Committee, I'd like to bid you welcome to this season's New Year's Social. Drink, dance and be merry!'

The room broke into applause and cheers. Hugo smiled down from his podium, exchanging waves and greetings with the crowd. He nodded to the back of the room, towards Charlie and Felix – and suddenly, his eyes alighted on Lauren. She saw their expression change, first to confusion, then, slowly, to recognition. His lips parted. Lauren's head spun. She ripped her gaze away and reached out a hand, afraid she might stumble. Just then, someone grabbed hold of her and Charlie.

'Hey, girls, why aren't you dancing?' cried Minky Coombes. She and Portia were swigging booze out of a pocket flask. They were clearly already wasted.

'Yeah,' Portia chimed in. 'This music is ah-mazing!'

'And there are so many boys! Enough for everyone to snog.'

'Thanks for the invite, but I've already got a boy.' Charlie squeezed Felix's hand. 'We're gonna stay here for a bit.'

'Well come on then, you!' Portia insisted, tugging at Lauren's sleeve. 'You can't waste Alice Rochester's super-glam dress. You've gotta show off some moves.'

Lauren nodded, glad of the distraction. Trying her best to breathe normally, she slipped into the safety of the dancing mob.

'Whoa,' Felix smirked as soon as she was gone. 'So that's Lauren Taylor. I can hardly believe she showed her face tonight. She must be pretty embarrassed. I mean, everyone at this entire party has read her diary.'

Charlie swiped his arm. 'Yes, thank you, Felix, we realise that. Don't you think it's time everyone got over that and tried to be nice to the poor girl?'

Felix turned red. 'Yeah, I guess,' he mumbled. 'I was just saying . . .' He reached for Charlie's hand again. Just then, Hugo Rochester appeared at their side.

'Look at you two, all cosy and romantic,' he said, kissing Charlie on the cheek.

She grinned. 'Hey, Rochester. Nice little speech. I never knew you were such an accomplished MC.'

'Piss off.'

'Ooh, touchy!' Charlie squeezed his shoulders. 'By the way, Georgie Fortescue says hi. She couldn't come tonight 'cause she's still suspended. But you know she's coming back to school next week, right?' She looked at him intently.

Hugo nodded. But he seemed distracted; his eyes were scanning the hall. 'Yeah, that's great. Um, listen, I have to ask: that was Lauren Taylor you were just chatting to, wasn't it?'

'Maybe . . .' Charlie folded her arms.

'Oh. Cool. Hey, would you do me a favour? Will you . . . will you invite her to my birthday party next weekend?'

Felix nudged him. 'Why? 'Cause you think it's a sure thing that you'll get in Lauren's pants? I wouldn't count on that, since she's never even kissed anyone.'

'Shut up,' Hugo exclaimed. 'No, that's not it. She seems sweet, that's all.'

'Hmmm . . .' Charlie narrowed her eyes. 'Are you sure that's all? I know I'm not Lauren's BFF or anything, but no way am I inviting her if this is some kind of trap.'

'Of course it's not a trap!' Hugo spread his hands. 'Who do you think I am? I mean, obviously I was flattered by her little declaration, but she wrote it in her diary, for fuck's sake. People say weird shit in their diaries the whole time. We've never even met. She just sounds kind of quirky – I like that.'

'Well . . . OK, I'll bring her. Or at least I'll try. But if I find out that your intentions are less than honourable, you'll have me to answer to.'

'Ooh,' Felix laughed. 'My girlfriend's serious. Better not mess with her.'

'Fucking right,' Charlie grinned.

'Mini fish and chips?' interrupted a waiter. He thrust a canapé tray into the middle of their group.

Charlie turned to take one, and checked herself, noticing the waiter's face. He was about eighteen, tall and lean, with piercing eyes. 'Oh,' she stuttered, confused. 'Hi.'

The boy looked at her blankly.

'I-I'm sure I know you,' Charlie said. 'From somewhere.'

'You must have snorted too much coke,' the boy replied tersely. 'I've never seen you before in my life.'

Charlie's eyes narrowed. 'But you look so familiar.'

'I'm sure there's a perfectly logical explanation for that. Maybe you've seen me in Asda. I work there.' He ran his eyes over the group, and his lip curled into a sneer. 'Or maybe not. I can't imagine you lot slumming it. I'm sure Marks and Spencer is much more your scene.' With an eye-roll, he swung round and walked off.

Charlie watched him, raising a chip to her mouth. Then, suddenly, she dropped it. She'd realised who he was.

Chapter 18

'Another Pinot Noir for the lady,' said the waiter, depositing a massive goblet of red wine in front of Dylan on the polished oak table. The candle next to it wavered, then steadied. 'And a Laphroaig for the gentleman. Excellent choice of whisky, sir. May I bring you anything else?'

'No.' Jasper yawned.

'Are you sure?'

'Yes, yes, you can leave us,' Jasper said, wafting his hand as if at some kind of irritating fly. He took a sip of his honey-coloured drink and turned back to Dylan.

'How annoying. I do hate pesky staff. Anyway, as I was saying, our old yacht was nice, but our new one is far superior. It's two hundred feet, upholstered in white leather, and has its own state-of-the-art cinema. We're planning on sailing it round the Caribbean at Easter.'

'Mmhmm. Cool. Great.' Dylan nodded, pretending to pay attention. She studied Jasper's lean, handsome face, which had so impressed her when they'd first met: the chiselled jaw, the ice-blue eyes, the confident mouth. Jasper had suggested tonight's date at the Chesterton Arms, Hasted's poshest bar, so they could spend some quality time together, as he'd put it. But so far, all he'd done was insist on choosing her wine, brag about the von Holstadt family assets, and act as if they hadn't even had a fight the other day in town.

'. . . but Uncle Friedrich wouldn't calm down,' Jasper was chortling. 'He whipped off his pants and jumped straight into the Mediterranean, stark naked in front of all the natives! It was literally hil-ah-rious. Ha, ha, *ha*!'

'Oh, yeah, funny,' Dylan laughed, sipping from her bucketful of wine.

Jasper smiled at her, pulled his chair closer and slid his hand over her leg. 'By the way, I'm not sure I told you, but you look stunning tonight. Really. Stunning.'

'Thanks,' Dylan murmured, blushing as he tucked back a piece of her hair.

'You know, maybe I'll ask Daddy if you can come.'

'Where?'

'On our trip round the Caribbean. On our yacht.'

'Oh, wow. But . . . do you think he'd mind?'

'I don't see why not,' Jasper whispered, leaning in to kiss her neck.

'Mmm,' Dylan sighed. Just as her eyes were sinking shut, they fell on a familiar figure at the bar. 'Hey, weird. Isn't that Seb?'

'Doubt it. Where?' Jasper twisted round. 'Oh. Yeah. It is.'

'Looks like he's here all by himself.'

'Ignore him. Seb's a strange bird. He's always going drinking alone. Anyway—'

'Not on a Saturday night, though! It's sad. Let's get him to join us.'

'No! Tonight's supposed to be just us, we're supposed to be—'

'Seb!' Dylan waved, pretending with only a flash of guilt not to hear her boyfriend. 'Over here!'

Seb, who'd been leaning on the sleek ebony bar, looked around in surprise, and waved.

'Come join us!' Dylan called above the room's civilised hum. 'Pull up a chair, we have plenty of space.'

'Shhh!' Jasper hissed. 'Please, do you have to be so American? In England, we don't yell and scream in bars.'

'What do you do, then? Brag about your family's fleet of ships and act rude to the waiters? Hi, Seb!' Dylan exclaimed, before Jasper could respond.

'Hello, you two. Am I interrupting?'

'No! Of course not. Join us. How come you're here all by yourself?'

Seb tugged at his velvet jacket lapel. 'Didn't have anywhere else to be. You two are out. George Demetrios is watching Arsenal replays. T and Rando have gone clubbing in London.'

Jasper, who had been leaning back in his seat and glaring at Seb, now uncrossed his arms. 'Oh, really? What club?'

'Dunno. Sonia invited them somewhere. One of these trendy, expensive places with a stupid name.' Seb sat down and put his book on the table.

'Ovid's *Metamorphoses*,' Dylan read. 'Looks like some light entertainment. What's it for?'

'Nothing, really. Our Classics teacher mentioned it the other day, so I thought I'd get a copy. It's really cool. Have you read it?'

Shaking her head, Dylan scanned the back of the book. '"One of Latin literature's greatest epics, full of myth, legend and transformation." Sounds interesting.'

Jasper jabbed her thigh with his knee. 'No it does not, you silly. I don't understand you, Seb man. You're such a geek. Spending Saturday night reading two-thousand-year-old Latin texts? That is a waste of life.'

'Excuse me, but I think you'll find it's the opposite,' Seb retorted. 'How can history and mythology and literature be a waste of life? They're the things that connect us to past generations. They make us think about our place in the universe. They give humanity a purpose.'

'Oh god, stop it with the intellectual crap,' Jasper groaned. 'This isn't Radio Four – you don't have a rapt nation to impress. You know as well as I do that school isn't about learning things. It's about getting decent grades, getting into a good university and landing a prestigious job so your parents have something to brag about while you party and jet-set for the rest of your life. School's just for show. Do the minimum work for the maximum effect – that's the way to play the game.'

Dylan and Seb were staring at him.

'Hold on, do you actually believe that?' Dylan asked, her forehead creased.

'Of course I do. 'Cause it's true, babe. And you can stop

it with the disapproving frown,' Jasper grinned, pinching her waist. 'Oh, hang on.'

Digging in his pocket, he jumped to his feet. 'Phone call. Gotta take this. Be right back.'

As Jasper retreated to the bar, Dylan regarded Seb over the rim of her glass. 'Does he always talk to you like that?'

'Oh, you know Jas.' Seb shrugged. 'Sensitivity isn't his strong point. Neither is giving good advice.'

'What do you mean?'

'Come on, have you not met him? Jasper's always telling people to do ridiculous things. Like, the other day he told T that the best way to get over Alice was to shag as many girls as possible. Really emotionally mature, right? He said that guys who'd only slept with one girl were basically gay.'

'He said that?' Dylan demanded. She stared at Jasper, who was now talking loudly and gesticulating with his phone-free hand. 'What the fuck? What a sexist, homophobic, chauvinist, arrogant—'

'Wait! Uh . . .' Seb looked alarmed. 'Don't lose your temper. Maybe he didn't say exactly that. I might be remembering wrong.'

Dylan chuckled. 'Too late. You've given him away now. But come on, you've known him for ever – does he really think stuff like that?'

'I don't know. Maybe *think* is the wrong word. Maybe the problem is that he *doesn't* think.'

'Maybe.' Dylan sighed. 'You know, sometimes I feel like he doesn't even realise what he's saying. I mean, he can be so amazing and nice and sweet, and then other times

119

he treats me like such a . . . misfit. As if I don't feel different enough already.'

'Tell me about it.'

'Huh?' Dylan fixed her cornflower-blue eyes on Seb's face. 'How do *you* feel different? I'm American. I just moved to this country. I don't know anything about all this British stuff. But you were born and raised here. You're a true-blue Hasted House boy. You're one of them.'

'Yeah . . .' Seb sighed. There was a long pause, as his gaze slid past their table to the empty air. 'I guess it seems that way, doesn't it? That's the way I've always wanted it, at least . . .'

Dylan blinked. Seb wasn't making any sense. Maybe he was drunk. Maybe he was stoned. Before she could snap him back, the song playing overhead finished. A sudden quiet descended.

'No!' Jasper's phone call carried across the bar. 'I can't. I need it before Monday – or it's over.'

Dylan's forehead creased.

'Please.' Jasper's voice was quieter but still audible. 'This weekend. You have to. Or how am I . . . ?'

The music kicked back in, swallowing the rest of the sentence. Seb drained his drink. Jasper dipped his head. Dylan squeezed the edge of their table, feeling it press into her palm. The more she knew of each and every one of the so-called friends she'd made in this country, the more she realised how much she had to learn. And now, her very own boyfriend was proving to be no exception to the rule.

Chapter 19

'I win!' Tally squealed, slamming her shot glass on the stainless-steel bar at LaLa Lounge half a second before Alice. 'Oh yeah, oh yeah, go me, go me,' she chanted, her tiny silver dress glimmering under one of the club's many disco balls. 'Now you have to do a dare! You have to do whatever I say. I'm gonna think up something reaaaally good.'

'Stop gloating!' Alice giggled, swatting her arm. 'Just tell me what I have to do.'

'Or *who* you have to do.'

'No way! We're keeping this decent. Or at least PG.'

'Oh, are we now?' Stroking her chin, Tally cast her eyes along the trendy crowd at the bar. 'Hmmm . . . Now who should I make you go talk to? Him? No . . . Him? No . . . Ooh, that guy's all on his lonesome. And he's cute. Don't you think?' She was pointing to a swarthy type with a crop of curly black hair.

'Are you mental?' Alice demanded. 'No way am I chatting up anyone wearing that amount of hair gel.'

'But he's adorable.'

'Tals. Get some glasses. He looks like a total slimeball.'

'Fine! Picky, picky. I'll choose someone else, then. But you only get one pass, and that was it. Hmmm . . . There! Him,' Tally said. This time she was pointing to a redhead with designer stubble and a check shirt. 'Hoxton-style hotness. You can't ask for fairer than that.'

Alice shrugged. 'Yeah, he's OK. Scratchy-looking beard, though. Plus, he probably takes longer getting ready in the mornings than any girl – that's what these metrosexual types are like. But whatever . . .' She heaved a long-suffering sigh. 'What do I have to do?'

'You have to snog him. For at least five seconds!' Tally insisted, raising her voice over Alice's protests. 'And you're not allowed to say it's for a dare. That's cheating.'

'OMG, you are *so* mean. Let me just buy you a few cocktails instead,' Alice wheedled, grabbing her purple Chanel wallet out of her evening bag. She dangled it in Tally's face. 'Come on, you know you want to . . .'

'I do not! And by the way, are you refusing a challenge? Because you know what the penalty for that is: three back-to-back tequila shots. Hello, hangover.'

Alice rolled her eyes. 'Fine, I'll kiss your stupid ginger. But if he's a weirdo, you have to come save me.'

'Promise.'

Alice squared her shoulders, gulped the rest of her martini and checked out her reflection in the mirror behind the bar. She flicked her ponytail, sucked in her cheeks and sidled towards the target. He was just paying for a drink.

'Hey,' she purred, wedging herself next to him.

Redhead Man gave a start. 'Hey yourself.'

'Nice-looking . . . cocktail.' Alice raised her eyebrows suggestively. 'What's in it?'

'Vodka and soda.'

'Oh. Simple yet classic. I like your style. Is it good?'

'Of course it's good. It tastes like vodka and soda.' Redhead grinned. He had an Irish accent, and it was kind of sexy.

'Can I try it?'

'I guess. If you want.' He nudged the glass towards Alice. Ignoring it, she stood on tiptoe and drew his face towards hers.

'Hey, what are you doing?'

'I'd prefer to taste it this way.'

Before Redhead had time to reply, their lips met. He tasted warm and alcoholic, and his stubble was actually kind of cute. *One . . . two . . .* Alice counted to herself. It was totally okay snogging someone who wasn't Rando. In fact, it was refreshing to get him out of her head. *Three . . .* She was hardly even thinking about him. *Four . . .* Hardly at all. *Five.*

'Done!' She pulled away.

Redhead was gaping at her. 'Wow.'

'Yeah. Anyway, gotta go. See you later.'

'Wait!' He made a grab for her hand. 'Don't go. Let me at least buy you a drink.'

'I already have one. Nice meeting you, though. *Ciao.*' Wiggling her fingers in farewell, Alice pushed her way back to Tally.

'Did it!' she crowed. 'Mission accomplished. Congratulations, please.'

'High five, darling! So . . . was he good?'

Alice shrugged. 'I've kissed better. But I'm sure he could be trained. Most guys can.'

'So true,' Tally giggled. 'You know, the only one of my boyfriends who didn't need training was Rando. He was the most romantic kisser in the world. He had the most incredible soft lips . . .' She sighed, and her eyes went big and dreamy.

'Um, babe . . .' Alice twisted her fingers into knots. 'I thought you said you were over Rando.'

'I am! *So* over him. Tonight we're celebrating new beginnings. Which is why I'm treating us to a bottle of champagne. Dom Perignon!' Tally called to the bartender, pulling a wad of crisp new banknotes out of her clutch bag.

'Hey . . . Where did you get that money?'

'Duh. From a cash machine. Get ready – we're drinking to new boys, new loves, new— *OhmyGod*,' Tally gasped. Her colour drained. She went as pale as candle wax, and her hand flew to her neck.

'What's wrong? Tals, are you OK?'

'I . . . I . . .' Tally's breathing was shallow. She stood on tiptoe, scanning the area near the DJ booth. Then, all of a sudden, she shut her eyes, trembling. 'Thank goodness. It's OK. It's nothing.'

'*What's* nothing?'

'I just thought I saw . . .'

'Who?' Alice urged. She craned her neck towards the DJ booth. There was no one familiar in sight. Just a line of bouncers, their arms folded, their eyes scouring the crowd. 'Who?'

'No one you know. Just someone I . . . I used to . . .' Tally shook herself, and smiled. 'Whatever. It wasn't him. Let's drink.'

Alice frowned. Tally's hand dropped from her neck, and Alice now saw what she'd been holding: that weird gold pendant she'd worn night and day since she'd reappeared from her New Year mystery tour.

'Cheers!' Tally cried, handing her a frosty, bubbling glass.

Alice hesitated. Then, 'Cheers!' she grinned.

She was having fun. She was actually having fun for the first time all week. And nothing was going to spoil her night.

Chapter 20

'Tristan!' Sonia screeched. She sashayed across the polished black dance floor at LaLa Lounge, tugging Bella Scott behind her. 'At last. I thought you'd never get here. We've already had two drinks each and been forced to fight off chavvy imposters. I don't know why the doorman let them in. Oh!' Sonia stopped short. Behind Tristan, a familiar figure was emerging from the cloakroom, trying to tame his wavy hair. 'Rando. I didn't know you were coming.'

'Nice to see you too,' Rando snorted, stooping to kiss her cheek.

'But . . . but what are you doing here?'

Rando shrugged. The truth was, he didn't really know the answer to that question. Well, he knew the practical answer – that Tristan had begged him to be his wingman and had finally succeeded in dragging him along. He just didn't know why he'd given in. Being in an over-trendy, overcrowded club with Alice's depressed ex-boyfriend – not to mention Alice's insane ex-lackey – wasn't his idea of fun. 'I hope my presence doesn't mess up your plans.'

Sonia's eyes bulged. 'My *plans*? What plans? I don't have any plans. How could it mess up my plans? Hmph. I just don't think it's very gentlemanly to show up late *and* with an unexpected guest, that's all. But if you're lucky, we just might forgive you. Ooh, and by the way, T,' she cooed, poking Tristan in the chest with a French-manicured nail, 'I just adore your baby-blue shirt. It's the same colour as Bella's earrings. Speaking of Bella, doesn't she look *stunning* tonight?'

'*Don't!*' Bella pleaded under her breath.

'*Shhh,*' Sonia hissed. 'T, pay attention! Doesn't Bella look amaaazing? Don't you just love her dress?'

'Oh . . .' Tristan nodded, his chestnut quiff bouncing up and down. 'Yeah, it's nice.'

'*See?*' Sonia dug Bella in the ribs. 'I told you. Short and tight – boys are sooo predictable. Tristan'll be gagging for it in no time. Oh, and don't worry, I'll keep Rando out of the way while you work your magic.'

'Shhh! He'll hear you.'

'As if.' Sonia rolled her eyes. 'No one can hear anything over this music. Now come on – we're going to the toilets so you can put on more make-up.'

'But I'm wearing enough make-up.'

'Of course you're not, you halfwit. You have to look flawless for the Big Seduction. Trust me, I know what I'm talking about – I seduced Seb Ogilvy last term, didn't I? And how many other girls do you know who've managed to snog him? Boys!' Sonia called, not bothering to wait for a reply. 'Run along and fetch us more mojitos. Bella and I are off to powder each other's noses. Toodle-oo.'

127

'Guess we'd better listen to the ladies,' Tristan chuckled, leading the way towards the bar. 'And sorry about your less-than-warm welcome. I don't know what Sonia's problem is – did she expect me to come all alone?'

'She isn't exactly brimming with charm, is she?' Rando snorted, skirting an eight-foot-tall bouncer. 'No wonder she and Alice fell out.'

'Oh god, please don't mention Alice tonight. I only want to think about happy things. Such as the number of incredible hotties in this place.' Tristan gaped at a dark-skinned beauty with crystals woven into her hair. 'She's a goddess. And so is she! And so is she!' He nudged Rando. 'Hello? Can I get a little enthusiasm?'

'Sure . . .' Rando shrugged. 'They're pretty.'

'Pretty? Is that the best you can do? Well I, for one, am planning on following your cousin Jasper's advice.'

'Oh, no.' Rando shook his head in mock despair. 'This can't be good. Which bit in particular?'

'The bit about playing the field, of course. I've been thinking: I'm young, I'm single, and it's not like I'm ugly or anything. Why shouldn't I have a bit of fun?'

'Totally, man. If you say so.'

'Gee, thanks for the enthusiastic endorsement.' Tristan folded his arms. 'Do you have a problem with casual sex, or something?'

'Not at all. Not if you think it'll help you get over Alice. Personally, it wouldn't help me get over . . . someone I loved. But . . .' Rando cleared his throat. 'Anyway. We're not talking about me.'

'No, but maybe we should be.' Tristan's forehead creased. 'Are you all right, mate?'

'Yeah. Fine. Why?'

'Dunno. You just seem a bit . . . down. You've been quiet all week, and you totally didn't want to come out tonight – I practically had to drag you on to the train from Hasted. I mean, if I didn't know how much you worshipped me, I'd take it personally.'

'Ha! Yeah, it's really personal. Ha, ha.' Rando handed his gold AmEx card to the bartender. 'Hey, look, the girls are coming back. And by the way, T, you may not have to look too far if you want to pull tonight.'

'Huh? What do you mean?'

'Come on – it's so obvious Bella Scott has the hots for you.'

Tristan's eyes widened. 'Are you serious?'

'Duh. What planet are you living on? And she's cute.'

Tristan looked at Bella. It was true – she was cute. Right now, there was a lovely flush on her cheeks as she met his eye and then glanced away, sipping her mojito. Why hadn't he ever noticed her before? And, now he came to think about it, she was cool. She was the one who'd persuaded her dad to let the Paper Bandits play at his star-studded Christmas party. That had been a pretty decent thing to do.

'Hey,' he said, 'how was . . . how was the, er . . .' His mind had gone blank. Which, besides being incredibly lame, made no sense; it wasn't as if he'd never chatted up a cute girl before. Maybe he was out of practice. 'How was the loo?' he blurted out.

Bella giggled. 'Umm, fine.'

Tristan swallowed. She had a soft, full mouth, and pearly teeth that sparkled when she smiled. 'Is this your first time at LaLa's?'

'No. I was here for the premiere of *Gorilla Sunrise* – my dad's latest film. They took over the whole place for the opening party.'

'Wow. I saw that film – it was awesome. You must get to go to so many cool things.'

Bella ducked her head. Her hair bobbed against her smooth, dimpled cheeks. 'I guess.'

A few steps away, Sonia smirked, stroking her own sleek black hair as she watched the scene unfold. Rando had disappeared from sight; he'd obviously got the message. Now all she had to do was find Alice and her plan would be complete. Her eyes swept the club.

Chapter 21

'Hey, Ali, remember this move?' Tally cried. She'd cleared her very own ring in the centre of the dance floor, and all around her, floppy-haired boys in loafers and open-necked shirts were watching, slack-jawed, as she gyrated in her silver minidress and swung her white-blond hair in manic circles. 'Remember we made it up in our dorm room in Year Nine, just after I started at St Cecilia's?'

'OMG, stop!' Alice giggled. 'I had totally forgotten about that. We were so ridiculous back then.'

'Shit, my dress is falling down!'

'As if you care. You love flashing your boobs. Eeek!' Alice squawked, pointing. 'Look who it is. Redhead Man. Standing alone like a loser. Is he, like, stalking me?'

'I bet he is. You're such a good kisser, he just can't forget about you. He wants to keep smooching, and smooooohing, and— Shit.' Tally gripped Alice's wrist.

'What's wrong? Think you've seen some random person you know again?'

'Uh uh. This time it really is someone we know. It's . . . Hey, Sonia,' Tally trilled.

131

Alice stiffened. Slowly, she turned round.

'Hi, Tally. Hi, *Alice.*' Sonia was standing in front of them, a self-satisfied smile on her perfectly made-up face. Her lips, coated in just the right amount of gloss, were twitching in a freakish, maniacal way. 'Fancy bumping into you.'

Alice narrowed her eyes. 'What are you doing here? How did you know we were coming tonight?'

'*Excusez-moi?*' Sonia batted her eyelashes. 'This is a public place. It is merely coincidence that both our parties happen to be present.'

'Both our parties?' Tally snorted. 'What, you mean you're not here all by yourself?'

'Ha. Ha. Ha,' Sonia laughed mirthlessly. 'I'm terribly sorry, I should have said – I'm here with some good friends of ours. I believe they're . . . oh yes, right over there.'

She pointed a jewel-laden finger across the dance floor, and Alice caught her breath. There was Tristan, talking to Bella Scott. Actually, talking was an understatement – he was practically drooling all over her. Alice's eyes narrowed. T seemed to have made a remarkable recovery since she'd last seen him, practically in tears at Tom's Deli. At that moment, he leaned in for the kill.

'Oooh, they're kissing, they're kissing! Scandal!' Sonia screeched. A demonic grin spread across her face. 'Oopsie, Alice darling, guess you didn't want to see that. I feel sooo responsible. Hmm, it looks like Tristan's moved on . . .' she paused for effect, 'since he dumped you.'

Tally charged forward. 'Shut the fuck up, you nose-job

junkie bitch! For your information, Alice dumped him!
She—'

'Tals, darling,' Alice cut in, 'don't waste your breath.
Sonia Khan isn't worth our attention. She has no idea how
relationships work. She's never been out with anyone for
more than two weeks. That's the threshold, before people
realise what a loser she really is. Take Seb Ogilvy. He only
kissed her once before he ran a mile in the opposite
direction.'

Sonia's smile wobbled. 'Oh, bravo, Alice. Always so clever
with the insults. No wonder Tristan dropped you like a
stinking turd. No wonder he's found someone else.'

Alice sniffed. 'You know what, Tally? I can't be bothered
to listen to this. If you need me, I'll be in the loo.'

'Ring me if you want me, babes. I'll be right here,'
Tally growled, 'giving this slimy, cow-faced cretin a piece
of my . . .'

The rest of Tally's sentence escaped Alice's ears. She
slipped away, weaving among knots of gyrating dancers
towards the dim wood-panelled corridor at the back of the
club. Here, in the quiet, she stopped and leaned against
the wall. A memory lapped at her mind. A memory of that
balmy, starry September night in the fields between St
Cecilia's and Hasted House, when she and T had shared
their first kiss. Alice closed her eyes. It was stupid to care
about Tristan getting off with someone else. After all, she'd
dumped him. And she wasn't in love with him any more.
Maybe she never even had been. She drew in breaths of
the club's thick, sweat-soaked air.

'Alice?' said a voice. 'Is that you?'

Alice's heart stalled. Electricity shivered through her body. She opened her eyes. Rando was standing less than three feet away.

'What on earth . . .' He blinked in disbelief. 'What are you doing here?'

'The same as you, I guess.' Alice strained to keep her tone light. 'Trying to enjoy my Saturday night.' She ran a hand over her dress. Her palms felt clammy.

'You look pale.' Rando took a hesitant step towards her. 'Are you OK?'

'Yeah. It's just a bit stuffy in here. Probably drunk a bit too much.' Alice's heart was pounding. Blood throbbed in every part of her body. She raised her face, and Rando's beautiful blue eyes locked on hers.

Suddenly she was in his arms. 'I miss you,' she whispered.

'I miss you, too.' Rando's lips were inches from hers. Alice savoured the scent of his skin, his hair, his clothes. It was as if seeing Tristan with someone else had made her appreciate who she really loved; had made her want to cling to him with both hands.

At that moment, the hall door slammed open. The noise from the dance floor swelled.

'There you are!' someone cried.

Alice jumped backwards. Redhead Man was charging down the corridor, waving a shiny, purple object above his head. He barged between her and Rando with a self-satisfied grin. 'You little tease. I've been looking for you all over the place.'

'Oi!' Rando started forward. 'What do you think you're—' Just then, his eyes fell on the wallet in Redhead's hand.

'You dropped this.' Redhead held it out to Alice. 'I guess you got too carried away jumping on me to notice. Not that I'm objecting to a snog from a smoking-hot girl. And now you can snog me again as a thank-you for bringing it back.' He winked.

'Alice . . .' Rando said. 'What's going on?'

'Nothing. Just—'

'Who is this guy? Have you been kissing him?'

'If you mean me,' Redhead butted in, 'then I hate to break it to you, mate, but the answer is yes.'

Rando ignored him. He peered at Alice, his face taut.

Alice took a deep breath. 'Yes. I kissed him. But—'

'Forget about it.' Rando held up his hand. 'You don't have to explain yourself to me. We're not together – you can do what you want. Just do me a favour, and don't make a complete fool of me again, OK?' He swung on his heel, his fists clenched.

'Rando, stop! Please, let me explain. I . . . Wait!'

Rando spun back round. 'Why should I wait? What do you have to say to me? Nothing's any different to how it was before. Or . . .' He stared at her. 'Or is it?'

Alice looked into his eyes. They were glinting with the same steel as last weekend, when he'd demanded they come clean. To Tally. To Tristan. To everyone.

She dropped her gaze. 'No,' she mumbled. 'But please, I—'

The noise from the dance-floor boiled up again. She raised her face, and saw she was speaking to no one. The door slammed. Rando had gone.

Chapter 22

'You can't be serious!' Mimah exclaimed, almost spilling the perfume she'd been sampling in Space NK, Hasted's only decent make-up shop. Ignoring the saleswoman's glare, she gripped her phone to her ear. 'Sonia actually had the nerve to turn up there? What a little sneak.'

'Tell me about it. I came this close to breaking her pert little plastic-surgeoned nose for her,' Tally said on the other end of the line. 'And then, when Alice went to the loo, she actually tried to win me over. She was like, "I have nothing against you, Tally Abbott. I've reserved a special place for you in my new crew." As if. What a psycho.'

Mimah cackled. 'I can't believe I missed all the drama. I mean, Bella Scott and Tristan Murray-Middleton is serious gossip, too. Did they shag?'

The shop assistant's eyebrows puckered.

'I don't know.' Tally was whispering now. 'Alice wasn't up for a confrontation, so we left and went to get chips at Vingt Quatre. That place is always packed, even at two in the—'

'Oh, hang on. I've got a text,' Mimah interrupted. She detached her phone from her ear. It was from Charlie. Again.

137

Mimeee! R U coming to meet me or not? Hurry up!!!

'Ugh,' she groaned into the receiver, 'I think I should go. My little sister won't stop messaging me. She wants me to meet her in Asda.'

'Asda?' Tally exclaimed. 'Since when did Charlie go ghetto?'

'My question exactly. Apparently she needs advice on something.'

'Aw, that's sweet. Must be nice to have a little sister who looks up to you. Sometimes I wish I wasn't an only child.'

'And sometimes I wish I was,' Mimah said, as her phone beeped yet again. 'Listen, I'll see you and Al back at school tonight, OK? Bye.'

She hung up. Around the corner, Asda was buzzing. Townies were battling each other down the aisles, rushing to get the best deals on their weekly shop. An old lady with blue hair ran over Mimah's foot in her hurry to grab the last pack of cherry Bakewells. Mimah rolled her eyes.

I'm here, she texted Charlie. *Where the hell r u?*

Three seconds later the reply came.

Go to the info desk. Good luck.

Mimah grimaced. Good luck with what, exactly? Getting out of this place alive? Maybe Charlie was still hung-over from Friday night's Social, she thought, scanning the area around the information counter. No sign of her sister. She'd just decided to pack it in and go home when, suddenly, she saw him. He was standing behind the desk, wearing a blue shirt and a red tie. Mimah's jaw dropped. He *worked* here.

At that second, Aidan glanced up. 'Can I help you?' he began; then his neck tightened. 'Well. Look who it is. Miss Rags-to-Riches. Never thought I'd see you in a commoners' shop like this.'

Mimah took a step back. Her phone beeped.

Did u find him?? Have a good talk. Thought u guys needed one. C xxx

Mimah's legs went numb. 'Listen, I didn't know you worked here. I was just . . .'

'Sightseeing?' Aidan suggested. 'Interesting. Once again we bump into each other when I'm doing a job and you're loitering about enjoying yourself. Coincidence, or just the status quo?'

'Stop it, please,' Mimah implored.

'Stop what? Speaking the truth?'

'OK, I know you're pissed off with me. And I know I shouldn't have lied to you. But please, do you have to start off our first conversation in weeks by ranting about rich and poor and class and all that rubbish? It just makes you sound like you have a skyscraper-sized chip on your shoulder. And I know you're not like that. Not really.'

'Well, thanks for your faith in my character. And for the sociology lesson,' Aidan sneered. 'It's easy to call that stuff rubbish when you're on the winning end, isn't it?'

Mimah took a deep breath. 'Look, I'm sorry. You're right. I didn't mean to go off on a rant like that. And I won't bother you if you don't want me to. I just want to know if you're OK.' She paused. 'Are you?'

Aidan sniffed. He straightened the clipboard on his desk.

''Cause I heard you quit tutoring. And – and I was worried.'

'Oh, really? About what? That you'd no longer have an outlet to assuage your social conscience? It's tough for you rich kids, isn't it?'

'Yeah,' Mimah snapped, 'it is. You know what? Forget it. If you don't want to talk to me, that's your decision. But I wish you could just say so, and not be so fucking nasty. I did something shitty and I've admitted it. How long are you going to punish me?' Heaving her bag over her shoulder, she strode away from the desk. The black hair swinging across her face only half obscured her look of frustration and disappointment.

'Wait!' Aidan's voice reached her.

Mimah almost didn't turn around. When she did, he was tugging at his tie. 'I have a break now. I was gonna go for a walk.' He shrugged. 'You can come. If you want.'

She stood motionless for a moment. Then she gave a nod. 'OK.'

In the warmer months, the Hasted riverfront came alive, its pub gardens and piers buzzing with couples and families. But in the dead of January, all was quiet. The grey water flowed beneath the grey walkway under the grey sky. Boat masts spiked the air, matched in sharpness by the trees' bare branches. Aidan marched with his hands in his pockets, his eyes trained straight ahead. Mimah paced next to him, struggling to keep up despite her lacrosse-toned legs. Neither of them spoke for several minutes. Finally, Aidan raised his head.

'Maybe I shouldn't have been so unfriendly back there. But you caught me by surprise. Actually, I don't even know what I'm doing here with you – I promised myself I'd never talk to you again.'

Mimah glanced at his face.

'Do you have any idea how humiliating that was, turning up at London's poshest party as a waiter and seeing you were one of the guests? Serving you stupid little canapés on a silver tray? I thought I was gonna fucking die.'

Mimah bit her lip. 'I can imagine. Honestly, you don't know how sorry I am. I'm sorry I lied, I'm sorry I *kept* lying, I'm sorry for everything. But I knew you'd pigeon-hole me as soon as I said I went to St Cecilia's. You'd have judged me – admit it.'

'Of course I would have judged you! Everyone judges everyone else all the time. But you should have let me get to know the real you, not some stupid fake version.'

'I wanted to come clean once we got to know each other better, I promise – but by then it was too late. Anyway, you did know the real me! OK, so you were missing the rich-boarding-school bit, but just because my family has money doesn't mean my life is perfect. You have no idea what I've been dealing with for the past year.'

'OK, so tell me. What?'

'I . . . I don't really want to talk about it. But the point is, why should I be defined by my background?'

'That's a ridiculous question. Our backgrounds make us who we are.'

'I don't think that's true,' Mimah said slowly. 'I think

we make ourselves who we are. I mean, who we *really* are.'

'I wish I could believe that.' Aidan strolled to the water's edge. His shoulders were stooped inward towards his chest – as if he were hunching away from the world. As if, Mimah thought, he were hunching away from her. 'You know, I thought we actually had something, you and me.'

'We did! We still can. Maybe, if we just gave it another chance—'

'It won't work.' Aidan stared into the current. His eyes crinkled against the white winter light. 'I just can't trust you. I'm sorry.'

Mimah blinked. Her eyes were dry – she'd cried her fair share over Aidan – but his hollow voice hit her like a stone. 'OK. Just tell me one thing. Why did you stop going to tutoring?'

'That's none of your business.'

'But I mean, was it because of me?'

He was silent for a long moment. Then he sighed. 'No.'

'Then *why?* You were going to pass your maths GCSE and be an engineer and do great things.'

'Yeah, right,' Aidan scoffed. 'That was just a stupid dream.'

'How can you say that? You're clever – really clever. If you work hard and study, you can do anything you want.'

Aidan barked out a laugh. 'Is that what they tell you at school? That's the problem with you rich lot. You think that just because people *deserve* to get something, they'll get it. I hate to break it to you, but that's not the way things work in the real world.'

The wind gusted. Mimah pulled her parka tight. In a few short weeks, Aidan seemed to have given up on everything. His career. His ambition. Her.

'OK, I admit,' she burst out, 'being successful is easier for people who go to good schools and have money behind them and parents who know people. But that doesn't mean you can't do it. It doesn't mean you should just . . . quit.' She touched Aidan's sleeve. 'I believe in you.'

He glanced down at his arm, where her hand lay. Then he turned his eyes full on hers. 'I think you're the only person in the world who does.'

They stood there staring at each other.

Ring ring. Ring ring.

'Shit.' Aidan tore his gaze away, fumbling for his phone. 'Hello, Mum? Where are you?' His face tightened. 'Fuck. Not again. No, look, don't do anything. Just hang on. Just a few minutes. I'm coming. I'll be right there.' He hung up. 'I have to go.'

'Where?'

'Nowhere. Don't follow me!' Aidan flung over his shoulder, as he bolted away. 'And don't come looking for me again. This is the last time we can meet.'

'What? Why?' Mimah cried after him.

But Aidan's figure was already receding along the walkway. The flowing of the river was her only reply.

Chapter 23

Charlie nudged her tray along the salad bar in the Dining Hall, wrinkling her nose at the selection of rubbery Cheddar cheese, wilted broccoli florets, waxy lentils and tinned corn. The dinner ladies never put on a particularly good show on Sunday evenings, and they clearly hadn't chosen tonight to up their game. She sprinkled her mixed greens with dry-looking grated carrot, and headed for the nearest empty table. Mimah had just majorly bollocked her for interfering with Aidan, and she wasn't in the mood for socialising.

'Charlie baby!' a voice cackled in her ear. 'Your day just got a hundred times better! Guess who's back.'

Charlie turned round, and found herself staring into a grinning, make-up-laden face. 'George!' she exclaimed.

'Miss me?' Georgie Fortescue giggled, pinching a lettuce leaf off Charlie's tray.

'Of course. Like mad.'

'Good. Because I missed you, too. Home wasn't exactly a party.' Plonking herself into one of the Dining Hall's antique wooden chairs, Georgie hugged her bony knees to her chest. She narrowed her kohl-smothered eyes.

'Actually, Charlotte, I have a bone to pick with you. Why didn't you phone me more while I was suspended? Were you ignoring me or something?'

'What do you mean?' Charlie blinked. She ground some fresh pepper on to her food.

'You know what I mean. I left you three voicemails yesterday after the Social, and you didn't return a single one of them. I was dying to know how it went. Not to mention desperate to speak to someone other than my parents.'

'I wasn't ignoring you, I promise. I was just . . . hungover. Poor you. Was your mum being mean?'

'Of course she was,' Georgie snapped. 'Since when has Mummy not either ignored me or been a total cow?'

Charlie cast her friend a sympathetic look. The Fortescues owned diamond mines in South Africa, and they'd never had much time for their youngest daughter. They'd packed her off to boarding school at age six, and only just tolerated her presence during the Christmas, Easter and Summer holidays. Most of their love was lavished on Hattie and Lavinia, Georgie's stunning older sisters, who were both overachievers at uni in Bristol.

Georgie was still frowning. Charlie squeezed her arm. 'I really am sorry if I neglected you. I'm so happy you're back – school's been utterly shit without you.'

'Hmmm . . .' At last Georgie smiled. 'It better have been, biatch. Right, tell me all about the Social.'

'Oh, you missed nothing – it was way boring without you there.' Charlie laughed, but her grin felt tight. The

145

truth was, the Social hadn't been boring – it had been super-fun. And actually, it had been sort of refreshing not to have Georgie around. She and Georgie had only become friends over the past six months. Georgie had always been the most rebellious girl in their year, and her wild ways had appealed to Charlie in the dark days after her father left. But now, mistrust had snaked into Charlie's mind. Georgie was moody. She was unpredictable. And worst of all, she could be cruel. The Lauren Taylor diary fiasco had proven that beyond any reasonable doubt. Charlie hadn't seemed at all bothered that she'd almost ruined Lauren's life. In fact, she seemed to think the whole thing was a joke.

'Was there any gossip?' Georgie was looking at her intently.

'A bit. Nothing important. Minky Coombes snogged Henry Hollister. Izzy Bruin snogged Freddie Chiswell. Ooh, and James Pearce-Gibbon went down on Augusta Chapman in an empty Geography classroom! That's what Felix told me, anyway. Scandalicious! Can you imagine if Mrs Gould had caught them?'

'Big fucking deal.' Georgie tossed her brittle blond hair. 'You know I don't give a shit about any of that. What about Hugo?'

'I hardly saw Hugo. He was the MC. He was running round all night.'

'Well I hope you kept an eye on him for me.' A spiteful grin spread over Georgie's face. 'I almost forgot, how did Lauren Taylor survive? I bet she hid in the loo for the entire party and cried her little blue eyes out with embarrassment. What a loser. Hugo must think she's so lame.'

'Ha.' Charlie gave a constipated laugh.

'Ooh, Charl, I can't wait till Hugo's birthday party next weekend,' Georgie babbled on, her voice rising to a squeal. 'Last week he sent me a message saying he was looking forward to seeing me after my suspension. He is sooo sweet. We are so gonna get together at his party. It's finally gonna happen, I just know it! And then we can all go on double-dates.'

'Hooray!' Charlie cried.

But her tummy twisted. She was supposed to be inviting Lauren to Hugo's party. She'd promised him she would. And there was no way she could tell Georgie about that little plan. She swallowed. Things were going to get messy.

Chapter 24

Alice slumped down the Tudor House stairs in the pre-dawn midwinter darkness, rubbing her eyes and yanking her hair into a loose ponytail.

'Whoever invented Monday mornings was obviously a massive sadist,' she yawned, laying her head on Tally's shoulder. 'I need sustenance. Do you think we've got time for a sneaky cup of tea before Chapel?'

'I'll make you one if you like. Are you feeling all right, babe?'

'Yeah, apart from my massive sore head. I shouldn't have drunk so much on Saturday night. And I can't stop thinking about that redhead I snogged. Ugh. Rank.'

'Alice Rochester!' snapped a thin, reedy voice. The Ho was standing in the doorway to Tudor House's kitchen, glaring down at Alice like a bird of prey. 'Stop gossiping about your sex life and get a move on. You've got three minutes before Chapel. I hardly think that now is the time to start listing your weekend's conquests.'

'My conquests?' Alice's jaw dropped open. 'But . . . but Mrs Hoare, I wasn't—'

'Coats!' ordered the Ho, her beady eyes practically

spitting embers. 'Get your coats and get to Chapel, now. And don't contradict me, Alice Rochester. I believe I know what I heard.'

Alice's cheeks were practically purple as she and Tally grabbed their coats and pashminas from the cloakroom.

'That is so inappropriate,' she hissed, stomping into the frigid morning. 'She has no right to listen in on our conversations. And is it just me, or was she basically calling me a slapper? The Ho, calling *me* a ho!'

Felicity Foxton followed them, gnawing the end of a piece of toast.

'Hey, Ali,' she said, struggling into her coat and tamping down her hair. 'Did you have a good weekend?'

'Yeah, fine,' Alice sighed. She was so not in the mood for Felicity Foxton and her hideous frizz-head.

''Cause my brother said he saw you in the VIP queue for LaLa Lounge on Saturday night. He said you looked mega-cute.'

Alice rolled her eyes towards Tally. 'Oh, really?' She flashed a fake smile. 'I don't think I know your brother. Was he at LaLa's?'

'No, he was on his way to Kitts. On Sloane Square.'

'OMG, Kitts! That is so great. Hope he had fun.' Alice blinked at Felicity a few times. There was a long silence.

'Um, well, OK! See you later,' Felicity said at last, clearing her throat. She quickened her pace to walk ahead of them down the avenue towards Chapel.

Alice snorted. 'Ugh. I wish people wouldn't talk to me

all the time. '*Hey, Ali, Ali, my brother saw you on the weekend. Fuck off. What's she trying to do, impress me?*'

'Duh,' Tally said. 'People are always trying to impress you. Don't tell me you're not used to it by now.'

'But I mean, seriously, Kitts?' Alice scoffed. 'That place is so two years ago. Felicity Foxton is such a wannabe. Also, someone should tell her to shave her head. It looks like she's wearing a wig made of pubes.'

Tally burst out laughing. 'Babe, put the claws away, Flic isn't that bad. You're just in a grump because of the Ho. And because of, you know . . . Saturday night. Which is totally understandable, of course.' She gave Alice's shoulders a squeeze. They'd reached the yard outside Chapel, where girls were queuing up by year, waiting for the doors to open. 'I just wish there was some way I could cheer you up.'

'There is,' Alice said. 'It's easy. Go kill Sonia Khan.' She nodded towards a knot of about a dozen sixth-formers a few paces ahead. Sonia was standing in the centre, her high-pitched voice carrying right to their ears.

'Yah, girlies, I promise you, my seventeenth is going to the most exclusive party of the season. I'm only inviting the prettiest people in school. But don't worry – you've all made the cut, of course.'

Alice made a retching sound in Tally's ear.

'Sounds amazing,' Flossy Norstrup-Fitzwilliam squealed. 'And I just love the theme – Arabian Nights. What boys are you inviting?'

'All the hottest and most eligible ones, obviously. I've

had Penny de Claire send invitations to a hand-picked list from Hasted House, Glendales, St Vincent's and Gormley Hall.'

'Hang on, hang on,' Emilia Charles gaped. 'Penny de Claire is planning your party?'

'Wow,' said Cherry Rupert-Greene. 'She is a-mazing.'

'I know.' Sonia twisted her hair while stroking the diamond pendant that sparkled round her neck. 'Daddy said I should have the best. He likes to think of me as his little princess. And since it's going to be a bash full of gorgeous people, I've asked Bella to be my right-hand woman while I'm planning it – because she's absolutely stunning. Yes, you are, Bells. Yes, shut up, you are!'

'This is unbearable,' Alice whispered.

'Tell me about it,' Tally replied. 'I never thought Sonia could reach new lows of arse-kissing. But she has.'

Sonia's voice carried to them again, even louder than before. 'And I'll tell you who else thinks Bella's gorgeous.' In the dramatic pause, she cast a smug glance towards Alice and Tally. 'Tristan Murray-Middleton.'

'Wait, really? How do you know?' breathed Flossy Norstrup-Fitzwilliam, her big blue eyes bulging.

'Because on Saturday night, he and Bella—'

'Stop!' Bella said. Her face was beet-red. 'Sonia, please.'

'Oh, sorry, darling – I didn't mean to embarrass you. But you should be proud. Tristan Murray-Middleton is one of the biggest hotties around. You're lucky to have shagged him.'

'You shagged?' Cherry gasped.

'Sonia!' Bella cried. 'How could you tell everyone?'

Sonia slapped her hand over her mouth. 'Oopsie. I didn't mean to tell. It just slipped out. Mistake.'

Back in their part of the queue, Tally touched Alice's arm. 'Babe, are you OK? You shouldn't be hearing this. Do you want me to step in?'

'No,' Alice whispered. Her face was drawn, but calm. 'Let them have their stupid gossip. I don't need to make a fuss – I've got my self-respect.'

The group around Sonia and Bella was now screeching with excitement.

'I can't believe you slept with T!' burst out Emilia Charles. 'What was it like? Where did it happen?'

'Are you going out with him now?' clamoured Felicity Foxton.

'No, I . . . don't know,' Bella stammered, half giggling, half trembling. She shot her eyes towards Alice, clearly torn between the thrill of all the attention and the fear of payback. 'I mean, he's really hot and nice, but I didn't—'

'Jealous!' interrupted Cherry Rupert-Greene. 'Has he got a hot body from all that football?'

'Is he a good kisser?' asked Emilia.

'Ohmygod,' gushed Flossy, 'this is big.'

Sonia tittered. 'Yeah. I hear it *is* pretty big,' she snickered. Flossy, Emilia, Cherry, Felicity and the others erupted in giggles.

'Right, that is *it*!' Tally growled. And suddenly, before Alice could stop her, she hurled herself towards Sonia, tearing through the queue. Girls stumbled backwards in alarm. 'Shut up about Tristan, you stupid anorexic cow! You filthy worm! I warned you on the weekend, if you keep spreading gossip and upsetting Ali, I'll break your nasty little reconstructed nose for you right here, right now. Just try me.' Tally's lip was curled. Her body was taut and coiled, ready to spring.

Sonia stood perfectly still, a smug smile playing on her mouth.

'My, my, what a performance,' she sneered. 'That's right, Tally Abbott – threaten me. Try to intimidate me. That's the way you and Alice Rochester work, isn't it?' She turned to her audience. 'See why I'm not friends with Alice and her minions any more? They're manipulative and vicious and violent. They're practically criminals. I don't know why anyone likes them any—*Help!*'

Sonia fell backwards as Tally's hands landed on her chest. The two girls tumbled to the ground, shrieking and slapping and clawing.

'My hair! My make-up!' Sonia squawked, dragging herself out of the fray. As she stumbled to her feet, her hands cupped over her nose and her pashmina trailing down her back, she tripped over something.

'Wait, what . . . what's this?' she stammered, picking it up. 'Where did it come from?'

Everyone looked. In Sonia's hand was a massive wad of cash, at least three inches thick.

'Whoa,' exhaled Cherry Rupert-Greene.

'Shit,' muttered Emilia Charles. 'That must be at least a thousand pounds.'

153

'Give it here,' commanded a voice. 'It's mine.'

Everyone turned. Tally was holding out her hand. 'It fell out of my pocket. It belongs to me.'

'But . . .' Sonia sputtered, 'but what's it for? Where did you get it?'

'From the fucking bank,' Tally snapped, snatching the money and stuffing it into her pocket. Sonia stared at her. Then, slowly, her eyes shifted to Alice, whose jaw was hanging on its hinge. Sonia smiled to herself. Obviously she wasn't the only one confused by Tally Abbott's suspicious behaviour. And if she couldn't win Tally over to her side, she was going to have to resort to other methods of dealing with her instead.

Chapter 25

Seb twisted and turned in front of the mirror, attempting to examine his outfit from every possible angle. It was Friday evening, and he had the dorm room to himself. Tristan, along with the rest of the gang, had rushed off to the Dining Hall for fish sticks and mashed potatoes, but Seb couldn't think about food.

Nervously, he hummed along to the 1930s jazz crooning out of his iPod dock. He was listening to Duke Ellington's 'Mood Indigo', which was the only thing that could calm him down when he was scared out of his wits. He listened to it before exams. He'd listened to it before his driving test in the autumn. And he was listening to it now, before his date with Will Larkin. Which was – he shuddered – tomorrow night.

Taking a deep breath, Seb drained his engraved silver whisky flask. Then he read Will's text for the fiftieth time.

Still on for drinks 2moro? Lemme know, looking forward. I've got a few venues in mind.

Wonderful. A few venues. How unhelpful could you get? Seb looked down at his slim corduroy suit and striped skinny tie. Maybe he should wear drainpipe jeans and a check shirt instead. Or a tweed jacket. Or a plain old American Apparel T-shirt. He nodded to himself. Yeah, low-key, that was probably the best option – nothing said 'loser' like trying too hard. Which meant it was a good thing that Will couldn't see him now, deciding on outfits an entire twenty-four hours in advance.

Sticking his hands in his pockets, Seb turned back to the mirror. If only his blue eyes didn't look so terrified. If only his hair wouldn't stick out in every conceivable direction. If only he didn't look so . . . uptight. Loosening his tie, he threw back his shoulders.

'You're cool,' he mouthed to himself. 'You're hot. You're gonna be great.'

'What. The. Fuck?' guffawed a voice.

Seb leapt a foot in the air. He whirled around. Tristan was standing in the doorway.

'How – how long have you been there?'

'Long enough to see you acting like a freak,' T grinned. 'Oh, mate, I have so many questions about what the hell you're doing. Like, why on earth are you listening to your relaxation music while you're all dressed up in that suit? And why, oh why, are you talking to yourself?'

Seb yanked off his tie. 'Look, man, shut up. I've got to go to this . . . do tomorrow. With my dad. Some ballet thing – yeah, he's really into funding ballet at the moment. His new girlfriend – or one of his new girlfriends, I should say – is a choreographer.' Seb silently congratulated himself. This sounded plausible. And the part about the girlfriend, at least, was true.

Tristan was tapping his foot. 'All right, that explains the suit. And the talking to yourself? Don't tell me you're going senile.'

'No, man. Practising my small talk. Small talk's an art, you know. One that I've perfected, if I do say so myself.'

'Oh, right, Sebastian Ogilvy, the small-talk maestro.' T flopped down on his bed. 'Shame you're not here tomorrow night, though – I was thinking we could go to the pub in Hasted and have a few pints. I need a quiet one after last weekend.' He rubbed his hair and looked at Seb expectantly. 'So, are you going to ask me or not?'

'About what?'

'About Bella Scott! About my wild weekend. I've been waiting all week to have a chance to chat. You haven't asked me about it once.'

Seb chuckled. 'Dude, when did you turn into such a girl? I didn't want to pry – I thought if you wanted to talk about it, you'd bring it up. And anyway, you've been hiding out in the Library all week.'

'That's 'cause I've got mental amounts of work to do. This term sucks. You know, the only person who doesn't seem massively stressed out is Jasper. I just saw him at dinner and he was completely off his face.' T made a joint-smoking motion with his fingers. 'He's stoned the whole fucking time these days. And then whenever he turns up to class, he's got his prep done. What is *up* with that?'

'Dunno. Maybe the weed fairies are writing his essays

for him.' Seb shrugged out of his suit jacket. 'So, go on then, how was it? Last weekend, I mean.'

'It was cool. Yeah.' T grinned. 'It was nice. Bella's a nice girl.'

'And?'

'I dunno. Her parents were away in LA, so we went back to her place. We didn't even really chat – we just got right down to business. She's got a great body. A lot curvier than Alice. Kind of . . . softer.'

'That's not difficult,' Seb laughed.

'And then I left in the morning. Didn't stay for breakfast. You know, it's weird sleeping with someone where there are no emotions involved. I mean, I know some people do it all the time . . .'

'*Jasper*.' Seb coughed.

'Exactly. But I never had. It's quite liberating, actually. It's cool to know that you can have fun with someone without caring about them. There's no angst, no worrying about what it *means*. It's just physical.'

'So I'm guessing you're not gonna take it any further. Bella Scott isn't gonna be the next Mrs Murray-Middleton?'

'Nah.' T shook his head. 'I'm not into finding another girlfriend right now. Like I said, I just wanna have fun.'

'Does *she* know that?'

'I guess so. I mean, I haven't called her.' T scratched his head. 'Why, do you think I should?'

'Um, I think it'd be nice . . . Like, you could send her a text or something. You know, so she doesn't feel bad.'

'Hmm. Yeah.' Tristan glanced at his phone. 'I dunno. I've been working on a song about it, though. I only have lyrics so far. You want to see them?'

'Sure.'

T handed Seb a piece of paper, obviously torn out of his rough book. It was dirty and crumpled, and looked like it had been travelling in his pocket for days.

ONE-WOMAN FOOL

Babe I think you're pretty,
Babe I think you're cool
But babe, I gotta warn you
I'm no one-woman fool.
I won't buy you flowers,
Roses white or red.
Won't even cook you breakfast
If you wake up in my bed.

I might buy you dinner
If you let me spend the night
But baby, I'll be moving on
As soon as it gets light.

I'm not a fucking bastard –
I just have a lot of flings.
Wild like an eagle
I just wanna spread my wings.

So baby, we can hang out,
But remember this one rule –
Don't try to tie me down –
I'm no one-woman fool.

Seb cleared his throat. 'Interesting. Yeah. I like the rhythm. Rando'll have a fun time on the drums. And it's, er, really . . . sensitive.' He grinned. 'Maybe don't show it to Bella, though, OK?'

'Hmmm . . .' T scratched his chin, clearly not listening. 'I might try to come up with some kind of chorus. Maybe I'll take a little break before I finish my prep.'

Seb turned around and, in the mirror, watched as Tristan plucked a few chords on his guitar. Then his eyes flicked back to his own face. For as long as he could remember, he'd been a spectator at the show of his best friend's life. He'd witnessed T's loves. Watched his sports. Listened to his songs. He knew it was time for a change. And however tomorrow went, he was going to have some stories of his own.

Chapter 26

Georgie Fortescue stomped across Quad, her face thunderous, her silver-studded boots echoing off the crumbling stones.

'I have the worst news ever,' she grumbled, accosting Charlie Calthorpe de Vyle-Hanswicke at their regular meeting spot outside the Dining Hall.

'What is it, darling?'

'My parents are grounding me for the entire weekend. They're saying that since I got suspended I can't go out at all, not even with a curfew. It's practically child abuse.'

'That's awful!' Charlie exclaimed, as the two friends descended the sweeping, red-brick steps on to the Great Lawn. It was Saturday lunchtime, and lessons had just finished for the weekend. Girls were scurrying across school, lugging satchels full of prep, heading to sports practices, and rushing back to their dorms to change out of their uniforms. Charlie blew a strand of jet-black hair out of her face. 'Tonight is literally the worst night they could choose to suddenly become disciplinarians. You've been looking forward to Hugo's party for ages. Isn't there anything you can do?'

'No. My house is like a fucking prison. My parents are gonna be watching TV in the living room all night, and if I try to sneak past, they'll see me.'

'Hang on, I've got an idea. How about you tell them you're staying at mine?'

Georgie rolled her eyes. 'Excuse me, imbecile, but does the word "grounded" mean nothing to you? Oh no, I forgot – your dad's absent and your mum's a zombie on drugs who doesn't even *notice* what you do, let alone care.'

'What the hell?' Charlie stopped dead. Two red spots were burning on her cheeks. 'How can you say that? Why do you have to be so . . . so bloody mean?'

Georgie folded her arms inside her ratty poncho-style jumper. In the harsh daylight, you could clearly see how much foundation she'd caked on to cover her acne. 'Look, I'm sorry, OK? I didn't mean it. I'm just in a bad mood. My life sucks.'

'That doesn't mean you should try to make my life suck too! I'm meant to be your best friend.'

'You are!' Georgie linked her arm through Charlie's and walked on, gripping her in a vice. 'I'm sorry. I'm sorry, I'm sorry, I'm sorry! Now, can you stop being so fucking high-maintenance, please? I need you to do me a favour.'

Charlie sighed. 'What?'

'Make sure you tell Hugo how distraught I am that I can't be there tonight. I'm about to text him myself, but I want him to be thinking about me all night long. So keep mentioning my name. God! I can't fucking believe I'm missing his party.' Georgie shot a death stare at a

passing Year Seven. Then, suddenly, her expression bright-
ened. 'Ooh, by the way, Charl, I've got him such an
awesome present. I spent loads of money on it – I practically drained my bank account.'

'Oh, George, are you sure that's a good idea?'

'Of course it's a good idea. I've liked Hugo for ages.
It's about time he knew it.'

'If you say so.' The girls had reached the front hall of
Locke House, and Charlie detached her arm from
Georgie's. 'I'm just going to get my wallet. See you back
here in five?'

'OK. But hurry up. I'm hungry for lunch.'

Upstairs, Charlie pushed open the door to her dorm.
Lauren was sitting at her desk, hunched over a textbook,
chewing the top of her pen. Charlie felt a pang of guilt.
She'd hardly exchanged three sentences with Lauren since
Georgie had come back. She'd told herself it was to protect
Lauren. But if she was honest, she knew it was to protect
herself, too. Anyway, now that Georgie wasn't coming to
the party tonight, she might be able to grant the birthday
favour that Hugo had asked.

'Hey, Lauren?'

'Yeah?' Lauren muttered, without looking up.

'Got a sec? I wanted to ask you something.'

'OK . . .' Lauren twisted round. 'What?'

'Well, there's this party in London tonight. I was
wondering . . . I was wondering if you're free. I mean, if
you wanted to come.' Charlie almost laughed. This was so
awkward; it felt like she was asking Lauren on a date.

'Wait.' Lauren's face was confused. 'What?'

'A party.' Charlie sat down on her bed. 'I'm inviting you . . . to a party . . . in London. Got it?'

'Yeah, I thought that's what you said.' Lauren fiddled with a strand of her yellow hair. 'Whose party is it?'

'Oh, just some girl from another school,' Charlie lied. No way would Lauren come if she knew it was Hugo's party. 'I'm . . . uh . . . not really gonna know anyone there. So I thought it'd be nice if you'd keep me company.'

Lauren was looking at her suspiciously. 'What about Georgina Fortescue? Won't she be there to keep you company?'

'Oh. No. She's grounded.' Charlie flashed a quick smile. 'So you don't have to worry. Come on,' she added. 'It'll be fun. It's neon-themed – everyone's gonna be wearing crazy dayglo stuff.'

Lauren was silent for a moment, thinking. From outside, the laughing voices of Isabelle Bruin and Augusta Chapman floated through the open window. In the corridor, a group of girls were chattering, their footsteps receding over the squeaky old floors. Everyone but her had somewhere to go. She glanced at her Spanish textbook, then out the window at the now-empty front garden, and then around at the quiet, half-deserted dorm. Finally, her eyes landed on Charlie again. She twisted her pen between her fingers, trying to make up her mind.

Chapter 27

'What do you think of these, darling?' Piper Taylor called, pointing to the pair of sparkling diamanté-encrusted shoes on her feet.

'Nice!' Dylan exclaimed. She and her mom were in Christian Louboutin on Mount Street, one of London's chicest shops at one of its most exclusive Mayfair addresses. This afternoon had been the perfect bonding experience – a late lunch at Bar Boulud in Knightsbridge, followed by a spending spree. 'But what are they for? Do you have a party or something?'

'Darling, I have my wedding, silly!' Piper did a twirl. 'I was thinking I could wear them on the big day. They'll definitely go with the dress. See?' Reaching into her Hermès bag, she took out a sketch of her wedding gown, which was being custom-designed by Stella McCartney.

Dylan stared at the drawing. She tried to imagine her mother in that white pouf, in those shoes, walking down the aisle with Victor Dalgleish in just a few months. She still couldn't believe her mom was marrying such an insincere, slimy, self-obsessed sleaze. But she'd sworn to herself that she'd be nice about him. At least in front of her mother.

She smiled. 'I think they're beautiful. You'll look absolutely great.'

'Thank you, darling. They are adorable, aren't they? Well, I suppose I might as well take them. If I change my mind I can always buy something else.' Piper smiled, handed her platinum AmEx card to the salesgirl and glanced at her watch. 'Wow, it's past six thirty – time flies. What time did you say you were going out?'

Dylan shrugged. 'Not sure. I'm seeing Jasper, but we haven't made a plan yet.'

'Now why am I not surprised? It's a mystery to me how you and your sister ever get anything done – you're both allergic to commitments. You refuse to make any kind of plan till the very last minute.'

Dylan shrugged. 'All of my friends are like that. Making plans is lame. It's like, really uptight.'

'Whatever you say.' Piper pulled on her gloves and opened the shop door. 'Well, since you're so relaxed and spontaneous, how about we dash over to the Connaught for a quick mother–daughter drink? They have a lovely hotel bar.'

'Wait, really? You mean you'll let me have a glass of wine?'

'In your dreams,' Piper snorted. 'I'll have a glass of wine. You can have a lemonade. I realise you probably drink with your school friends, but not with me.'

Dylan grinned and rolled her eyes. 'Well, OK. Since I'm at a loose end . . .'

Around the corner at the Connaught, a top-hatted doorman directed them through the lobby to the stylish art-deco bar, where leather banquettes curled around low tables, and flickering candles reflected in the gleaming marble floors. The buzz of conversation was growing steadily louder as the evening crowd filtered in. Dylan checked her phone twice before placing it on the table. She should be hearing from Jasper any minute. In fact, she should have heard from him already.

'Isn't this a treat?' Piper said, crossing her long, slim legs and picking up her glass of Beaujolais. 'Cheers, darling.'

'Cheers.'

'Now, tell me, how are things with Jasper?'

'Fine . . .' Dylan sipped her lemonade, suddenly alert. She eyed her mother over the top of the glass.

'Remind me, what was his last name again? Van something?

'Von Holstadt.'

'Oh, yes, Holstadt. Vic says they're a *very* good family. Very impressive. Old German royalty,' Piper added in a whisper.

'Yeah, whatever. I guess.'

'Well, you may be all casual about that sort of thing right now, Dilly, but when you get older, you'll realise how important it is. Now, dear . . .' Piper patted her pale blond hair. 'I've been wanting to have a talk with you. I think it's very nice that you have a boyfriend. I just hope you're being safe. Are you using condoms, or something else?'

Dylan spluttered out her mouthful of lemonade. '*Excuse* me?'

'It's very important to protect yourself, darling. If you're having intercourse with Jasper, you have to be safe. Do you want me to take you to the doctor so you can go on the Pill?'

'Mom!' Dylan glanced in panic at the group of young people who had just colonised the next table. 'Please.'

'OK, OK, just trying to help. If you're mature enough to have sex, you should be mature enough to talk about it.'

'Well can we talk about it *another* time?' *Like, never,* Dylan added to herself.

'Of course, dear. I didn't mean to embarrass you. But if you need anything, just know I'm here. Remember, I have a lot of experience myself.'

'Oh my god.' Dylan shut her eyes. 'I cannot believe this conversation. I'm going outside to make a phone call, OK?'

'Sure. But don't be long. Victor's whipping up a stir-fry and we're planning to watch that *Downton Abbey* boxset he gave me for Christmas.'

Dylan drained her glass, wishing it contained a strong shot of something, and bolted outside into the chilly evening. She punched in Jasper's number.

'Hello?' He picked up on the eighth ring, and his voice was croaky.

'Jasper?'

'Dylan? Hey, baaabe.'

'Are you sick? You sound kind of sick.'

'Me?' Jasper giggled. 'No way, man. I'm high. Heehee!'

Dylan sighed. 'Oh, OK. Well, what time do you want to meet?'

'Meet?'

'Yeah. It's almost seven thirty. Should I just come over to your house and pick you up?'

'Sure you can go to my house.' Jasper giggled. 'I'm sure my parents would love to see you.'

Dylan made a face. 'What are you talking about?'

'I'm in Hasted, babe. I'm not in London. George Demetrios and I are watching reruns of *The Inbetweeners*. Heehee! Oh, wait, I love this scene. George, George, pause it.'

'Jasper!' Dylan barked. 'Get with it. What do you mean, you're still in Hasted? We had plans!'

'Chill, babe. Take a chill pill, heehee! Since when did you get so plan-crazy? Oh, hold on, I've got a call waiting.'

There was a series of beeps on the line. Dylan was shaking, both from frustration and from the cold. She'd left her coat inside. She should just fucking hang up. She was about to, when Jasper's voice came back on the line.

'Tals, gorgeous! Have you got the goods? When can we meet?'

'Hello?' Dylan frowned. 'It's still me.'

'Oh!' Jasper cleared his throat. 'Ummm . . . sorry, I thought—'

'I can tell what you thought!' Dylan snapped. She took a deep breath, trying to keep her voice calm. 'Jasper? I

169

have two questions: one, why are you calling Tally Abbott "gorgeous", and two, why the hell are you meeting up with her when you were supposed to be seeing me?'

'I'm not . . . Dill, gorgeous, it's not like it sounds. I—'

'How dare you call me gorgeous! You know what? I can't talk to you right now. Call me when you're not stoned out of your brain. And when you're ready to keep our plans.'

Dylan shoved her phone into her pocket. Her head was pounding. *Have you got the goods?* What was Jasper talking about? Money? No, he had plenty of that. Booze? No, he could just go buy some. Drugs? Dylan slapped her hand to her mouth. Was Tally dealing drugs? She always had been a bit wild. And after all, no one knew where she'd disappeared to over New Year. She could have fallen in with any number of shady people. Dylan took a deep breath. Her teeth were chattering with cold. She couldn't think about this right now. She had to go back inside. She had to explain to her mom that her plans for tonight were off. Grimacing, she imagined herself crashing Piper and Victor's romantic *Downton Abbey* fest, trying desperately to fend off another 'safe sex talk' attack. This was going to be the lamest Saturday night ever.

Just then, Dylan spotted a skinny, blond figure in the square in front of the hotel. She squinted. Was it . . . ? 'Seb!'

He whipped around.

'Hi!' Dylan grinned. 'We have to stop bumping into each other like . . .' Her words died as she clocked the look of panic on Seb's face. Before she could ask what was wrong, a tall, strawberry-blond boy bounded across the street.

'Hey!' he said, touching Seb's arm. 'Sorry, am I late?'

'N-no,' Seb stammered. He shot his eyes towards Dylan. 'I was early.'

'Cool. Is this a friend of yours?'

'Yeah. But . . . I just bumped into her. Shall we—'

'Hi! Will Larkin,' the boy interrupted, flashing a thousand-watt grin. 'Nice to meet you.'

Dylan introduced herself, trying not to stare. This Will Larkin character was totally beautiful. He had high cheekbones and eyes the colour of the Caribbean sea. For some reason, she felt like she'd seen him somewhere before. Maybe he was one of the Ogilvys' family friends.

He turned back to Seb. 'Listen, man – before we go in, I have a confession to make.'

'Oh? What?' Seb's foot was tapping the pavement. He stuck a cigarette between his lips, but his hand was shaking so badly he could barely light it. Dylan's forehead creased.

'There's this party I promised I'd go to later on. One of my co-stars in *Much Ado About Nothing* – it's her birthday. Do you want to come? There'll be loads of celebs there – good people-watching, I promise.'

'Um . . . Yeah, maybe. Sounds fun.' Seb shuffled his brogues on the pavement.

'Cool. Shall we go inside, then? I booked us a table. Oh, wait, finish your cigarette.'

Dylan sighed. 'Well, I guess I'd better disappear, guys.

I'm with my mom. Lame, I know. Anyway, nice to meet you, Will. Have a fun night.'

Both boys waved. And then, just as she was turning away, Dylan heard it – Will's voice, soft as a murmur: 'Seb, listen, it's great to see you again. I was super-excited when I met you at Lucian Scott's party – but I thought you'd never call.'

Dylan's eyes darted back to them. Will was reaching out to touch Seb's hand, his fingers lingering hesitantly a few centimetres away. And Seb's cheeks were glowing a deep, translucent red.

Her mouth dropped open. In a rush, she understood.

Chapter 28

By the time their martinis arrived, Seb was so stressed out he was practically paralysed. He replayed the scene on the hotel steps again and again in his head, struggling to work out how likely it was that Dylan *knew*. His mind felt like a pendulum on speed – one second he was convinced she'd realised everything; the next, he was certain he was safe.

Across the table, Will popped a big green olive into his mouth.

'It's absolutely astounding, rehearsing at the Globe,' he was saying. 'Have you been there? To the Globe? It's this massive Elizabethan theatre that they've reconstructed to look just like it did in Shakespeare's day. But duh, I'm sure you knew that – I remember at Sir Lucian's party, you told me you were interested in history. Anyway, I was absolutely shocked when I got the part – I was up against so many brilliant Shakespearean actors. But I think Nigel – that's our director – was looking for fresh young faces. The new generation in theatre. Know what I mean?' His olive stone landed in the saucer between them.

'Oh. Yeah. Right.' Seb gulped his cocktail. Will was even better-looking than he'd remembered. He was wearing his unruly reddish-blond hair swept back from his face, accentuating his wide mouth and his sky-blue eyes. But Seb couldn't concentrate on that. He couldn't concentrate on anything.

'The rest of the actors are an absolutely brilliant bunch,' Will went on. 'They're all totally up-and-coming. Jenna Vance plays my love interest – she just got cast in the new Ryan Gosling film. And then there's Corey Benson, who's in like, every single BBC miniseries ever made. Corey is *such* a brilliant guy, actually – he's twenty, only a year older than me, but his career's miles ahead of mine. Have you seen him in anything?'

'Umm . . .' Seb polished off his martini. 'Sorry, who?'

Will frowned. 'Listen, are you OK?'

'Of course! I'm fine.' Seb produced a grin. 'Sorry. I just guzzled that martini a bit too fast.'

'Really? Because I feel like a bit of a weirdo. I mean, no offence but I've been nattering away for the past ten minutes and you're just . . . sitting there.'

'Oh god, I'm sorry. I'm really sorry, I'm listening, I promise.'

'All right, no need to go all apologetic on me. If you're nervous, it's fine. First dates are always weird, aren't they? That's why booze was invented.' Will chuckled. 'If you're freaking out, just drink more.'

'Yeah. Ha, ha. My philosophy exactly.' Seb rubbed his head. 'Oh, and try not to bump into people you know before the date even starts.'

'You talking about that girl outside?'

'Yeah.' Seb squeezed his eyes shut. 'God, it's so awful. Why did she have to be there? I can't believe it.'

'Awful?' Will gave a bemused laugh. 'What are you on about? Are you embarrassed to be seen with me?'

'No! It's not that – it's nothing to do with you. It's just, I don't know, she might . . . *tell* someone.'

'Tell someone? Who? The date police?'

'Yeah. Well, I mean, our friends – which is basically the same thing. If anyone found out, it'd be the worst thing that ever happened to me. I don't know what the hell I'd do. Shit.'

There was no reply. Seb looked up.

Will's face was stony as, slowly, he set down his glass. 'Excuse me,' he said, 'but what exactly are you trying to imply?'

'H-huh?' Seb fiddled with his napkin. He'd obviously made some kind of mistake.

'Are you . . . are you trying to tell me you're not *out*?'

'I . . . I . . . Well, no. Are you?'

Will's face darkened. 'Of course I bloody am! I'm not ashamed of who I am. For fuck's sake!' He shoved his drink away. 'Typical. I'm on a date with a closet case. I am so *over* this – guys who sneak around and practically faint whenever I mention meeting their mates. It's pathetic. I mean, how do you even do it? How can you call people your friends if they don't even know when you're dating someone?'

Seb just looked at him. He bit his lip.

'Whoa, hang on.' Will leaned way back in his chair.

'Have you ever even dated anyone at all? Is this your first ever date? Oh my god – it is, isn't it? Brilliant. This just gets better and better.'

Suddenly, Seb jumped up.

'I should just go!' he blurted out miserably. 'You're right, I'm sorry, I never should have come.'

Seizing his jacket, he squeezed out of the banquette, trying to swallow down the well of anguish in his chest. How could he have been so stupid? All his ridiculous fantasies about this date – how he might have actually met someone who liked him and understood him. How he might actually have a life. And now here he was crawling back home to Daddy's house, everything over after one drink.

He reached the exit. Cold air from the lobby hit him in the face. Laughter spilled from an incoming group. And then, without warning, a hand landed on his shoulder.

'Seb. Wait.'

He turned. Will had followed him and was slightly out of breath, his eyes distressed.

'I'm sorry. I'm really sorry. I didn't mean to attack you like that. I'm a total dick.'

'Forget about it.' Seb tried to push past him. 'You're not. I should have—'

'What? Confessed this was your first ever date? Sent me a CV of your boyfriend credentials?' Will sighed. 'God, I shouldn't have lost it like that. I forget how it can be, for some people. I forget how hard it is. I mean, not to be vain or anything, but I'm an actor with a pretty face

– people almost *expect* me to be gay. And you're what, seventeen and at boarding school? There's probably like, one pupil who's ever come out in the entire history of that place, and people still talk about it. Right?'

Seb gave a caustic laugh. 'Something like that.'

'Yeah, well, exactly. So . . . I'm sorry.'

'Forget it.' Seb took another step towards the door. 'It's not a big deal.'

'It is. But please: stay anyway?'

Seb looked at Will. His confident movie-star swagger had disappeared, and in its place was an earnest look. His eyes, behind their beautiful blue, were imploring, and almost a little afraid. After a few seconds, Seb dropped his shoulders. 'Well, I guess I didn't really want to go home and watch black-and-white movies by myself anyway . . .'

'So you'll stay?'

'Yeah. For now.'

'Excellent,' Will beamed. 'I'll make it up to you, I promise. And I'm gonna convince you to come to that party later, too. Because I told everyone in the cast that I had a date tonight, and if I turn up solo, I'll look like a total loser.'

Seb grinned.

'Will Larkin!' a voice cried at that moment. A woman pushed past Seb and threw her arms in the air. 'So it is you! I thought it was.'

Will's eyes widened. 'Oh, Zaza! Wonderful to see you! Mwah, mwah.'

'Mwah, darling! So, you're opening in *Much Ado* soon.

Nigel's been spreading the most marvellous buzz about you.'

'Oh, has he? I must tell him off when I next see him, then – I'm sure he's exaggerating.'

'Not at all! We all know how talented you are. In fact, hold on – I'm emailing my assistant right now to call your agent and set up a meeting.'

'Wow, that would be brilliant.' Will shot Seb an apologetic glance. '*Sorry,*' he mouthed. '*Networking. Be right there.*'

Seb nodded. 'See you at the table.' Back in his seat, he chewed his lip. The Dylan dilemma was still nagging at his mind. He couldn't just leave it – who knew what conclusions she might jump to? And more important, who knew who she'd tell? But what was he meant to say? *Please don't think I'm gay?* He weighed his phone in his hand, racking his brain.

Hey, he wrote, *sorry if I was awkward earlier on. U caught me by surprise.*

His phone beeped in reply.

No worries.

Cool. Ummm so it's kind of a secret I'm out with a friend 2nite. T thinks I'm with my dad. Can u keep it to yourself? PLEASE?

Sure. On one condition.

Seb gulped. What condition? *What condition?* His heart was practically jumping out of his chest. A second later, his phone beeped again.

Invite me to that glam celeb party you were talking about. Sounds fun! And I'll keep quiet about anything you want. ☺

Seb pulled at his hair. What was the smiley face for? Was Dylan talking in some kind of code? And how the hell was Will going to react to this? Surely he couldn't just invite some random to gatecrash their date.

But he had to. There was nothing else he could do.

Chapter 29

Lauren Taylor smoothed her little black dress, trying to ignore the fluttering in her tummy as the taxi chugged into a pristine Kensington square and halted outside an enormous house.

'Whoa.' She turned to Charlie Calthorpe de Vyle-Hanswicke. 'Whose party did you say this was again?'

'Hmm? Oh, don't worry, the cab's on me,' Charlie said, burying her face in her handbag and pretending not to hear the question. 'Hey, look, they've got disco lights. Sounds like loads of people are here already.'

'Yeah.' Lauren trembled as Charlie led the way up the front steps. Bass notes, punctuated by squeals and cheers, were throbbing out through the house's stunning Victorian facade. For some reason, she had a funny feeling about this party. But she couldn't explain why. Probably just nerves.

The door swung open.

'Charlie! Hurrah!' cried a boy Lauren didn't recognise. He was wearing a neon-yellow T-shirt, neon trainers and at least twenty neon plastic tubes round his neck. 'Coats in the utility room. Drinks downstairs. Presents can go in the— Hold it, hold it.' The boy was blocking Lauren's way. 'Who are you?'

'Oh, um, I'm with Charlie. She said it would be OK if I came. I didn't mean to—'

'Jonno!' Charlie cut in, grabbing Lauren's arm. She rolled her eyes. 'Can you please stop terrorising my friend?'

'I'm not terrorising her. I was only about to offer her some face paint. She doesn't look nearly neon enough.'

Lauren glanced down at her outfit. 'Oh. But I'm wearing neon tights, see?' she said, pointing to her bright pink legs.

'First of all,' Jonno said, 'those are not neon – they are merely garish. And second of all, that's the only element of colour in your entire outfit. The rest is black.'

'Oh god,' Charlie groaned. 'You'll have to excuse Jonno. He's a bit pedantic, as you can see.'

'It's not my fault! Our host specifically told me – if they haven't made an effort, ambush them! Not that I'm complaining – it's a pretty good job, checking out each and every girl who comes through the door.'

'Perv. I suppose you do have a point, though – Lauren isn't looking particularly festive.' Grinning, Charlie swiped a tube of face paint off the hall table. 'Come on, let's brighten her up.'

'Whoa, wait, what are you doing?' Lauren squealed.

'Just a little makeover . . . Jonno, you get the orange. I've got the yellow and pink.'

'Help! I'm under attack!' Lauren giggled, fidgeting as Charlie drew a sun on one of her cheeks and Jonno produced a zigzag pattern on the other.

'Much better,' Charlie said, standing back to admire her handiwork.

'Agreed. And now,' Jonno added, placing a neon-green halo over her hair, 'you're allowed in.'

'Oh god, I feel like such a freak,' Lauren said, as she and Charlie edged past a cluster of people in the hall, trying not to disturb a row of valuable-looking oil paintings, and started down a flight of stairs.

'What do you mean? Look at those girls – they're wearing way more neon crap than you. Don't be uptight – you have to get into the spirit of things.'

Lauren raised her eyebrows. Getting into the spirit of things wasn't exactly easy when you'd been forcibly kept *out* of it for so long. But before she could mention this, they reached the bottom of the stairs and emerged into a huge state-of-the-art kitchen, heaving with party guests. People were everywhere – dancing on chairs and sprawling on countertops and pouring beer down each other's throats. Lauren's eyes darted to and fro.

'Hey,' she said, tapping Charlie's shoulder, 'you thought you wouldn't know anyone here, but there are plenty of St C's girls. There's Portia, and Minky and— *Ohmygod.*' Lauren's throat constricted. Something had caught her eye – an enormous banner hanging above the doors to the garden, its letters screaming down at her: *HAPPY BIRTHDAY HUGO!*

'Charlie . . .'

'What?'

'Wh-whose party is this?'

182

'Hmm? Oh, I—'

'Is it Hugo Rochester's party? *Is it?*' Lauren cried.

Charlie glanced at the banner. 'Lau, I was gonna tell you, I promise, as soon as— Wait! Where are you going?'

'Where do you think? I'm leaving! I can't believe I fell for your stupid see-through story. I can't believe I thought you actually liked me. Get out of my way.'

'Wait! Calm down, you don't understand . . .'

'Oh, I think I do, you bitch! You brought me here just so you and your nasty friends could laugh at me. Where's Georgina Fortescue? I bet she's hiding somewhere, waiting to jump out with a video camera.'

'No, no, I promise, Hugo asked me to bring you. Hugo—'

'Hello! Do I hear my name?'

Lauren froze. There, standing right in her path, was Hugo Rochester himself.

'Oh, hi,' he exclaimed, staring at her. 'It's Lauren, right?'

'Yeah,' Lauren mumbled, keeping her eyes somewhere below his chin. 'S-sorry for gatecrashing your party. I didn't know . . .'

'Gatecrashing? Nonsense! I'm so pleased you could come.'

Pleased? Warily, Lauren raised her gaze. 'You . . . are?'

'Of course. That's why I asked Charlie to invite you. Hey, Charl.' Hugo gave Charlie a hug, then turned back to Lauren. 'Anyway, I'm Hugo. I don't think we've ever formally met, but I've heard your name. From Charlie,' he added hastily. 'Not, like, through gossip or anything. All good things, of course.'

For a second, Lauren couldn't even form words. She just stood there, her mouth hanging open. Hugo had asked Charlie to invite her? Charlie had been saying nice things? Maybe she was being naïve – maybe it was all a big lie – but Hugo actually seemed genuine. And his almond-brown eyes were so earnest and sweet. . . 'O-oh. Thanks,' she stammered. 'I mean, it's nice to meet you too. I mean, happy birthday.'

'Thanks! Actually my birthday's not till next week. But I like to string it out for as long as possible, so I managed to convince my parents and Alice to keep out of the house for the weekend. Nice face paint, by the way. Suits you.' Hugo smiled.

There was a silence as Lauren gazed at his soft, full lips. Charlie nudged her.

'The face paint was my handiwork, I'll have you know,' she cut in. 'Mine and Jonno's. Lauren didn't realise how seriously we take our themed parties here.'

'Oh, she'll learn,' Hugo chuckled. 'Gosh, you girls don't even have drinks. Can I get you something? I could concoct one of my famous pot-luck cocktails . . .'

Lauren grinned tentatively. 'Sounds adventurous.'

'Oh, it is. You'll have to come supervise, though. I don't want to add anything you hate. Like curaçao or pineapple juice or something.'

'Actually, I love pineapple juice.'

'Aha! Then we'll have to hunt some out.'

'Be right there, guys,' Charlie called, as Lauren and

Hugo strolled off together towards the bar. She took out her phone, hoping for a message from Felix – he'd said he'd be here around now – and saw, with a flash of guilt, a text from Georgie instead.

Guess what babe! Sneaked out of my prison!!! Coming 2 Hugo's. See you v sooooon xxx

Charlie's eyes widened. The message had been sent half an hour ago. Georgie would be arriving any second.

At that very instant, a pain shot through her arm.

'Ow!' she yelped.

'Oh, did that hurt? Good.'

Charlie wheeled round. Georgie was standing behind her, dressed entirely in fluorescent orange spandex. It made her look even bonier and pastier than usual. Charlie bit her lip, trying not to crack up.

'Babe!' she cried, putting on a thrilled voice. 'You're here! But why'd you hit me?'

'Like you don't know,' Georgie snapped.

'Huh? What are you talking about?'

'I'm talking about *that*.' Dragging Charlie into a corner, Georgie pointed a shaking finger at the fridge. Hugo and Lauren were standing close together, examining a bottle of vodka. Hugo's hand was hovering near the small of Lauren's back. At that moment, Lauren glanced up at him and they both smiled. 'Just look at that. Don't pretend it's not your fault – Jonno told me you brought Lauren Taylor here. He said you were being all cutesy and giggly with her upstairs. And now Hugo's all over her. What kind of fucking friend are you?'

'Oh shit, I'm sorry. I'm really sorry. Hugo asked me to invite her, and it's his birthday so I didn't think I could refuse. I should have told you, but I didn't want to upset you.'

'So you wait till you think I'm not coming and then you sneak around behind my back? Disloyal cow.' Georgie dropped her voice to a fierce whisper and stuck her face right into Charlie's. She was wearing about twenty layers of foundation, and so much eyeshadow she looked like a raccoon. 'You know how into Hugo I am. You're so mean. And when the hell am I supposed to give him his present? I bought him the new special-edition Xbox, plus four new games. I was so excited.' She brandished a gift-wrapped box at Charlie.

'Oh no, hon, I told you not to spend so much. You—'

'Hon? Don't you dare call me "hon"! You've ruined everything.'

Charlie sighed. 'George, please be reasonable. I don't think I ruined anything. I'm not trying to be mean, honestly, but I think if Hugo liked you he'd pay more attention to you. And if he's not into you, you can't buy his love with expensive presents.'

'Oh my god. How dare you fucking preach to me?'

'I'm not! I'm just trying to help. You've been delusional about Hugo for long enough. And I've been encouraging you, so it's my fault too. There are plenty of guys who'd be happy to go out with you. Just not him.'

'Shut. Up!' Georgie's face was livid. Her lips were trembling with fury. 'We are finished, Charlotte Calthorpe de

Vyle-Hanswicke. Game over. Consider this your official notice as my BFF.'

'*What?*' Charlie laughed. 'You can't fire a friend.'

'Just watch me. And by the way,' Georgie threw over her shoulder as she swept towards the staircase, 'you'll regret betraying me. Because you're nothing without me. Nothing!'

'Oh, really? At least I'm not wearing dayglo orange. At least I don't look like a radioactive Oompa Loompa!'

A group of Malbury Hall girls standing nearby tittered. Georgie's face flushed crimson. 'Careful, Charlotte. You'd better watch your back.'

'Ooh, I'm scared,' Charlie jeered. But inside, her stomach churned. She knew what Georgie was capable of. She knew it only too well.

Chapter 30

Dylan slipped through the unmarked doors of Shoreditch House, east London's coolest members' club, and sidled through the stylish cement-clad lobby. The scent of expensive candles hovered in the air. Tasteful, minimalist furniture glowed in the dim light. Over by the front desk, an intimidatingly gorgeous hostess was flirting with a pair of banker types, flashing her red-lipsticked smile at them while she toyed with the buttons of her silk polka-dot blouse.

Dylan cleared her throat. 'Excuse me?'

No response.

'Excuse me!' she practically shouted, her voice bouncing around the hall.

The receptionist glared down at her. 'Can I help you?'

'Yeah, I'm here for Jenna Vance's party?'

'Name?'

'Dylan Taylor. But I don't think I'm on the list.'

'Um,' the receptionist sniffed, 'if you're not on the list then you can't go up. It's a private party. And this is a private club.'

'I know. But would you . . . would you mind looking

under Will Larkin's name? I think he put me as his plus-one.'

Heaving a sigh, the receptionist grabbed a clipboard and flicked through dozens of sheets of paper. Finally, she shrugged. 'Sixth floor,' she said, and turned pointedly back to the bankers.

Dylan tugged at her short flower-patterned skirt as she rode the lift upstairs. Maybe she shouldn't have come. She obviously wasn't cool or pretty enough for this place; she was just some loser who'd been stood up by her boyfriend on Saturday night, who couldn't even get the receptionist's attention and who had to crash someone else's date in order to get an invitation.

Just then, the elevator doors slid open. Dylan's mouth dropped. She was on the roof. Straight ahead of her, a swimming pool glowed electric green under the night sky, surrounded by blazing outdoor heaters and strings of lanterns. Silhouetted against its shimmering light, droves of people were flitting to and fro, knocking back cocktails, throwing their arms around each other and laughing. It was the most beautiful party Dylan had ever seen – a tropical jewel in the middle of a January night.

She took a deep breath and ventured forward. She had to find Seb. He was her life raft in this sea of strangers. She squeezed along a hallway and into a huge glass-walled room, even more packed than the pool deck. Glamorous people seemed to be sprouting everywhere – even Alice Rochester and Tally Abbott might have been intimated by this crowd. In the middle of it all, a fire flickered in an open fireplace, sending a delicious smell of woodsmoke into the air.

'Tuna tartare?' A waiter offered Dylan a canapé tray.

'Thanks!' She reached out to take the last piece, but just as she did, a boy's hand darted in ahead of her.

'Hey!' she cried. Without thinking, she jerked his sleeve. 'That is way rude.'

'Ow!' the thief exclaimed, wheeling on her. Dylan caught her breath. The boy was gorgeous – the kind of gorgeous that makes you stop and stare with your tongue hanging out. He had longish seventies-style brown hair that wisped around his face, and luminous olive skin. His eyebrows were raised.

'What'd I do?'

'You, uh . . . you stole the last hors d'oeuvre! I was just about to take it.' Dylan blinked. She could hear exactly how lame she sounded.

'Seriously?' The boy was staring at her. 'I help myself to a free canapé, and you hit me? I mean, sorry if I didn't realise your name was written on it. Get a life.'

Checking his sleeve for damage, he walked off. Dylan gaped after him, her cheeks burning, blood rushing to her head. She was about to chase him down and give him a piece of her mind when, suddenly, she chuckled. No temper tantrums. That was the rule. Anyway, this was a party full of theatre people, meaning the boy was probably some kind of self-obsessed, attention-seeking egotistical actor. Not worth her time. And why did she even care if some random hottie was rude to her? She had a boyfriend anyway.

At that moment she spotted Seb. He was standing at the bar, alone.

'Hey!' she called in relief, pushing her way over.

Seb wiped his lips. An empty shot glass was sitting on the counter in front of him. 'Hi. So you found it.'

'Yeah. It was quite the challenge, though. I don't think I've ever been this far east in London. Cool area – it reminds me of New York. You know, kind of gritty and industrial?'

'I suppose.' Seb stuck his hands in his pockets. His eyes looked a bit bloodshot. 'Listen, I need to talk to you.'

'Yeah. I was thinking the same thing.'

'I held up my end of the deal,' Seb went on, jumping in before Dylan could speak. 'I invited you to this party. Now promise me – promise me again – that you won't tell T I'm not with my dad.'

'Of course, I promise! But . . .' Dylan stepped closer to him. 'But can I ask you a question?'

'What?'

'That's not what you're really worried about, is it?'

Seb eyed her uneasily. 'What are you on about?'

'You're not worried about T knowing you're not with your dad. You're worried about him finding out who you're with instead.' Dylan paused. 'Listen, I don't want to pry or anything, but I just got this . . . feeling. Back at the Connaught. About you and Will.'

Seb clenched his jaw.

'Don't worry,' she said. 'It's no big deal. If you're gay, I mean.'

191

'Shhh!' Seb hissed. He gripped his empty shot glass. Dylan saw that his hand was shaking. 'Of course it's a big deal. And anyway, I'm not gay.'

Dylan folded her arms.

'Oh god, I knew it – you're gonna tell everyone, aren't you?'

'Of course not! I already said I wouldn't tell anyone. And I won't – not even Jasper. I mean, Jasper may be my boyfriend, but he's not exactly the most sensitive, tolerant person in the world.'

Seb barked out a laugh. 'You can say that again. Can you fucking imagine if he knew? If any of them knew?'

Dylan pursed her lips. 'OK, I get why you're worried. But listen – you don't have to be worried in front of me, OK? I think it's totally cool if you're gay. Honestly. And I think it's awesome that you're on a date. But I understand why you don't want those stupid, immature boys to know. If you don't want me to tell, I won't.'

'Really?' Seb bit his lip. 'You promise? You really, honestly promise?'

'I promise. And when I make a promise, I never break my word.'

Seb looked at her. Then, after a moment, he nodded. 'I believe you. I don't know why, but I do. And you know what else?' he added. 'I think Jasper's lucky to have you.'

'Oh, please.' Blushing, Dylan buried her face in her cardigan. 'Can we change the subject now?'

'Be my guest.'

'Great. So . . .' Dylan grinned. 'How long have you been dating Will?'

'Is that what you call changing the subject?'

'Well, we're not talking about *me* any more, are we?'

'Fine.' Seb sighed. 'Actually, this is our first date.'

'Oh no!' Dylan's face fell. 'You're joking.'

'Nope.'

'Shit, I'm so sorry! I'm totally gatecrashing.'

'It's fine. It's not like we're having an intimate dinner – we're at a party. To be honest, I'm pleased to have someone I know here.' Seb grinned. 'I mean, who the fuck are all these people?'

'Good question,' Dylan giggled. 'This is like, the glammest crowd ever. Come on, let's get your date to rescue us.'

Outside, they skirted the pool and emerged into a covered trellised area where the party was more raucous. Will was shaking his hips to the R&B blasting out of hidden speakers, holding a glass of champagne in each hand.

'Hey,' Seb shouted in his ear, 'you remember Dylan, right?'

'No. I've completely forgotten her, even though we only met three hours ago.' Will grinned, kissed Dylan on the cheek and handed her one of his champagnes. 'Here. Had a spare. Hello again.'

'Hey, thanks! Listen, I am so sorry to interrupt your evening. I had no idea tonight was your first date.'

'You told her?' Will raised his eyebrows at Seb. 'I mean, you told one of your friends that we're on a *date*?'

'Yeah. Well, I mean, she guessed . . .'

Will smiled. 'Hey, by the way, guys, I want you to meet someone. Core!' he called. 'Come here. Seb, Dylan, this is Corey Benson, my newest and bestest friend.'

'Nice to meet—' Dylan began. Then, all of a sudden, she froze. She'd seen Corey before – he was the dickhead who'd stolen her tuna tartare. He spotted her at the same moment, and flicked his eyes away.

'Corey's my castmate in *Much Ado About Nothing*,' Will went on, throwing his arm round Corey's shoulders. 'He plays Benedick – the main love interest. 'Cause he's sooo fit,' Will added with a grin. 'No, but seriously, he's the star.'

'I am not!' Corey protested.

'Yes you are, man – it's not a subjective thing. You have the most lines of anyone in the play. And you're brilliant.'

'No I'm not, *you're* brilliant.'

'No, you are.'

'No, *you* are.'

'No, you are.'

'Oh god,' Dylan groaned, before she could stop herself. 'Actors trying to out-humble each other? I've never heard of anything less genuine.'

Will guffawed. 'Me-*ow*.'

Meanwhile, Corey Benson's mouth had dropped open. 'Oh my god, that's the second time you've snapped in my face. What have you got against me?'

'Second time?' Will said. 'When was the first?'

'Inside. This little spitfire attacked me for taking the

last canapé. I mean, literally attacked me. I probably have a bruise.'

'Oh, please,' Dylan scoffed. 'I brushed your sleeve. And you stole it right from under my nose.'

'Well, well, well,' Will tutted. 'Core, nicking hors d'oeuvres from a lady is unpardonably rude.'

'See!' Dylan crowed. 'Even your best friend agrees with me. Next time maybe you'll curb your canapé aggression.'

'Look who's talking!' Corey exclaimed. 'The American. As if you don't come from the most aggressive nation on earth.'

'Oh, how original,' Dylan snapped. 'The American thing again. I am so fed up of being called aggressive just because of my accent.'

'It's not just because of your accent – it's because you're actually fucking aggressive. Although the accent does help.'

'Whoa, whoa!' Will cried. 'Guys, claws in. Back down.'

'I will if she will,' Corey said.

Dylan folded her arms and glared at him. Suddenly, his mouth twitched. She squinted. There seemed to be a sparkle in his eyes.

'Hold on,' she exclaimed. 'Are you . . . are you mocking me?'

Corey smirked. 'What gave you that idea?'

'*Are* you?'

'Has anyone ever told you you're hilarious? You take everything so seriously.'

'Shut up!' Dylan could feel herself starting to smile. She raised her hand to swat him, but before she could—

'Um, excuse me?' someone said, tapping Corey's shoulder.

They all looked. A semicircle of girls had burst out of the crowd, and were jostling around him.

'Yes?' he said.

'Uh . . . sorry to bother you. I'm Ellie.'

'Hi, Ellie. I'm Corey.'

'I know!' A high-pitched giggle escaped from Ellie's throat. 'I'm a friend of Jenna's from home. She's told us all about rehearsing with you. And . . . and I just love your work! Can I get your autograph?'

Dylan snickered.

'Of course you can, Ellie,' Corey beamed, pushing forward and blocking Dylan out. 'And I'm happy to give your friends autographs, too.'

'Ooh, thanks! Can you sign right here?' Ellie pulled her strappy top down even lower than it already was and presented her cleavage in Corey's face. 'I have an indelible marker.'

'Oh, um, sure,' Corey said, trying to speak over Dylan's increasingly loud chortle. He took the pen and dashed off his signature across Ellie's chest. 'There you go.'

'Eeeee!' Ellie screamed. 'Thank you thank you thank you!' Before Corey could stop her, she grabbed his head and planted a big wet kiss on his mouth. 'I just kissed Corey Benson, everyone! Corey Benson is a *god*. And he signed my boobs. OMG! Corey's name is tattooed on my boobs!'

The gaggle of girls rushed off, shrieking.

'Whoa,' Seb muttered.

'See?' Will said. 'I told you Corey was famous.'

'Fucking hell.' Corey rubbed his head. 'Sorry about that.'

'Oh, don't apologise,' Dylan said. 'You can't neglect your fans. It wouldn't be right. After all, you are a *god*.'

'Shut up.'

'But it's true. You stud muffin.' Dylan burst out laughing. Her long blond waves tumbled over her face.

Rolling his eyes, Corey flicked at a strand. 'How did your hair get so long?'

'Uh, it grew that way?'

'Right. Couldn't afford to have it cut?'

'I could ask you the same question, seventies boy.'

Corey chuckled. Dylan looked into his face. She could see exactly why that Ellie girl had wanted to kiss him. His eyes were somehow earnest and teasing at the same time. His skin was a perfect light-olive colour. His lower lip was full and pouty . . .

She shook herself. She had a *boyfriend*. And Corey was famous – he couldn't possibly like her.

As if reading her mind, he stuck his hands in his pockets and jerked his head towards the dance floor. 'So, I think I'm gonna go join the rest of the cast for a bit. Do you guys want to come?'

'Actually . . .' Will cleared his throat. 'I'm kind of warm. It's hot in here, isn't it? Seb, do you want to get some fresh air?'

'Ohhh . . .' Corey winked. 'Yeah, you guys go. I'll introduce Dylan to everyone.'

Before Seb knew what was happening, Will had plucked his sleeve and led him away from the party, on to a quieter part of the roof. Here, away from the heaters and the sweaty crowds, the night air washed over them, bathing their skin like water. Seb looked at his hands, white against his dark jacket. Suddenly, his heart was racing.

'That was funny,' he said, to break the silence. 'Are you sure we should have left those two? They seem to sort of hate each other.'

'Actually, I thought Corey kind of liked your friend. Or if he doesn't, he should. He usually turns into a primping peacock in front of girls. And girls fawn all over him, of course. But Dylan didn't. She's cool.' Will took a step closer to Seb. 'Tonight's been really fun, hasn't it?'

Seb nodded. His hands felt clammy. 'Y-yeah. It's funny about Dylan,' he babbled. 'We never really talked before last weekend. Not properly, anyway. She's cool.'

'Mm. Have you seen the view from over here?' Will took Seb's hand and drew him to the very edge of the roof. 'Pretty, isn't it?'

'Beautiful.'

But Seb wasn't even looking. All that mattered now was Will's hand, warm and strong around his. Slowly, he turned his face, and slowly, deliberately, Will leaned in. Their lips met. The lights of east London gleamed down below.

Chapter 31

'Ninety-seven . . . ninety-eight . . . ninety-nine RSVPs!' Sonia squealed, gloating over the names on Penny de Claire's latest party list, which had just arrived in her inbox. It was Sunday night, and she and Bella Scott had colonised one of the squishy red couches in the otherwise empty Tudor House common room. 'My party isn't for another two weeks and it's already massive. I bet I'll have at least a hundred and fifty people. Eat that, Alice Rochester.'

'Yeah,' Bella Scott murmured. She was staring at her phone. 'Hey, Sone? Do you think Tristan's away?'

'Away?' Sonia snorted. 'Of course he's not away. It's the middle of term.'

'Oh. Yeah. You're probably right.'

'For goodness' sake.' Sonia rolled her eyes. 'Don't tell me you're still moping over T?'

'I'm not moping! I'm just upset. I don't understand why he hasn't been in touch. I haven't heard from him since . . . since we *did* it.'

'Darling,' Sonia said, gritting her teeth, 'I hate to sound like a broken record, but boys like to wait a while. They never contact you straight after they've shagged you.'

'But it's been over a week now,' Bella moaned. 'I thought they were supposed to wait two or three days. I thought there was like, a rule.'

'Yes, well, he's probably busy. Tristan's a very popular boy, and boys get distracted easily. Now, darling, do you want to start boring everyone to death? Hmm? Because if you do, by all means keep talking about this. I'm your friend, so I don't mind, but I feel I should protect you from alienating everyone else.'

Bella wiped her nose. After a few seconds, she nodded. 'You're right. I know you're right. I'm going to forget about it now. See? Happy face!'

'Excellent, darling. Now, come help me choose harem wall hangings. Should I go for red velvet, maroon crushed velvet or orange silk?'

'Oh, orange silk, definitely,' cackled a voice. 'Sounds sooo cool.'

Bella and Sonia jumped.

'A-Alice,' Bella stammered.

'Dylan, did you hear something?' Alice said, glancing behind her. 'I didn't. Oh, maybe that's because I don't speak to bitches who've slept with my cast-offs.'

Bella's lip trembled. 'But . . . but Ali, I didn't . . . I never wanted to upset—'

'*Or* bitches who suddenly decide to become BFFs with my ex-friends,' Alice cut in.

Bella's cheeks burned with mortification.

Sonia jumped up. 'Come along, darling, enough of this tripe. Let's go upstairs where we can talk in peace.

Now that Dylan's vacated my room, it won't stink of halitosis.'

Mechanically, Bella got to her feet. As she followed Sonia from the room, she glanced desolately back at Alice and Dylan, who had flopped on to a couch.

'OK, fire away,' Dylan said once they'd disappeared. 'Tell me the latest—'

'Hang on,' Alice interrupted. Uncurling herself from the sofa, she crept across the common room and placed her hand on the door. 'Ha!' she cried, wrenching it open.

Sonia, who had been crouched on the threshold, sprang to her feet.

'You idiot,' Alice scoffed. 'You think I was friends with you for five whole years and didn't learn your eavesdropping tricks? Get away from here. Go!'

'Oh, right, because I still take orders from you. And for your information, I wasn't eavesdropping. I couldn't care less what you two crones have to say to each other. I was looking for something. Oh look! There it is.' Grabbing a mauled pencil from the floor, Sonia dangled it in Alice's face. Then she turned and pranced up the stairs.

Slamming the door, Alice joined Dylan on the couch. 'Right. Now that the rats have been flushed out, we can talk without being spied on.'

'Good. So, I want the update on Rando.'

'Yeah, right. If by "update" you mean "utterly boring and dead-end overanalysis by yours truly", be my guest. I haven't heard from him since LaLa Lounge. I think he hates me.'

'Aw, babe, I doubt it.'

Alice shook her head. Suddenly, her eyes brimmed with tears. 'Oh Dill, I just miss him so much. I've never felt so strongly about anyone. I know it's stupid – we were only together for like, a week.'

'But I guess time doesn't matter, does it? You can probably be with one person for a whole year, and not feel as much as you do in one week with someone else.'

'That is not helpful.' Alice dabbed her eyes. 'Oh god, now my make-up's running. I can't believe I'm crying.'

'Listen, Ali, if you're so miserable without him, maybe you should try to get back together.'

'I can't! You don't understand,' Alice hiccuped. 'First of all, he'd never want me again now. Not after he saw me with that guy at LaLa's. You should have seen his face – he thinks I'm a prick-tease and a slapper. And also, Tals and I are getting on really well – she's my best friend – she'd never forgive me if I got together with Rando. I'd lose everything.' Alice sniffled. 'See? It's impossible. And the worst part is, I think . . . I think I love him. I wouldn't feel like this if I didn't.'

'Feel like what?' said a familiar husky voice as the door banged open again. Mimah burst in. 'Hey, Al, what's wrong?'

'Oh, nothing.' Hastily, Alice wiped her eyes. 'Allergies.'

'In the middle of January?' Mimah said suspiciously. 'Oi, Dylan, have you been upsetting my mate?'

'No!'

'I heard some pretty intense murmuring from outside. Are you sure everything's OK?'

'Y-yeah,' Alice faltered. 'Don't be a drama queen. We were just talking about . . . about—'

'Jasper,' Dylan cut in.

'Oh really?' Mimah grinned. 'I love a bit of Jasper gossip. Do tell. And shove up.'

Mimah squashed on to the couch. Alice gave Dylan's arm a grateful pinch.

'Wait a sec. I'm fed up of people listening in. Let's turn on the TV so no one can hear us.' Dylan zapped the remote control, huddling closer to the others as noise filled the room.

'So,' she whispered, 'I'm super-pissed-off with Jasper. I was supposed to see him on Saturday night, but when I called him at like seven p.m., he was too stoned to meet up.'

'Bastard!' Alice gasped. 'That is so rude. I hope you told him off. Dill's an expert at keeping Jasper in line,' she added to Mimah.

'Yeah, well, I was about to yell at him, believe me. But then he put me on hold, and when he came back on the line, he obviously thought he was talking to Tally. And he said something totally weird.'

'What?' Alice was sitting bolt upright.

'He goes, "Hey, Tals, have you got the goods? When can you meet me?" How bizarre is that? It's like she's his drug dealer.' Dylan laughed. 'Not really, but you know what I mean.'

'Yeah.' Alice's eyes sharpened. 'What else did he say?'

'Um, excuse me,' Mimah interrupted. 'Drug dealer?

What are you, an idiot? Don't you mean secret lover? I mean, no offence, Dylan, but Jasper von Holstadt isn't exactly famous for his fidelity. And we all know what Tally's like – lovely, of course, but not one to resist temptation. He was probably talking about condoms or something.'

'What the—' Dylan grimaced. But before she could say any more, soaring music from the TV flooded the room. Some kind of romantic period drama was unfolding on the screen. A young man emerged from a woodland path, riding a white horse.

'Hey, look,' Mimah squealed, 'it's that guy, Corey Benson. I keep seeing him in everything. He is so cute!'

'Ohmygod!' Dylan seized Alice's knee.

'Ow!' Alice snapped. 'Just 'cause Corey Benson's cute doesn't mean you can rip my leg off.'

'Sorry. But guess what? I met him. No, even better, I *hung out* with him on Saturday night.'

'What? When?'

'After Jasper stood me up.'

'That is so unfair!' Mimah moaned. 'What's he like?'

'Hold on,' Alice cut in. 'I totally don't believe you. Exactly how did you end up hanging out with a fit, eligible celebrity?'

'Oh . . . umm, well . . .' Dylan kicked herself. There was no way she could explain this without giving away Seb's secret.

'Hesitation!' Alice cried. 'You're so obviously lying. Attention-seeker!'

'No way!' Dylan protested. 'I promise. I was with . . .

my mom. And Victor Dalgleish. They were going to this media party and I tagged along.'

'Hmm . . .' Alice teased. 'You went to a party with your mum on Saturday night? Oh, sure. Where exactly was this "party"?'

Luckily, before Dylan had to flounder any more, Mimah's phone rang. And kept ringing.

'Hellooo . . . are you gonna get that?' Alice said.

Mimah stared at the screen. 'But who the hell is it? I don't know the number.'

'Oh, then don't pick up. I never pick up numbers I don't know. It might be some weird stalker.'

Mimah knit her eyebrows together. Then she pressed the phone to her ear. 'Hello?'

'Jemimah?' said the voice on the other end.

'Oh my gosh.' Mimah scrambled off the couch. 'Aidan?'

'*Oh no*,' Alice mouthed. She tugged at Mimah's jumper. '*Don't talk to him.*'

'Thank god you picked up.' Aidan was breathing hard. 'I'm so worried, I don't know what to do. She's missing. She hasn't been home since yesterday and I . . . I—'

'Aidan! Hold on. Calm down. Who are you talking about?'

'My mum!' Aidan sounded like he was actually sobbing. 'She keeps going on benders. I didn't know who else to call. My younger brother's useless and my friends . . . You're the only one I can trust. Fuck, she could be lying in a ditch somewhere. Where has she been all night? I need to find her!'

'OK, calm down. Have you reported it to the police?'

'No.' Aidan took a deep breath. 'That's a good idea. I should do that. Shouldn't I?'

'Yes. Call them now. And . . . Aidan?'

'Yeah?'

'Do you want me to come see you tomorrow? I can skip a few classes. I mean, if you need someone.'

There was a silence before Aidan spoke. 'Are you sure?'

'Of course I'm sure.'

'OK. That'd be . . . Yeah. Thanks.'

When Mimah hung up, Alice was staring at her. 'What the hell was that about?'

'Aidan. He's in trouble. I have to help.'

'No, you don't. Be careful, Mime. Don't get in over your head.' But Alice might as well have saved her breath – her words evaporated in the inattentive air.

Chapter 32

Charlie Calthorpe de Vyle-Hanswicke clattered into the Geography classroom and threw herself into the last available seat just as the start-of-lessons bell rang. Their teacher, Miss Clifton, gave her a stern look.

'No running, Charlie.'

'Sorry,' Charlie said breathlessly, trying to ignore the fact that Georgie Fortescue was leering smugly at her from the end of the row. 'Didn't want a late mark.'

'Then you should organise yourself better so that you have time to walk to lessons.' Miss Clifton was young and surprisingly pretty for a teacher. Not to mention quite stylish. She mostly wore pencil skirts with crisp blouses and black heels. Quite a radical look in a staff room filled with frumpy dresses and crocheted cardigans, Charlie thought with a smirk.

As soon as the teacher's gaze was distracted, she leaned forward to the seat in front and tapped Lauren Taylor's shoulder. 'Hey. You disappeared this morning – didn't see you at breakfast.'

'Oh. Hi,' Lauren whispered. 'Yeah, I was just finishing up the homework.'

'Oh god, that prep was impossible, wasn't it? The bit where you had to do a diagram of the different methods of rock formation? It took me hours.'

'Me too. I spent way too long trying to draw a lifelike volcano. I even sketched little trees on top of it.'

'Uh, I don't think volcanoes have trees, you dummy.'

'Yeah, they do. Don't they? Just not near the top, where they'll get covered in molten lava.' Lauren groaned. 'Oh god, I hope Miss Clifton gives marks for artistic merit.'

Charlie snorted. 'Don't worry, I'm sure she will, since this is a *Geography* lesson.'

'I'm getting such bad grades here. I just can't get used to the way you guys do things. And the teachers are so much meaner than at my school in New York.'

'Girls!' Miss Clifton was clapping her hands. 'Finish up your conversations. Homework in, please. Pass your sheets to the end of each row for collection. Thank you.'

'I've only been to New York once,' Charlie whispered, adding her meticulously drawn prep to the stack that was heading towards Georgie. 'My dad took our whole family there about three years ago. But we hadn't realised it was Thanksgiving. Everything was closed, so we ended up eating room-service turkey in our hotel suite.'

'A true New York experience.'

'Do you miss it?'

'Yeah. A lot. Mostly when—'

'Miss Clifton?' Georgie Fortescue's voice pierced the room. She was waving her hand in the air.

'Yes?'

'Someone in my row hasn't handed in their prep. I'm missing a set of diagrams.'

'Are you sure?'

'Yes, I've counted three times.'

Miss Clifton folded her arms. 'All right, who hasn't done the homework? Come on, own up.'

No one raised a hand.

'Girls, really, I detest dishonesty. If you come clean, you can have till lunchtime to produce something. Otherwise it's detention.' The teacher waited a moment before rolling her eyes in annoyance. 'Right. Georgie, go through the papers.'

For several seconds, the classroom's silence was punctuated only by rustling. Finally, Georgie looked up, her face contorted into a mask of horror. 'Miss Clifton, it's Charlotte Calthorpe de Vyle-Hanswicke! Hers is the one missing.'

'What?' Charlie exclaimed. 'No way! I handed mine in.'

'But it's not here,' Georgie said innocently, rattling the sheaf of papers. 'And I wouldn't make it up. I mean, I'm Charlie's best friend.'

Charlie's jaw dropped. 'You . . . you—'

'Miss Clifton!' Lauren interrupted. 'Georgina's lying. I saw Charlie hand in her homework.'

'Lauren! Calling your form-mate a liar is a very serious accusation. Besides, I don't see how you could have seen Charlie do anything, since you're sitting with your back to her. Or should be, at least.'

'But it's true,' Charlie insisted. 'I definitely handed it in. Other people saw me.' She nudged her neighbour. 'You saw me, Gussie, didn't you?'

'I don't know . . .' Augusta Chapman fiddled with the zipper of her pencil case. 'You handed me the pile to pass along. I just assumed yours was in it.'

'It was! Georgie must have hidden it. She's sabotaging me! She's annoyed at me so she probably stole it and—'

'Uh, Miss Clifton?' Georgie interrupted. Her eyes were wide. 'I think Charlie's acting a bit paranoid. I'm only saying this because I'm her friend, but . . . I'm kind of worried. I mean, paranoia, lashing out? You remember what happened last term . . . with her sister . . . *The drugs,*' Georgie added in a loud whisper.

Gasps echoed through the class.

'How dare you!' Charlie cried, leaping up.

'What? Oh, sorry, sweetie, I thought everyone knew about the thing with the pills and—'

'That's quite enough, Georgina,' ordered Miss Clifton. But she looked shaken. 'Charlotte, sit down. I want you to stay behind after class – we need to talk. And I'm giving you detention so you can do the prep.'

'But Miss Clif—'

'I said that's enough.'

'But it's so unfair! I did the prep. Georgie stole it. Search her if you—'

'*Shut up,* Charlotte! Do you realise how ridiculous you sound? Everyone, quieten down. We have to get on with the lesson.'

The teacher turned, rigid with annoyance, and started writing on the whiteboard. Georgie shot Charlie an evil grin.

'*See*,' she mouthed. '*You're nothing. Nothing.*'

'*Fuck you*,' Charlie mouthed back. Clenching her fists, she glared into space. Finally, she ripped a piece of paper out of her rough book, scribbled a note and dropped it over Lauren's shoulder.

Lauren jumped. Then, as stealthily as she could, she unfolded the paper.

Can you believe that bitch??? First she tries to destroy you, now me. OMG I am gonna kill her. I need distraction before I do it RIGHT NOW.

Lauren chewed the top of her pen. Then she scribbled a reply.

Try ignoring her. She only wants attention. She's obviously a major psycho. Umm, I kind of have some news – might distract you.

What? Charlie wrote.

Promise you won't tell anyone.

Promise. Cross my heart. What????

Lauren bit her lip. Then she tore out a new piece of paper, scrawled something on it and, twisting stealthily, dropped it on Charlie's desk.

'Miss Clifton!' Georgina Fortescue chimed.

'Yes, Georgina? Do you have a question about the environmental effects of limestone erosion?'

'No, Miss Clifton. I probably would if I could pay attention, but I'm actually finding it really difficult to concentrate. I think there are people passing notes.'

'Georgina, no one likes a tattle-tale,' Miss Clifton sighed. But her eyes swept the classroom. 'Charlie Calthorpe de Vyle-Hanswicke! I see that note in your hand. Don't you think you should be on your best behaviour right now? Please stand up and read it to the class.'

Charlie gulped. 'But . . . I don't even know what it says.'

'I suppose you'll find out with the rest of us, then.'

Charlie rolled her eyes. Getting to her feet, she unfolded the paper and scanned the handwriting. Her eyes shot open. 'Uh, Miss Clifton, this is private.'

'If it's so private, then it should have waited till after class. Read it out, please. That's the rule.'

Charlie wiped her palm against her grey school skirt. Then, with a glance at Georgie Fortescue, she cleared her throat.

'Hugo Rochester texted me during Chapel. He said it was lovely talking to me at his party. He was like, 'do you wanna maybe meet up this week?' Eek! Do you think it's a date??? Advice please!!!'

The classroom erupted before Charlie had even finished reading.

'OMG!' squealed Minky Coombes. 'Hugo asked Lauren out.'

'I told you he fancied her!'

'That's *definitely* a date!'

'Hugo never goes out with anyone!'

'Girls!' bellowed Miss Clifton.

'Ohmygod, this is the story of the century!'

'*Girls!* Settle down.'

But the whispers continued. The only silent person in the room was Georgie Fortescue. She glowered at her desk, stabbing her fountain pen into the wood.

Chapter 33

'Thanks for coming,' Aidan said, his face pinched and tired as he opened the door to the ground-floor flat that he shared with his mum.

'Of course.' Mimah stepped – or rather climbed – over the threshold, picking her way round a mound of yellowing magazines. The boxlike front hall was so crammed with stuff – food cans and old shoes and broken suitcases and spiny umbrellas – that you'd be lucky if you didn't fall and break your neck. Aidan's flat had been cramped during Mimah's last visit, too, but it was now in far worse shape.

'So . . .' Aidan said. He led the way into the tiny kitchen and hovered in the middle of the floor, cupping his elbows in his hands. 'Uh . . . do you want some tea?'

'Oh, yes thanks, that'd be lovely.' Mimah winced at the formality of her own voice. It was weird to be acting like this after their phone call last night. How could you break down in front of someone like that – be so raw, so vulnerable – and then go back to offering them tea? She toyed with the faux-fur collar of her parka. It was also weird being back here, in this flat. The first and only other time she'd been here, she and Aidan had made love all afternoon, the pale December sun seeping through the crack in his bedroom curtains, dust motes swirling in the intimate half-light.

She cleared her throat. 'So, um . . . how's the Asda job?'

'Yeah, fine. Y'know. It's a job.'

'Yeah. And are you still working at that garage too?'

'On and off.' Aidan was filling the kettle over a sink piled with dirty dishes. Suddenly, he slammed it down. 'Fuck this. I have to get out of here.'

'Oh. But I just got here.'

'I know. But I need some fresh air. Come on.'

Aidan grabbed his tattered sheepskin jacket. Out in the street, their footsteps sliced through the cold, still air. They walked without speaking through two or three roads like Aidan's – narrow, run-down, lined with squat terraced houses. Mimah glanced at his profile, sharp and unfathomable.

'Do you want to tell me about you mum?' she asked. 'What did the police say?'

'They're looking for her.' Aidan pursed his lips. 'They sort of know her, around the police station. She's . . .' He stopped.

'She's what? Go on.'

Aidan didn't reply.

'It's hard, having to take care of your parents, isn't it?'

Aidan laughed sardonically. 'Oh, right. How would you know? Been watching too much gritty TV?'

'For fuck's sake!' Mimah cried. 'What is your problem? You ring me when you're upset, you say you want my help, and then when I try, you dismiss me like I'm some stupid sheltered princess. Either take me seriously or don't take me at all, OK?'

Aidan stared at her. 'I . . . I'm sorry. But honestly, can you blame me for not taking you seriously when you say things like that? I know nothing about you, except that you go to boarding school and you're filthy rich. Not to mention fucking clever and probably destined for a career as an astrophysicist. What can you possibly know about problems, and taking care of your parents and . . . and anything else!'

Mimah smiled ruefully. 'A lot. Because I have those problems myself.'

Aidan blinked at her.

'Look,' Mimah sighed. 'I thought I came from just another normal, happy family. You know you hear these things, about your friends' parents splitting up, or fighting all the time, and you think, *That would never happen to me?* Well, it did. My father? I used to practically worship him. I thought he was the cleverest, most amazing guy in the world. And then, one day last year, I found out he wasn't who I thought he was at all.'

'How do you mean?'

'He'd been cheating on my mum. He'd been . . .' Mimah swallowed. 'He'd been using escort services.'

'Whoa.' Aidan's eyes widened. 'Like, prostitutes?'

Mimah nodded. 'And he was a big-shot, high-powered magistrate from a society family, so the papers fucking loved it. That's actually how we found out.'

'*Whoa*,' Aidan repeated.

'Yeah. My mum kicked him out. And then she totally broke down. It's like she's lost the will to be a real person. I can't remember the last time she got properly dressed, never mind left the house. She drinks all the time. At first, I thought that was normal – everyone in our set loves a bit of a tipple. But not like this. And she takes pills. Loads of them. Antidepressants, sleeping pills, whatever other kind of pill they've come up with. And then last term I found out my little sister was taking them too. Not legitimately, I mean – not because she'd been prescribed them. She'd been stealing them from our mum. And when she got caught, I took the blame. My school almost expelled me. Then they decided I could stay if I did community service and showed how sorry and reformed I was. And that, in case you were wondering, is how I ended up tutoring you. The end.' Mimah folded her arms. 'OK. Hit me with yours.'

Aidan, whose face had grown more and more shocked during Mimah's speech, now laughed incredulously. 'Fuck. I'm not sure I can top that story. No, but seriously . . .' He rubbed his nose. 'I'm really sorry. It sounds awful.'

'Yeah. It's not the best. But what happens happens. You gotta deal with it.' Mimah shrugged. 'Anyway, your turn. Don't tell me I blabbed all that for no reason.'

Aidan stared ahead of them, down the long, grey pavement. They'd left Hasted's residential pocket behind, and were walking down a street scattered with launderettes, kebab shops and off-licences.

'Well, you've probably guessed already. My mum's an alcoholic. At least she doesn't pop pills though – I suppose I should consider myself lucky about that.' He glanced at Mimah, and sighed. 'I dunno. Sometimes I think the drinking's why my dad disappeared. Or maybe it was the other way round – maybe that's when she started – I was too young to remember. Anyway, we've always managed. I took care of her and of my younger brother. I worked after-school jobs. I forged signatures on our school report cards. I did the cooking and cleaning. I tell myself that's why I did so badly in lessons. But I always intended to get out. Leave this shithole behind. Do something where I could make some fucking money and buy myself a better life. That's why I went to tutoring. It's why I met you.'

He looked again at Mimah. She was nodding, her almost-black eyes glittering under her fringe.

'For a while, I thought it would work. Mum seemed to be getting better. She actually got a job and I thought she'd stopped drinking. I'm a fucking idiot,' Aidan snorted. 'Over Christmas, I found out how wrong I was. I came home one day, and there she was, passed out in the bathtub, surrounded by bottles, and I thought . . . I thought she was fucking dead.' He blinked. 'I took her to the hospital, and they made me prove I was over eighteen and didn't have to go into child welfare or any shit like that. God, it was what I'd been dreading my whole fucking life. Anyway, she just kept drinking. I had to watch her round the clock. And that was when I realised – I was never getting out of here. Nothing was ever going to change. Tutoring, studying, trying to better myself – it was all a stupid dream. I'm trapped here and I always will be.'

He halted. They'd reached the top end of Hasted Common. A chilly wind ruffled his unkempt hair, underneath which his eyes were as hard and brittle as glass.

'Hey.' Mimah touched his arm. 'I think there are ways of getting out, you know. You can't let your mum ruin your life. And I'm sure she wouldn't want that, if she realised what she was doing. I think when people are ill like that, they have no idea how they're affecting anyone else. You could get her some help. There are treatment places . . .'

'What? Stick her in rehab? No way am I doing that to her.'

Mimah sighed. In front of them, the community centre squatted above the common like a looming reminder of their past. She nodded towards the Starbucks a few doors down. 'Hey, come on, I'll buy you a coffee.'

'No you won't. I don't need you to buy me anything. What, you feel all sorry for me now that you've heard my sob story? Well I think I can afford my own latte, thanks.'

'God, would you chill?' Mimah rolled her eyes. 'I thought we were getting past all that crap. I was only offering 'cause it's my turn. You treated me to fish and chips last time. Remember?'

'Oh. Yeah.' Aidan raised his eyebrows. 'Guess I shouldn't be so touchy. Thanks.'

Once they had their coffees, they turned back on to the Common and wandered over the short, spiky grass.

'Can I admit something?' Aidan said.

'Sure.'

'You know another reason why I wanted us to get out of my house, earlier on?'

'Why?'

'Because it reminded me of that time we were there together. I mean, the first time, when we . . .'

'Yeah.' Mimah sipped her drink. 'I know.'

'Oi! Aidan!' cried a voice, breaking in on their privacy. Just up ahead, a group of boys were kicking a football around.

Aidan waved. His face changed from brooding to chummy in a split second, as if he'd pulled down a shutter and hidden all trace of his real life.

'Get this!' the boy called, booting the ball.

'I'd better join them,' Aidan said, 'just for a second. Otherwise I'll never hear the end of it.'

'Why? Scared they'll tease you for being with a girl?'

'And not just any girl – a pretty, obviously posh girl. Wait here.' He thrust his coffee cup at Mimah and ran towards the game.

'What do you mean, wait here?' she cried. 'No fucking way.'

Dropping both cups on the ground, she darted forward, racing Aidan towards the ball. 'Got it!' she cried, tackling him and galloping with it across the grass.

'Oooh, Aidan, looks like your girlfriend's better than you!'

'Looks like she's better than everyone,' someone else

yelled, sending out a long, admiring whistle as Mimah dodged two attackers in a row.

She ran and wove with the ball, twisting round to grin at Aidan as the wind streamed through her hair. And across the field of his friends, Aidan smiled back.

Chapter 34

Alice flicked through the racks of dresses at Whistles, Hasted's only clothing shop that didn't cater either to tacky townies, frumpy housewives or the droves of tourists that came here to marvel at the quaint old town. It was Wednesday afternoon, and she was supposed to be playing badminton back at school for Electives Day. But she'd made a quick getaway as soon as the bell had rung for lunch. The only reason anyone ever chose badminton was because the teacher, Miss Gill, was a massive pushover and hardly ever noticed when girls were absent. And today, Alice was on a mission. Jasper's parents, the von Holstadts, were holding a lavish charity gala in London at the weekend. The whole crew was going to be there, and she needed a new dress. A beautiful, floaty, feminine dress to remind Rando what he was missing.

Alice plucked a yellow silk number off the rack, held it up, made a face and put it back. She pulled out a black feather-trimmed dress instead. This could work. It was fun. Sexy. And the feathers might remind Rando of soft, downy duvet days . . . All it needed were a few accessories – dangly earrings, maybe, or the gold bangles her older brother

Dom had brought back from his gap year building villages in Nepal. She headed for the dressing room. Just as she was untucking her top, she heard the shop door swing open.

'Are you sure you don't mind shopping with me, darling?' came a girl's high-pitched, upper-class voice. 'I know how tiresome it can be for you poor menfolk.'

'Of course not. I have a free period anyway. It's nice to get out of school. And to see you.'

Alice stiffened. It felt like someone was sitting on her lungs. The second voice – she knew it. It touched something in her, like a tremor in the earth quivering through the surface of a lake. Carefully, slowly, she peeked out from behind the curtain.

There he was – Rando – standing at the rack where she'd just been browsing thirty seconds before. And next to him was a girl. Alice squinted. A pretty, slim girl with caramel-coloured hair and stylish tan knee-high boots. She squinted even harder. It wasn't anyone she knew.

As she watched, the girl brushed Rando's arm. 'What do you think of this? I've had my eye on it for a while, but I wanted to get a man's point of view.'

'Nice, I think. I can't really tell. Looks a bit big, though, doesn't it?'

'It's not my size, silly! I'm just talking about the style. Here, look.'

Alice's fingers tightened over the white changing-room curtain. The bitch was pulling out the same dress *she* was about to try on.

Giggling flirtatiously, the girl swirled round, holding it against her body. 'So?'

'Hmm . . .' Rando cocked his head. 'I'm not sure about the feathers. Might be a bit much. But if anyone can pull it off, you can.'

'Oh, stop!' the girl simpered, swatting him. She turned to the sales assistant. 'Have you got this in an eight?'

'A young lady's just trying the eight on, actually. But she shouldn't be long.'

'Oh, how irritating. Never mind, we'll wait. We've got time, haven't we, Rando?'

'Absolutely.'

'Let's hope that other young lady doesn't buy it. I might have to fight her off if she tries. Oh, isn't girls' shopping just full of politics? Ha ha!' Unbuttoning her pristine camel-hair coat, the girl settled on to a bench right outside the changing rooms, and patted the seat next to her.

Alice drew back from the curtain, her heart racing like a trapped bird's. She stared at herself in the mirror. Her face was taut with horror. There was no helping it – she was cornered. She was going to have to go out there and face them. And the longer she kept them waiting for the dress, the weirder it was going to look.

One . . . two . . . three. Snatching back the curtain, she strode towards the saleswoman, keeping her eyes straight ahead.

'Thanks, I've decided not to bother with this dress, actually. I suddenly realised I'd seen loads of uncool losers wearing it. Yeah, it seems to be popular with the wannabe crowd.'

Rando had stood up. 'A-Alice?'

'Hmm? Oh! Hello.' Alice put on her most charming, uninterested smile. 'What are you doing in a ladies' boutique? If you're looking for a present for your mum, you might try the dress I just gave back. It would probably suit a more . . . mature woman.'

'Actually,' cut in the sales assistant, 'this young lady wanted to try it on.'

Alice slapped her hand over her mouth. 'Oops. No offence.'

'Rando?' said the caramel-haired girl. She was shooting daggers at Alice. 'Who's this?'

'Oh, uh, sorry, I should have introduced you.' Rando scraped a hand through his hair. 'Alice, this is Tiki Hardinge-Smythe. Tiki, this is Alice Rochester. Alice is . . . a friend of mine.'

The word 'friend' hung in the air between them. Alice could feel her fake grin start to curdle.

'Well,' she said, with one last effort, 'lovely bumping into you. Absolutely lovely. Gosh, it's almost three, I'd better head back to—'

'Hey, you!' barked a deep, rough voice. The door banged open, rattling on its hinges, and a tree-sized man wearing a black leather coat burst into the shop. Three paces, and he'd crossed the entire floor.

'You are Alice Rochester, correct?' His accent sounded eastern European.

Alice gaped up at him. Words seemed to have fled her brain.

'Answer the question!'

'Whoa, hang on just a minute,' Rando interrupted. 'That's no way to talk to her. Who the hell are you?'

'Rando, shhh!' Tiki hissed.

The thug stuck out a beefy hand and shoved Rando backwards. 'Listen to your woman. I know who you are. But I am not interested in you.'

'You know who I am?' Rando scoffed. 'Yeah, right. Pardon me if I don't believe you.'

'You are Thomas Randall-Stubbs. You are her ex-boyfriend.'

'Wh-whose ex-boyfriend?' Rando stammered, his swagger deflating. He glanced nervously at Alice.

'Natalya's. Natalya Abbott.'

'You know Tally?' Alice whispered. 'How? Who are you? What do you want with her?'

The stranger carved his features into a smile. 'Never mind that. You just give Natalya a message from me.'

'Wh-what message?'

'You say, her friends are looking for her. You tell her, it is not too late. OK?' Without waiting for an answer, the giant pounded across the shop and slammed the door behind him.

For a moment, everyone remained rooted to the spot. The saleswoman let out a little moan.

'Ohmygod!' Tiki whimpered, her glossed lips trembling. She clung to Rando's elbow. 'What the hell was that? And who on earth is Natalya Abbott? She sounds like bad news.'

Rando squeezed Tiki's arm and turned to Alice. 'Are you OK?'

She nodded. 'Yeah.'

'Why was that . . . that *mobster* looking for Tally? What could he possibly want? Do you have any idea?'

'No,' Alice whispered. Her insides felt like that static you sometimes saw on old TVs. 'But I'd better go. I have to give her the message. I have to find out what's going on.'

'Do you want me to help? It might not be safe out there. Let me walk you back to school.'

'No.' Alice cast a split-second glance at Tiki Hardinge-Smythe. 'I'm fine. He's gone. And anyway, he said it was Tally he wanted, not us.'

'Be careful!' Rando called, as she reached the door. 'Who knows what the fuck Tally has got herself into?'

Without replying, Alice walked numbly into the street. Rando's question mirrored her thoughts exactly.

Chapter 35

Alice burst through the front door of Tudor House, almost impaling Bella Scott on the row of coat-hooks nailed in the foyer.

'Move!' she shouted.

'Ow,' Bella squeaked, making herself as small as possible. She watched, her blue eyes wide, as Alice bolted up the stairs and charged down the hallway, her face even more hard and angular than usual.

When she reached her room, Alice kicked open the door, dumped her coat and handbag and looked round. The place was empty.

'Tally!' she cried, sticking her head into the corridor. 'Tally! Where are you?'

There was no answer. She pushed open the door to the toilets, scanned the room and headed for the showers. Tally was just emerging from one of the stalls.

'There you are! We need to talk. Right. Now.'

'Babe, what on earth—! You look like you've seen a ghost.' Tally was wrapped in a powder-blue robe, with a towel twisted over her hair. Around her neck glistened the small gold disc she'd been wearing ever since New Year, its strange symbols gleaming. 'Why are you so pale? What's going on?'

'Why don't *you* tell *me*?'

'Huh? Because I'm not the one who's acting weird! Are you OK?'

'No. I'm not.' Alice flicked her eyes up and down the row of stalls. 'Who else is in here?'

'No one. I mean, it was empty when I came in. And I wasn't in the shower for very long.'

'Good.' Alice sank against one of the sinks. The back of her head was reflected in the steamy mirror behind it. 'Do you . . .' She took a deep breath. 'Do you have any idea what just happened to me in town?'

'Hmm,' Tally grinned, tapping her chin. 'Well, since I was playing basketball this afternoon instead of skiving off at the shops, and since I'm not a psychic: no.'

'Be serious!' Alice cried, her eyes burning. 'Enough smart-arsing about, OK? For once in your life, can't you give a straight answer?'

Tally fell back a step. 'Whoa, babe, chill. Just tell me what you're ranting about, OK? What happened?'

'A man . . . no, not a man, a . . . a . . .' Alice took a deep breath. 'A *giant*. A Russian giant hunted me down in town today. He said he knew you. He—'

'A giant?' Tally interrupted. Her face was alert, like an animal's. 'What do you mean, giant?'

'I mean exactly what it sounds like! A fucking big, massive, brick-shithouse man.'

Tally blinked. 'How tall was he?'

'How *tall?* What do you want, a precise measurement? Excuse me for not whipping out my tape measure!'

'OK, I just . . . Never mind. What happened?'

'He was looking for you. And he seemed dead set on finding you, too. He knows everything about you, Tals. He knew who I was, he knew who Rando was, he—'

'*Rando?* What was Rando doing there?'

'I . . . I don't know. He was just there, OK? That is so not the point.' Alice gripped the porcelain lip of the sink. 'He told me to give you a message. He said, "Tell Natalya her friends are looking for her." What friends, Tally? What sort of lowlifes are you hanging out with? It sounded like a threat!'

Tally's eyes had gone strangely bright. She stared through the steamed-up window into the twilit sky. Her delicate, birdlike fingers flitted towards the pendant around her neck.

'What did he look like?' she asked, her voice soft. 'I know you said he was tall. But what else?'

Alice's face was incredulous. 'Hmm, well, let me think . . . Oh no, wait! I've just remembered – I was too fucking petrified to start memorising his features.' She rolled her eyes.

'Think, Al. Think. It's important.'

Alice sighed. 'OK, he was wearing a black leather coat. He had quite small eyes. And brown hair. Cropped really short.'

'Brown? Are you sure?'

'Yes! What does it matter?'

Biting her lip, Tally looked at the floor.

'Tally! What is going on?' Alice leaned forward. 'You have to start telling me the truth. I'm your best friend. And I'm mixed up in this now. And I don't intend to sit around and let Russian mobsters threaten me!'

'He didn't threaten you! D-did he?'

'Not this time,' Alice said ominously. She folded her arms. 'Look, honestly, I only want to help. I'm worried about you. Please, tell me the truth. You didn't really go to Spain at New Year, did you?'

Tally was silent for several seconds. Then, finally, she shook her head.

'Why did you lie to me?' Alice groaned. 'No, hang on, I have a better question: where the hell is all your money coming from?'

Suddenly, Tally's expression closed, like a shutter blacking out the sun. 'I'm sorry. I can't answer that.'

'Why?'

'Because it's . . . a secret.'

'Oh my god.' Alice shut her eyes. 'I knew it. You're doing something illegal, aren't you? What is it? Are you dealing drugs? Is that it? Did you fall in with a bad crowd in Russia? Tally, are you in trouble?' Alice's voice rose higher and higher, until it hit a top-note of panic.

Tally burst out laughing. 'Oh babe, you are funny. You're so bloody melodramatic.'

Alice froze. Suddenly, her eyes were blazing. 'You know what? I think you'll find *you're* the one who's melodramatic. I'm not the one being chased by mobsters! I'm not the

231

one who disappeared for weeks and then suddenly re-appeared wearing a necklace covered in weird writing and carrying round wads of cash!' Alice was practically hyperventilating. 'You know what? I give up. You can keep your seedy secrets. But the next time some Russian thug thinks he's your friend, don't expect *me* to protect you.'

'Alice, wait,' Tally cried. 'Please don't be angry. You don't understand at all.'

'So make me understand. Where's the money from?'

'I already told you, I can't say.'

'Fine. You just let me know when you *can* say. Then we'll talk.' Alice swept out.

As the door slammed, echoing off the shower tiles, Tally leaned over the sink and bent her head, a single tear trickling down her face. Her locket dangled over the porcelain basin.

Meanwhile, in the very last shower stall, Sonia Khan wrapped herself tighter in her towel. So, she mused, grinning to herself, it looked like Tally Abbott, the golden girl, wasn't as pure as everyone thought.

Chapter 36

'Pass me a slice of mushroom, Gussie!' Minky Coombes called down the long, food-laden table.

'None left,' Augusta Chapman shouted from the opposite end. 'There's sausage, though. Or plain?'

'No way, you piggies! Mushroom's my favourite. I can't believe you've eaten it all.'

'Girls, please,' interrupted Mrs Gould, dabbing a drip of grease off her generous chin. 'Do try to keep it down a bit. We don't want to drive away the rest of the poor customers. Or they might not allow us back.'

It was Friday evening, and the Year Tens were out at Pizza Express in Hasted for one of Mrs Gould's famous 'treat nights'. The housemistress prided herself on these monthly dinner outings, where the idea was for the whole form to have good, wholesome, bonding fun – which of course was easiest when everyone was gorging on pizza, dough balls and ice cream.

'More lemonade, dear?' the teacher chirped. She offered the pitcher to Georgie Fortescue.

'No thanks,' Georgie said, with a saccharine smile. As soon as Mrs Gould turned away, she shot a savage glare across the table. Charlie Calthorpe de Vyle-Hanswicke glared back.

'Hey,' whispered Charlie, nudging Lauren Taylor, 'you've hardly eaten anything. Go on, finish that slice.'

'I can't. I'm too nervous.' Lauren twisted her napkin, which was already a damp knot in her lap. She'd spent at least an hour getting ready tonight, consulting with Charlie over outfits and make-up and hairstyles, and had finally decided on this: pink dress, black tights and leopard-print ankle boots. Her blonde hair was down around her face, and little pearl earrings glistened in her ears. 'Oh help, do you really think this is going to work?'

'Yes. You just have to be confident. If you look all guilty and shifty, then she'll think something's up. Trust me, it's all in the presentation.'

'Yeah. Yeah, you're right. What time is it?'

Charlie glanced at her delicate Gucci watch, which had been a present from her dad on her thirteenth birthday. 'Ten to eight.'

'Oh god.' Lauren took several shallow breaths and pushed her plate away. 'Do I look OK?'

'Yes, for the billionth time, you look great. Ready?'

'Ready.'

Stealthily, Charlie reached into her handbag. A second later, Lauren's phone buzzed against her dinner plate.

She grabbed it. 'Hello?'

'Mrs Gould!' Georgie cried, tapping the teacher on the shoulder.

'*Right on cue,*' Charlie muttered under her breath.

'Yes, dear?'

'Lauren Taylor's talking on the phone. I thought phones weren't allowed on treat nights. It's really rude, don't you think?'

'Yes, it is rather rude. Lauren!' Mrs Gould called, wagging her finger across the table. 'Put that away. No calls. I thought I made that clear.'

Lauren widened her eyes. 'Oh, hold on, Daddy,' she said into the phone, then held it away from her ear. 'Mrs Gould, I'm really, really sorry. But it's my dad. He's calling from New York.'

'Oh, your father?' The teacher's expression softened.

'Yeah. Do you mind if I go outside and talk to him? We haven't spoken in weeks – my mom doesn't let me talk to him when I'm at home. They're . . . they're not really on good terms. And I've wanted to hear his voice for *so* long. So, so long.'

Next to Lauren, Charlie burst into a suspicious-sounding coughing fit. 'S-sorry,' she gasped, keeping her eyes fixed on her pizza crusts. 'Must have gone down the wrong way.'

Mrs Gould was now gazing at Lauren with a moist, gooey expression. 'You poor dear. Divorce really does tear families apart, doesn't it? Yes, of course go talk to your father. And take as long as you need. We'll be here for a while – we haven't even thought about dessert yet.'

'But . . . but Mrs Gould—!' Georgie spluttered.

'Oh, thank you,' Lauren interrupted. 'Thanks so much, Mrs Gould. You're a real life-saver. Charlie can come get me when you're leaving.' She shot a look at Georgie, whose expression had suddenly shifted from confusion to dismay.

'*Good luck,*' Charlie hissed, with one last cough.

'*Thanks.*'

Outside, the cold air bit Lauren's skin as she flitted past the low red-brick buildings of Hasted High Street. She was so nervous, it felt like her legs had turned to rubber. It felt like a thousand tiny butterflies were fluttering in her chest.

The Four Horsemen pub was down a narrow side road. In the doorway, a group of smokers were huddled against the cold, puffing out clouds of smoke and icy breath. And a little apart from them, warming his hands in his pockets, was Hugo.

He spotted Lauren straight away.

'Hey!' he called.

Lauren swallowed. Hugo's eyes were bright and his cheeks were pink. Soft curls of blond hair twined out from underneath his grey wool hat. She still couldn't believe she was here. She still couldn't believe he'd asked her. In fact, she was having a hard time convincing herself it wasn't some sort of joke.

'I'm so glad you made it,' Hugo smiled. 'I was worried you wouldn't be able to get away.'

'Me too,' Lauren said, somehow managing to speak normally. 'It's all down to Charlie. I can only stay for one drink, though. I think I have about half an hour – at the most.'

'Not bad on a school night.' Hugo held open the door.

The pub was noisy and hot, and packed with beery, red-faced men. Over the bar, a TV was showing football, accompanied by a chorus of groans and cheers. Fruit machines blinked along one wall, next to a pinball machine and a table-football set.

'Uh, yeah, sorry for the venue.' Hugo rolled his eyes as he and Lauren crammed into a corner with their drinks, as far from the football fans as possible. 'This is practically the only pub in Hasted that serves Year Tens. Apart from Shock Box, and that shithole will probably be packed with school people. I thought it'd be nice to have some privacy.'

Privacy . . . Lauren took a sip of her rum and Coke. Hugo did seem genuine – how could he be trying to trick her, with eyes like those and a smile like that? But she still couldn't let down her guard.

'Don't worry, I think this place is kind of fun,' she said, trying to keep her voice steady. 'English pubs still seem cool to me. Sometimes I feel like England is one big theme park, full of . . . *English* stuff. And people with funny accents.'

Hugo burst out laughing. 'Well, that's lucky for me, I guess.' He ducked and covered his ears as a roar arose from the football crowd.

Lauren caught his eye and grinned. 'Your party was really fun.'

'Thanks. It's the first time I've ever had a big house party. I thought Alice and my older brother Dom had ruined my chances for ever. They've had some really wild ones. One time, Alice bought a vodka luge and it melted all over the kitchen floor and leaked into the basement.

My dad almost killed her. He was like, "That's it! There'll be no more birthday parties in this house. Ever again!"'

'How did you change his mind?'

'Oh, weeks of moaning and whining. I think he finally agreed just to shut me up.'

They both laughed. Hugo sipped his beer. 'You're the youngest, aren't you? In your family.'

'Yes. It's just me and Dylan.'

'Don't you find that hard? I mean, I'm the youngest too, and I always feel like my siblings do everything before me. And I don't just mean house parties. It's like, between them they're good at pretty much everything. OK, Dom was a bad boy at school, but all the teachers loved him anyway. And Alice is obviously Little Miss Perfect. How on earth am I supposed to look good when I'm up against that?'

'Tell me about it,' Lauren groaned. 'It's like that with Dylan, too, even though there's only one of her. She's smart, and she's good at art, and she's an amazing dancer. Plus, she's gorgeous and sexy and all the boys have always loved her.'

'I don't think you need to worry about that part, at least,' Hugo said. 'You're pretty gorgeous yourself.'

Lauren blushed.

So did Hugo. 'Oh, I almost forgot. I brought you something.'

'Really?'

'Yeah.'

'What is it?'

Hugo ducked his head. 'Oh, no, maybe I shouldn't have mentioned it. Now that we're here, it feels super-lame.'

'Show me!' Lauren grinned.

'OK, fine . . . But don't blame me if you think it's stupid.' Reaching into his coat, Hugo pulled out a small plastic package. 'It's sweets. They're pineapple-flavoured. You said you liked pineapple, at my party. And I saw them in the newsagent and thought I'd buy them, and . . . I'm an idiot.' He was wincing.

'No! This is so nice. Thank you.'

'Really?'

'Yes, really.' Lauren beamed. Weirdly, Hugo's awkwardness was making her feel more relaxed. She nudged him and nodded towards the table-football set. 'Hey, how about a match before I have to go?'

'Hmm.' Hugo smiled. 'If you like. But I'm warning you, I'm good. Really good.'

'Ooh, fighting words. You'll look pretty dumb if you lose after that boast.' Snickering, Lauren laid her coat across a radiator. She could feel Hugo staring at her pink dress, which was tight across the boobs before flaring out at the waist.

Just as they were taking up their positions, two men jostled out of the crowd.

'Sorry to interrupt,' said one of them, 'but we were about to play as well. How about we challenge you to a match? Us against you?'

Lauren raised her eyebrows at Hugo.

'Sure.' Grinning, he ran to the other side of the table.

Suddenly, there he was, right next to her. His shoulder brushed against hers as he gave the players a warm-up spin. 'What's our strategy?' he whispered in her ear, his breath warming her cheek.

Goosebumps ran up and down Lauren's body. 'Strategy?' she whispered back. 'Who cares? Let's just fucking win!'

'Good plan,' Hugo chuckled. 'OK . . . ready, steady, go!'

'Aaargh!' cried the men on the other side of the table, as they wrenched and twisted the handles, scoring three goals in quick succession.

'No way!' Lauren yelped. She tossed her hair, sending a cloud of perfume into the pub's sweaty air. 'Time to step it up, partner.' Baring her teeth, she fought and defended and attacked until, with a final flick of her wrist, the ball flew into the opposing goal.

'Score!' Hugo cried. 'Amazing play!' Seizing Lauren's waist, he spun her round and round and round until, all of a sudden, his face became serious. He gazed into her eyes. She stared back, her whole body trembling.

At that second, something buzzed in her pocket. She sprang away, fumbling for her phone.

You'd better get back. We're leaving in five! Gould is asking where you are.

'Text from Charlie,' Lauren murmured. Disappointment, mingled with relief, cascaded through her body. 'I have to go.'

'Wait.' Hugo grabbed her hand. Before she realised what was happening, he pulled her close and leaned in – and kissed her. Lauren closed her eyes, sinking into wonderful darkness, her mind switching off. She didn't even have time to think what this meant – her first kiss, her first anything. The only thing in the world was Hugo's mouth on hers, the firmness of his arm on her waist, the softness of his hair under her hand.

'I've wanted to do that for ages,' he whispered, drawing back a little.

Lauren swallowed. If only she could believe him. She wanted to, so badly. But she couldn't. Not after everything that had happened.

'Why?' she blurted out.

'Why?'

'Yeah. I don't understand – why don't you think I'm weird? Why don't you think . . .' Lauren could feel herself turning red. But she had to say it. 'The whole diary thing – me babbling on about how much I liked you, when we hadn't even met. I thought you'd think I was a freak. I mean, I almost can't believe you don't.'

She backed away a step and stared fiercely at Hugo, half daring him to crack up, admit that he'd kissed her out of sympathy. Or just plain spite – the stupid, pathetic new girl who had a giant crush on him, and zero experience with boys.

But Hugo only reached for her hand again. 'Don't be ridiculous. I mean, you wrote something in your diary. Something kind of stalkerish, I admit . . .' He grinned. 'But no, honestly, who doesn't write that kind of shit when they think it's private? I think it's cute. And anyway, it shows you have good taste, right?'

Lauren chewed her lip. 'Really? I mean, you actually like me, and you don't think I'm insane?'

'Really. I really, actually do,' Hugo murmured, brushing his nose against hers. 'Let me put it this way – if I'd seen you before you saw me, it probably would have been the other way round. *I'd* have written a whole diary entry about *you*.'

Lauren glided back along Hasted High Street beaming like the new moon, her feet hardly touching the ground. It seemed so simple, now that it had happened. One moment she'd been the girl who'd never kissed anyone. Now, she was the girl who'd kissed Hugo Rochester. The girl who Hugo Rochester *liked*. Turning round, she saw him watching her from the corner. She waved, and broke into a run.

Chapter 37

Sonia rifled through the pages of her Latin dictionary, crumpling them in her frenzy to find the right section.

'No wonder it's a dead language,' she muttered to herself. 'Why don't they have any words in here? Useless piece of crap!' Snatching up the book, she flung it towards the door of her room.

'Ow!' yelped Bella Scott, jumping backwards.

Sonia almost leapt out of her chair. Then a smile curved over her lips. 'Bellsy! I didn't know you were there. Just the person I was hoping to see. Have you done the Latin prep?'

'Yeah. Just finished it. And I was wondering if you felt like a trip to the Tuck In,' Bella said. The Tuck In was the school's new café, housed in its own modern glass and steel building, which had only been opened last term. 'I've got the biggest coffee craving ever.'

'Tell me about it. I've only drunk one non-fat latte so far today, and my ration is at least three. But the thing is,' Sonia purred, curling a piece of her glossy hair round her fingers, 'I can't go till I've finished this ridiculous translation.'

'That's cool. I'll wait.'

'Well, yes, of course you could do that. But there's no telling how long I'll be. Hmm . . . Oh, I have such a clever idea! Why don't you just let me copy your prep?'

Bella bit her lip. 'What, you mean word for word?'

'Umm, yes, darling, that's usually what copying means.' Sonia barely suppressed an eye-roll. 'Now, let's go get coffee, and when we come back, you can hand it over.'

'But I don't think I want to. I mean, it took me ages. I worked really hard to—'

'Darling! How can you be so selfish?' Sonia practically shrieked. 'Don't you know what a terrible headache I have? I can't possibly work any more, and it's only a bit of stupid homework. I'd do the same for you – you know I would. Isn't this precisely what best friends are for? How can I rely on you for anything if I can't even rely on you for this?'

Bella, who had taken a few steps backwards at Sonia's tirade, held up her hands. 'OK, OK. If you feel that strongly about it, go ahead and copy.'

'Wonderful!' Sonia beamed. Grabbing her cashmere coat and a lilac pashmina, she skipped down the stairs, and out the front gate of Tudor House. 'I knew you were a generous friend, sweetie,' she gloated, squeezing Bella's arm as they crossed the Great Lawn. 'And to show my appreciation, I'll treat you to whatever you like at the Tuck In.'

'Hi, Sonia!' called a voice.

Sonia squinted, then gave a condescending smile. 'Oh, hello, Emilia. Have you been in the art block?'

'Yeah.' Emilia Charles shifted her satchel from one shoulder to the other. 'How did you know?'

'Well, you're not exactly looking pristine, are you?' Sonia chortled. 'I can see at least three splodges of paint on your jumper. Not to mention that bit in your hair.'

'Oh.' Emilia's face fell. 'Well, anyway, I just wanted to say, I'm so excited about your party this weekend. Flic and Flossy and I have bought our Arabian Nights outfits. We're all coming as identical princesses, with different-coloured headdresses, and—'

'Sounds lovely!' Sonia beamed. 'But don't give away your whole costume, now. We wouldn't want to spoil anything. Bye! See you later. *Come on,*' she added under her breath, tugging Bella's arm.

Bella stumbled over the grass. 'How come you wouldn't let her finish? I thought you liked Emilia.'

'I do like her. I mean, she's all right – she's quite pretty, and she's quite cool, but that's hardly the point.'

'Oh.' Bella blinked as they walked through the doors of the Tuck In. 'What is the point, then?'

'Oh really, darling, has our whole party-planning process taught you nothing?' Sonia scanned the rows of cakes at the counter, then turned away, even though she was salivating for one of the cinnamon buns. 'Listen. When you have a social takeover scheme like mine – I mean, when you want to become the social leader of the year – you can't start treating everyone as equals. Otherwise, they'll forget that you're a level above them. What I did just now was communicate to Emilia that yes, she is worthy to speak to me, but no, she is not in the inner circle. The only people in the inner circle are you, and me.'

'Oh my god,' Bella giggled, 'you are so weird.'

'I am not weird!' Sonia huffed. She yanked a chair out from under one of the café's round steel-topped tables and plonked herself down. 'You'll see. And maybe in the future, you won't be such an amateur.' Bella frowned, but Sonia didn't seem to notice. 'Anyway, I'm very pleased with the way my party is shaping up so far. Now all I have to do is find out what skeletons Tally Abbott has in her cupboard, and expose them.'

'Oh god,' Bella groaned. 'Don't start going on about that again, please.'

'Do you think she's a Russian spy?' Sonia mused, stirring her latte. 'After all, her mother and grandfather still live in Moscow. That thug Alice met in town could have been her spymaster.'

'Right. A Russian spymaster in the middle of Hasted. Please, Sone – I thought you dismissed that theory yesterday. You said Tally wasn't subtle enough to be a spy.'

'Hmm, yes, true. But I haven't dismissed the drug-dealer theory yet. Tally's dad works in the City, and we all know that high-flying executives rely on coke to keep their energy up. I bet she's importing cocaine and supplying her dad and her stepmother as her primary customers. Yes! And she probably owes that man money.'

'Sone, I don't think—'

'Or wait, no! I've got it.' Sonia's face was now completely manic. She was waving her wooden coffee stirrer in Bella's face. 'She's a prostitute. Natalya Abbott is a hooker! That's why she had that massive wad of cash – she's been shagging all our male teachers, and probably most of Hasted House as well. The thug was obviously her pimp. I have to warn everyone.'

There was a clatter as Bella dropped her fork on to her cake plate. 'Sonia! Stop it right now. You're being completely insane. Those theories are nonsense, all of them. And anyway, I thought you said Tally was nice.'

'That was before she attacked me outside Chapel!' Sonia cried. 'Why do you keep sticking up for her? And Alice Rochester, too. You're such a sneak – I've seen you trying to say hello to Alice, and make up with her, and apologise for shagging Tristan. What is up with that?'

'I feel bad! Alice never did anything to me. I quite like her, actually. And it's your fight, not mine.'

'How can you say that?' Sonia gasped. 'You're my BFF! All my fights are your fights. All my problems are your problems. All my enemies are your enemies!'

Bella was shaking her head, her light brown hair swinging from side to side. 'You know what? I think you actually might be crazy, Sonia. You keep saying I'm your best friend, but all you do is criticise me, and torture me with your mental theories – and now you're saying I have to agree with every single thing you do? I'm not your clone, OK? And I'm not your slave either. You're kind of starting to freak me out. I'm sorry, but I have to go.'

'You can't go!' Sonia yelled, as Bella fled their table. 'Stay right here. And don't forget, I still want to copy your prep!'

Sonia's words echoed off the café's glass walls. A chorus of snickers rose up from the surrounding tables, and suddenly she realised that everyone in the entire place was staring at her. Grabbing her coffee, she pulled her pashmina round her face and stalked outside. She needed a cigarette. Turning off the Great Lawn, she trudged down a path lined with bare trees, until she came to a staircase set into a low stone wall. The sunken garden was the perfect smoking spot today – it was too cold for visitors, and only the hardiest, most wintry flowers were out.

Sonia picked her way round a clump of wind-ravaged rose bushes, towards the most hidden part of the garden. Then, suddenly, she stopped. Tendrils of cigarette smoke were curling around the side of a carefully pruned bush. Someone else was obviously here. A head of straw-like dyed blond hair came into view, followed by a ratty jumper, then a pair of skinny legs.

'Oh,' said Georgie Fortescue, before Sonia could back away. 'Hello. Thought I heard someone.'

'Well, you thought right,' Sonia said. She sat down on an ancient stone bench and dug out her pack of fags.

'You look a bit pissed off.'

'That's funny, since I'm absolutely fine.' Sonia sniffed. She was so not in the mood to open up to random Year Tens.

Gnawing at her thumbnail, Georgie Fortescue scuffed one of her black studded boots on the ground. 'At least one of us is, then.'

'Why?' Sonia rolled her eyes. 'What's wrong with you?'

'More like *who's* wrong with me. Charlotte Calthorpe de Vyle-Hanswicke. And Lauren Fucking Taylor.'

Sonia's cigarette froze mid-air. 'I thought you were friends with Charlie. And I thought you'd already fucked up Lauren's life.'

'Yeah, well, things are different now. Charlie betrayed me. She dumped me for that stupid blonde American bitch. And then they stole the guy I'm in love with. But they'll be sorry.' Georgie's eyes flashed. 'As soon as I work out a way to get my revenge.'

'Revenge, hmmm?' Sonia exhaled a thick grey cloud. 'You're not the only one with a grudge, you know.'

'Oh, really?' Georgie spat on the ground. 'Who's your beef with?'

'Lauren Taylor's sister, for a start. And Alice Rochester. And Tally Abbott, now that we're on the subject.'

Georgie chuckled. 'Not exactly an easy list.'

'They think they're such a cool, clever little crew,' Sonia went on. 'I've been trying to knock them off their pedestal all term. I thought that excluding them from my big birthday bash – the party of the season – would be enough. But a little extra humiliation might just sweeten the deal.'

'It always does,' Georgie smirked.

'Indeed. And you know,' Sonia said, tapping her chin, 'maybe one of the best ways to strike at someone is to do it from an angle they'd never expect.'

'What are you getting at? Explain.'

'What if . . .' Sonia dropped ash on the ground, 'what if we joined forces? You carry out my plot on Dylan and

Alice for me. No one would ever suspect you – you have no motive. You'd be perfectly safe from scrutiny and blame. And then, when that's done, I'll return the favour. Charlie and Lauren – out of your hair, courtesy of me. Just think about it. We'd be untraceable. The perfect crime.'

A slow grin stretched across Georgie's pale, pointy face. 'Interesting . . .' She smirked. 'I'm listening. What exactly did you have in mind?'

Chapter 38

'Hurry up or we'll miss the train!' Alice cried, crunching in her four-inch heels along the misty front drive of St Cecilia's.

'We will not,' Dylan said. 'We still have half an hour to get there.'

'Ow! You're treading on my dress,' Mimah whined. It was five o'clock on Saturday, and the girls were dolled up in red-carpet-worthy outfits, ready to rub shoulders with London's highest society at the von Holstadts' charity dinner and dance. Mimah snatched up the hem of her floor-length midnight-blue evening gown, darted ahead of the other two and yanked open the taxi door. 'Bagsy the front!'

'Oh that is *so* mature,' Alice snorted. 'Whatever. I actually *wanted* to go in the back. Dylan and I are gonna whisper about you all the way there.'

'Ooh, I'm worried. We're going to the station, please,' Mimah informed the driver, then twisted round to face Alice. 'Hey, do you think Magnus Bellamy will be there this year? Remember last year he was so desperate to pull Tally that he literally stalked us round the entire club? We had to hide in the kitchens.'

'Oh my god, yes!' Alice's expression had darkened at the mention of Tally's name, but now she burst out laughing. 'Magnus Bell-End. What a loser. As long as the Terrible Twins don't trap me into talking to them.'

'Fuck, yeah,' Mimah groaned. 'Olivia and Melissa Wyndham-Rhodes. They've got less than half a brain between them.'

'I know. One time, Livs asked me if England was the capital of Europe.'

Dylan's eyes widened. '*Who* asked you that?'

'Well, she once told me she had a photogenic memory,' Mimah interrupted. 'I think she meant photo*graphic*. And she definitely doesn't have one of those, either.'

Alice guffawed. 'We should start calling them the Twits instead of the Twins. I just wish the boys didn't think they were both so hot. George Demetrios literally follows them round with his tongue hanging out.'

Dylan sighed. 'I really wish I knew who all these people were.'

'No you don't,' Alice said. 'Trust us.'

'You'll know who they are after tonight, anyway.'

'I guess. But you guys don't understand – you know *everyone*. I'll never know them all, no matter how many of these things I go to.'

'Aw, poor little Dilly,' Mimah cackled. 'The little lost soul.'

'But sometimes I feel like I am!' Dylan insisted. 'I mean, those names – Wyndham-Rolls—'

'Rhodes,' Mimah corrected.

'Exactly. And Calthorpe de Vyle-Hanswicke, for goodness' sake! I mean, my last name's Taylor. I'll never fit in.'

Mimah made a face. 'I don't know what on earth you're worrying about. You're Jasper von Holstadt's girlfriend. His parents are the hosts tonight. You can't get more *in* than that. Unless Jasper really is shagging Tally Abbott,' she added with a laugh. 'In which case, you're pretty much out.'

'Mime!' Alice ordered. 'Be quiet. Don't wind her up.'

By now, the taxi had pulled up at the station. The girls climbed out and made their way on to the platform, walking slowly in their high heels. Dylan had gone quiet, and was biting her lip.

Mimah nudged her. 'Cheer up, Dill. I was only joking. No need to be a crybaby. I mean, what could Jasper possibly see in Tally – apart from her gorgeousness, sweetness, sexiness and charm, I mean?'

'Oh, ha ha ha,' Dylan snapped. 'Stop trying to make me paranoid.'

Mimah snickered. She glanced at the station clock. 'Ugh, we've got ten whole minutes. I told you we didn't need to leave so early, Ali. When are you going to stop being so anal about time?'

'And when are you going to shut up about it? Anyway, I wanted to buy a snack. I'm hungry.'

'You're always hungry.' Mimah took out her compact and slicked on a layer of red Chanel lipstick. 'Just don't spoil your appetite. Last year they served oysters and caviar blinis, and I want to scarf as many of those as—' Suddenly, the words died on her lips. Her eyes were fixed on something in her mirror. She snapped it shut and wheeled round.

'Mime? What's wrong?'

But Mimah wasn't listening. She was already pacing towards a bench on the platform a few feet away. A tall, dark-haired boy was slumped there, his head in his hands.

'Aidan?'

He lifted his face. 'Jemimah!'

'What are you doing here?' Mimah studied him, the small birthmark under her left eye lending her stare an added intensity. 'I've been texting and ringing you for the past two days. Why haven't you picked up?'

Aidan bit his lip. He was unshaven, Mimah noticed, and wearing a scruffy grey sweatshirt. Her eyes fell on the duffel bag at his feet.

'Mime.' Alice laid a hand on her shoulder. 'What's going on? Are you all right?'

Mimah took a deep breath. 'Yeah. Alice, I'd like you to meet Aidan. Aidan, this is Alice, one of my oldest friends.'

'Hi,' Alice said stiffly. 'We've met before, actually. Although I'm not sure you'd remember. You seemed more concerned with other things at the time.'

Aidan looked at Alice. His eyes took in her beige lace dress, her long legs and her shiny platform shoes. Finally, he met her eyes. 'Yeah, I remember. Lucian Scott's Christmas party. And you're right, it wasn't my best night. How are you doing?'

Alice blinked. Her mouth, which had been a thin, tight line, loosened a little. 'I'm fine.'

'Hey, Al, can you give us a minute?'

'If you want.' Alice folded her arms. 'But our train's gonna be here soon. Don't be long.'

'OK, *Mum*.' Mimah rolled her eyes and sat down next to Aidan, nudging his bag with her gold leather shoe. 'Going somewhere?'

'I could ask you the same question,' he snapped. Then he sighed. 'Sorry. You look nice. Really nice.'

'Oh. Thanks.' Mimah drew her coat tighter around her dress. Suddenly, she felt like some showy, inflated version of herself. The sheen of her freshly washed hair, the glitter of her jewellery, the bouquet of her perfume – it all felt brash and inappropriate on this grey station platform, with this grey figure by her side. She pursed her lips. 'Why haven't you been answering my calls? I've been worried about you. And your mum.'

'Thanks.' Aidan pulled the sleeves of his sweatshirt over his long, delicate fingers. 'Actually, my mum's fine.'

'That's great! You mean they found her?'

'Yeah. She's at the police station.'

'Since when?'

'Since a couple of days ago.'

'A couple of days? Why?'

Aidan turned his brown eyes straight on Mimah's. They were flickering with a strange light, and when he spoke, his voice was hard. 'The police picked her up on Wednesday. They said they found her rolling round on the riverbank,

255

soaked in booze, babbling away. No ID on her. Nothing. Just an empty bottle and a few pennies in her pockets. They stuck her in a cell to sleep it off. It took them till today to work out who she was.'

'So . . . ?' Mimah stared at him.

'So what?'

'So what the hell are you doing here? Aidan, wake up! Your mum's lying in a police cell, and you're sitting in the train station. Why?'

'Because I'm fed up!' Aidan tore at his hair. 'I can't fucking handle this any more, OK? Worrying myself sick about my mum, giving up everything I care about, watching her drink herself into the grave. She doesn't give a shit about me – why should I give a shit about her? I'm jumping on the first train that comes along. I am! And I'm not stopping till there's ten thousand miles between me and here.' His gaze burned into Mimah's. 'I'm following your advice.'

'*My* advice?'

'Yeah. You said to get out of here. You said to start a new life.'

'But I didn't mean like this!' Mimah cried. 'I didn't mean you should just pack up and sneak off – abandon your mum – abandon everything. Abandon me!'

'I wasn't going to abandon you.' Aidan's voice was quiet, urgent. In the distance, the tracks were rattling, the approaching train bleeding its electricity into the air. 'When I was far away and sorted out, I was going to call you. I had this plan . . .'

'Yeah, right. Doesn't sound like you've planned anything – except your own escape.'

'I promise. You were the only person I thought about. The only one I was going to tell. Believe me. *Please.*'

The train's echo was growing louder by the second. The rhythmic metallic clanging sounded like a hundred animals rattling a cage.

Mimah stared into Aidan's eyes. Suddenly, she grabbed his bag. 'That's it. Get up.'

'What are you doing?'

'Mimah!' Alice called. 'It's time to go. We have to get on.'

Mimah didn't reply. The train was now shooting into the station and she had to yell to be heard. 'It's not happening like this, Aidan. You're not just running away. If you want to start a new life, then start a new life – but it begins with going to get your mum. Come on. We're going to the police station. And then we'll talk.'

'We?'

'Yes. We!'

'Hang on . . .' Aidan's forehead furrowed. 'You're coming to the police station . . . dressed like that?'

'Who gives a shit how I'm dressed!' Mimah cried. And then, for no reason at all, she was giggling, even though there were tears streaming down her face. She wiped them away, shooting Aidan her fiercest possible look.

He broke into a grin.

'Mimah!' Alice shouted. She and Dylan were standing on the train, straining to hold open the doors. A toneless buzzer went off.

'*This train is about to depart. Please stand clear.*'

'Get on. Hurry up!'

'I'm not coming,' Mimah called back. She gripped Aidan's hand, watching as the doors slid shut. 'Go on without me. There's something I need to do here.'

Chapter 39

The Palm Court at Fulham's exclusive Hurlingham Club glowed with soft light from dozens of crystal lanterns. Jazz crooned from a piano, accompanied by the hum of small talk and the swish of evening dresses over the marble floor. Women glittering with jewels chatted to men in tuxedos while sipping champagne from elegant flutes and plucking shellfish off the oyster bar. And all along the room, beneath the domed glass ceiling, banners advertised the important work of the Angkor Hospital for Children in Cambodia. Jasper's parents, Prince Wilhelm and Princess Helena von Holstadt, had held this charity gala each winter for the past five years, ever since, as they liked to tell people, 'our grand tour of South East Asia opened our eyes to the suffering of the Third World'.

'Whoa,' Dylan said. She was standing in a corner with Seb, darting her eyes round the hall. 'Look at that woman. If her necklace is made of real diamonds, it's worth enough to buy about three US states.'

'Oh, it's definitely real diamonds. That's Nadira Fortnum. Bathsheba Fortnum's mother. She doesn't do fake.'

Dylan giggled. Champagne bubbles fizzed up her nose,

and she coughed. 'Who the hell is Bathsheba Fortnum? And why does she have such a ridiculous name?'

'It's a family name,' Seb said. 'Sheebs is all right. She goes to Malbury Hall – you know, the arch-rival of St Cecilia's. She's best friends with Messy and Olivia Wyndham-Rhodes.'

'You mean the twins? Alice and Mimah were talking about them earlier.'

'I'm not surprised – they're pretty gossip-worthy. And there they are,' Seb chuckled. He pointed to two identical girls, both stunning and both wearing extremely tight corsets, one in lime-green and the other in acid-pink. Their heels were so high they could barely walk, and they both had blond hair teased into gigantic bouffants. As Dylan watched, they stumbled over to Jasper and kissed him hello.

Seb swiped another glass of champagne off a passing tray, snickering as a photographer attempted to arrange Jasper and the twins into a tableau. 'The paps just love those two – double-trouble hotness. I guarantee you that photo will be in *Tatler* next month.' He shook his head. 'God, do you think Jas knows how sycophantic he looks? Just look at that cheesy grin.'

'You're so mean,' Dylan grinned, swatting Seb's arm. 'Poor Jasper. It's his parents' evening. He's supposed to be charming everyone.'

'And what a success he is.' Seb laughed. 'Come on, you've got to admit, Jas is a world-class schmoozer. Not that I'm criticising him. It's a useful talent – he'll be doing it for the rest of his life.'

Dylan frowned. 'What do you mean?'

'Well, it kind of comes with the territory, being defunct German royalty and all. The von Holstadts might not have any actual power any more, but the name still commands awe in a lot of social circles.'

'Hmm.' Dylan sighed and swirled her drink. She was still watching Jasper, who was now talking to a distinguished elderly couple as if they were his best friends. 'Look how comfortable he is, talking to anyone. I'm not sure I could ever do that. Do you think . . .' She swallowed. 'Do you think Jasper wishes he had the kind of girlfriend who'd be out there with him? I mean, someone gorgeous and glamorous, who'd-charm the pants off everyone in the room?'

Seb rolled his eyes. 'Oh, do shut up, Dill.' He grinned. 'I think Jasper likes it just fine having the spotlight all to himself. And he couldn't ask for a better girlfriend than you. Or a prettier one.'

'Oh, please.'

'It's true!' Seb looked at Dylan's long peach-coloured halter-neck dress, which showed off her shoulders and bust, and at her blond hair, which was piled on top of her head and garlanded with vintage lace. 'You look great. I'd totally dress like that if I were a girl. Hey, was that your phone?'

'Yeah.' Dylan slid her mobile out of her silk evening bag and scanned the message. 'Whoa! I don't believe this. Is he serious?'

'Who? What?'

'Look.' She shoved the screen in Seb's face. 'It's from Corey Benson! He found me on Facebook.'

'No. Way.' Seb grabbed the phone.

'And he's inviting me to the opening-night party of his play next week. The one he's in with Will.' Dylan widened her cornflower-blue eyes. 'But why? I thought he hated me.'

'Duh, well he obviously doesn't! He must totally fancy you.'

'Of course he doesn't! How could he possibly fancy me? He's a TV star. And a total babe magnet. Not that *I* fancy *him*, of course,' Dylan added. 'But what would he see in me?'

'What wouldn't he see in you? You're clever. You're funny. And you're so much hotter than those popsicle-thin TV-actress girls.'

'Excuse me?' Dylan's jaw dropped. 'Are you saying I'm fat?'

'Oh my god.' Seb whacked his forehead against his hand. 'I am so glad I'm not into girls. What is wrong with you? Of course you're not fat. Now can we talk about something that's not completely stupid? You have to come next Saturday. Will's already invited me – we can go together. It'll be great to have a wing-woman.'

Dylan fiddled with the big gold bangle around her wrist. 'I don't know,' she mused. 'It feels kind of weird just agreeing to go. I mean, I'm at my boyfriend's parents' soirée. I can't just text and say I'll go out with another guy.'

'Of course you can! Are you mental? Refuse a night out

with Corey Benson, just because you're dating *him?*' Seb jerked his thumb at Jasper, who was now leaning with his arm against a pillar, chatting to three waitresses. 'Look, you know what I think of Jasper. I think you're too good for him, for a start. And I don't think you should let him ruin your chances with Corey Benson.'

'What chances?' Dylan protested, rapidly typing on her screen. 'I wouldn't be ruining anything – this obviously isn't a date, because someone like Corey Benson would never go out with someone like me. There. Look, this is what I sent back.' She held out her phone.

'*Sounds fun thanks!*' Seb read. '*I'd love to come. But just as friends right? Cause I have a b/f.* ☺ God, you're an idiot,' he muttered. Dylan's phone beeped back.

'Give it to me!' she cried, grabbing it from Seb. They both stared at Corey's reply.

Umm obviously I meant just as friends. I'm inviting loads of people. Bring your boyf if you want. Maybe c u there. C.

'Happy now?' Seb asked.

Dylan had turned slightly pink. 'Yes, I am actually,' she sniffed. She bit her lip. 'Hey, where's Jasper?'

'Dunno. I saw him sneak off that way about a minute ago,' Seb said, nodding towards the lobby.

'Oh. Right. Well I'm going to go find him. I think I deserve a moment with my boyfriend at some point tonight, don't you?'

'Sure. If you want. But . . . maybe a different moment would be better. He kind of looked like he was on a mission.'

263

Dylan squinted at Seb suspiciously. 'What do you mean, a mission?'

'I don't know. Just . . . he was frowning. And walking really fast. Why don't you wait for him to come back inside?'

But Dylan didn't reply. Downing her champagne, she straightened her dress and strode the length of the atrium, weaving among gala guests, drinks tables and the palm trees that gave the room its name.

There was no sign of Jasper in the lobby – only the hushed sound of a door swinging shut. Dylan ran to it and slipped outside. The night-time grass, glittering with dew, was slowly unfurling itself where it had been flattened by footsteps. Slowly, silently, she followed the trail around the side of the building. Then she stopped, hugging the shadow of a pillar. There was Jasper. And there, right next to him, was a tall, blonde, beautiful, elegant girl. Tally Abbott.

Chapter 40

Alice slid a glass of white wine off the bar and hugged her arms across her beige lace dress. Next to her, a group of cute older boys were laughing and slapping each other's backs. She edged sideways, away from them. She wasn't in the mood to meet new people. And anyway, they were speaking in German – they obviously came from some random branch of the von Holstadt clan – and she had no clue what they were saying.

She sipped her drink. Feeling awkward in social settings wasn't something she was used to. And it wasn't something she liked. In the past, if she'd ever found herself alone at an event like this, she would have gravitated towards T. The two of them had always been partners in crime – having more fun than everyone else, and looking better while they did it, too. Alice's lips twitched. She thought back to that time a few years ago when she and T had dropped white Tic Tacs into all the Malbury Hall girls' drinks to fool them into thinking they'd been roofied. There had been a mass panic, and Alice and Tristan had almost been found out, but they'd got away with it in the end. Just like they always had. Alice's smile dimmed. If only she could go up to T right now – leap back over the months as if they'd never happened. But they had happened. And there he was, chatting up Bathsheba Fortnum, just like he had been all night.

Alice swirled her wine around the glass. Mimah had deserted her for Aidan. Dylan had disappeared somewhere with Jasper. And Tally – well, she couldn't face hearing any more lies from Tally just now. It looked like she was alone. And she might as well be alone outside.

The lobby was quiet. But not as quiet as Alice had expected. A soft voice was echoing off the marble floors. Her eyes fell on a figure by the door.

'I had fun, too,' Rando was saying. 'Yes, really. Hey, listen, Tiki? I can't get away right now. I'm at my aunt and uncle's charity bash. OK, I'll call you back later. OK, bye.' He put the phone down and turned round. 'Alice!' He jumped. Then he recovered himself. 'Hi.'

'Hey.' Alice started forward, refusing to meet his eye. Her hem swirled against her knees as she made for the exit.

'You're not leaving, are you?'

'Does it look like I'm leaving? With no coat and a half-full drink? I just want some air. It's hot in there.'

'Mind if I join?'

She shrugged. 'Yeah, of course, you can do what you want.'

The still, damp air outside felt like a curtain of freezing droplets hung over the earth. Piano music rolled out from the atrium, and the white walls of Hurlingham glowed in the mist.

'I've been thinking about you,' Rando said.

Alice rubbed her bare arms and stared straight ahead.

'I've been wanting to make sure you were OK. After that lunatic in town the other day. So . . . are you?'

'Depends what you mean by OK. I haven't spotted him again, if that's what you're asking. And Tally didn't suffer a dramatic breakdown or anything. Actually, she seemed to think it was pretty normal for a thug to show up looking for her. She hardly seemed surprised at all.'

'What? That's weird. But was she scared?'

'No . . .' Alice furrowed her forehead. 'She didn't seem to be, actually. She just kept asking for details – what he looked like, what he said. As if she was expecting him. Or at least, expecting *someone*.'

Rando frowned. 'Maybe she was just in shock. People do weird things when they're freaked out. But I'm glad she seems OK, I was worried for her. And . . .' he looked at the ground, 'I was worried about you, too. When you walked off back to school by yourself. I . . . I was going to call you, but I wasn't sure . . . I didn't want . . .' He took a step towards her.

Alice moved backwards. 'The person you were talking to on the phone just now – was it that girl you were with in town the other day? Tiki Hardinge-Smythe?'

Rando stopped. He ran a hand under the collar of his tuxedo jacket. 'Yeah. It was.'

'Oh. Right.'

'Listen, Alice, I—'

'I love this song!' Alice interrupted. The piano was playing 'Someone To Watch Over Me', an old jazz piece

267

that her parents liked to put on at home. She started humming along. Anything to prevent Rando going on about Tiki. Stupid Tiki, with her shiny hair and her stylish boots and her girlie-girlie voice. Suddenly, she shivered. 'Gosh, it's cold.'

'Here, have my jacket.'

'No thanks. A boy's tuxedo jacket? It'll look terrible on me.'

Rando laughed, revealing his adorable pointy teeth. Crinkles appeared around his glass-blue eyes. Alice swallowed.

'Of course it won't look terrible. Here.' Shrugging out of the jacket, he wrapped it round her, pulling her closer as he did so – whether on purpose or not, she couldn't tell. All she knew was that his hands were lingering on her shoulders, their warmth seeping through the fine black material. She stood there looking up at him, unable to move away, even though she knew she should. Even though she knew it was all too late.

At that moment, the door to the lobby swung open. The piano music swelled.

'Alice? *Rando?*'

They broke away from each other.

There, standing on the steps above them, was Tristan. His eyes were narrow, flitting from one to the other. 'What are you two doing out here?'

'Nothing.' Alice stood up straighter. Rando's jacket slid back on her shoulders. 'Just came out for some air. And I got cold.'

Rando cleared his throat. 'Cigarette?' he said, shaking out a pack.

T said nothing at first. Finally, he gave a nod. 'Yeah. Sure.'

The lighter flickered. Then there was silence. The cigarettes' white smoke dissolved in the misty air.

Chapter 41

Around the corner of the building, less than ten metres away, Dylan edged along the row of columns. She breathed carefully, silently, her eyes fixed on Jasper and Tally up ahead.

'Hey, darls,' Jasper whispered. He looked poised and elegant, his black-tuxedoed figure standing out among the white pillars. 'We've got to be quick. I don't want anyone to suspect.'

Tally smiled her perfect, glimmering smile, her white teeth shining in the moonlight. 'No one suspects. No one has any idea. I'm better at this than that.'

In the shadows, Dylan clenched her fists. But she couldn't make her move – not yet. She had to hear more.

'So,' Tally murmured, 'are we carrying on with this, or is it time to stop?'

'Why would we stop? I'm having a brilliant time. So far, this is practically the best term I've ever had. And I hope you're satisfied, too?'

'Oh, more than satisfied. It's just so easy, I can't believe we didn't think of this before.'

'You're telling me. You've been a lifesaver, Tals. You

really have. Except for that weekend when you went to LaLa Lounge and I thought you wouldn't pull it off. But you did. And I don't know how I ever managed before.' Jasper took a step forward.

Sweat condensed on Dylan's palms. This was it – Mimah had been right. And she was going to catch them at it if it was the last thing she did.

'By the way,' Tally whispered, 'how did it go last week?'

'Great.'

'So *Julius Caesar* worked out OK?'

'More than OK. A-star, baby, A-star.'

'See? I told you. I got the same thing.'

'I just love how predictable teachers are. Don't you?'

Dylan strained her ears. The conversation seemed to be taking a strange turn. It sounded like they were discussing schoolwork. Grades. That wasn't pillow talk. Not Jasper's kind of pillow talk, anyway. But still . . . something was happening . . . He was slipping something out of his pocket.

'Here.' He handed a package to Tally.

Dylan crept closer, squinting into the mist.

Tally examined the bundle for a second, before stuffing it in her clutch bag. 'Looks good. So what's on the menu this week?'

'Some Keats poems.'

'Easy. What else?'

'French. Have you done the subjunctive yet?'

'Of course.'

'Good. It's fifteen questions. Think you can handle that?'

For a moment, Tally didn't reply. She seemed to be thinking. Then she nodded. 'Fifteen's fine. But I want a hundred.'

'A *hundred?* Bit steep, don't you think?'

'No. But if you don't agree, you can always do it yourself. And I want fifty in advance. That means now.'

Jasper chuckled. 'You drive a fucking hard bargain, Tals. Which I respect, of course. Most girls are much easier than that.'

Dylan frowned. Without realising, she'd crept forward a few inches, and was staring fiercely at the scene. Jasper dug in his pocket again. At that moment, the fog thinned a little, the moon came out, and Dylan got a clear glimpse of what he held in his hand. The conversation raced back through her head. Suddenly, she gasped. With a cry of anger, she burst out from behind the pillar, her footsteps echoing down the misty portico.

'You idiots! You sneaking, dishonest idiots!'

'Who's there?' Tally squealed. 'Go away!'

'Dylan?' Jasper cried.

'Yes, that's right, you fucking moron,' Dylan yelled, shoving Jasper in the chest. 'It's me!'

'Ow, babe, that hurts!'

'Good.'

Footsteps sounded. From round the side of the building, Alice, Rando and Tristan came running.

'Dylan?' Alice panted. 'Tally? What's going on?'

'We heard a scream.'

'Are you all right?'

'No!' Dylan cried. She snatched the fifty-pound note from Jasper and waved it in Alice's face. 'Do you know what these two have been up to all term? Do you know why he's been meeting Tally in secret? Do you know why he's had so much time to get stoned and forget all about me? Oh, you'll love it. You really will.'

'Dill, calm down,' Jasper chortled. 'Don't lose your psycho temper. This is so not a big deal. And so not any of anyone's business.'

'It's my business! You're supposed to be my boyfriend – and who says I want to go out with a lying, sneaking cheat?'

'OK, Dill?' Tristan said. 'Take a deep breath. What are you talking about?'

'I'm talking about honour! Ever heard of it? Because these two obviously haven't. Yeah, that's right – Jasper's been cheating all term. Paying Tally to do his homework for him – paying her hundreds and hundreds of pounds.'

'That's ridiculous!' Rando protested. 'You can't just go around accusing my cousin of stuff like that.'

'Even when it's true?' Dylan shot back.

'Of course it's not true. I mean, yeah, Jasper cheats on homework sometimes – we all do. But an elaborate long-term scheme to cheat on virtually *everything*? No way. I think you're letting your imagination run away with you, Dylan.'

But Alice and Tristan just stared, their eyes slowly widening.

'Oh my god . . .' Tristan rubbed his face. 'Oh my fucking

god, Jas. No wonder you've been getting such good marks. No wonder you haven't been stressing.' He let out a stunned laugh. 'You know, this actually makes me feel better. You've been doing better than me because you're cheating – not because you're brainier! And all these weeks, I was thinking the world had turned upside down.'

Jasper grinned. 'Not so fast, mate. I mean, I've still been doing better than you, no matter what my methods were. I've said it before and I'll say it again – it's the results that count. And according to the results, I win.'

'Oh, right, you win at some stupid, petty cheating game.'

'Stupid?' Jasper spluttered. 'Petty? Don't you mean incredibly clever and apt? Tally needed money, and I needed not to work so hard. It's basic market forces, mate. Supply and demand. Bingo.'

T rolled his eyes. 'Alice, help me talk sense to him, please.'

But Alice had gone white. She was staring at Tally, shaking her head.

'Who are you?' she said. Her voice was low, dangerous. 'I feel like I hardly know you any more.'

'Ali, come on . . .' Tally darted forward. 'Don't be like that. I can explain. I needed—'

'Stop!' Alice held up her hand. 'Don't come near me. I've had enough of your lies. If you needed money, why didn't you just ask me for a loan? Why did you have to creep around behind my back? We're supposed to be friends – but you've got some secret life. Some secret, immoral, lowdown life!'

'Al,' Tristan objected, 'come on. You're being a bit harsh.'

'Am I?' Alice rounded on him. 'Just think if it was Seb – just think if your best friend had some sly, scheming secret. Wouldn't you feel betrayed? Wouldn't you be angry?'

'Yes, of course, but . . . but Tally's not Seb. Tally's different. We all know that. We've always known it. And that's why we love her.'

Inside, the pianist was playing a trill, the signal to go in to dinner.

'*You* love her, maybe,' Alice snarled. 'I do not. I'm finished with you, Tally Abbott. Come on, Dylan – let's go in and find our seats.'

But Dylan just stood there. 'No,' she said. 'I'm not coming. I can't. Jasper, you're dumped.'

'W-what?' Jasper stuttered. 'But Dill, babe, that makes no sense. You're being silly, you're—'

'Don't call me silly. Just be quiet and for once in your life listen to me, OK?' Dylan heaved a deep breath. Her lip was quivering, but her voice was perfectly calm. 'Over the past few weeks. I've put up with a whole lot of crap. I've put up with you cancelling on me. I've put up with you being stoned. I've put up with you being sexist and homophobic and snobby and arrogant and selfish. And I did it because I really, truly thought you were better than all that underneath. But now I realise I was wrong.'

'You weren't wrong! Dylan, come on. Let's talk. Please.'

But Dylan just shook her head. 'There's nothing to talk

about. You've lied and you've cheated, and you don't seem to care. It's like you don't even realise it's wrong. And that's not something I can forgive. So I'm sorry, Jasper, but this is the end.'

'Dill, wait! Please, come back. Stop!'

But Dylan didn't stop. She was already halfway across the lawn. Her shoulders were trembling, but her back was straight as it receded in the fog.

Chapter 42

Sonia sucked in her cheeks, straightened the bright pink sweatband around her head and slipped matching bands on to each of her wrists. Then she turned to face Georgie Fortescue. 'You're late.'

'I am not!' Georgie protested. 'We said one o'clock, and oh look – it's one o'clock.'

'It's two past one, actually,' Sonia sniffed, pointing a long-nailed finger at the clock in the gym changing room. 'And I like to start my workouts on time. I'm a very punctual person. Do you think one achieves a Hollywood beach body by cutting corners and acting like a sloth? No. One does not.'

'Um, whatever.' Georgie tossed her bleached blond hair. 'I'm sorry I delayed your sweat session, OK? Now can we get this show on the road?'

'I've been waiting to do that for two whole minutes,' Sonia said. Turning, she bent over her locker. She was wearing a pair of a bright pink leggings that perfectly matched her sweatbands, along with a pink sports bra and a purple spandex top. Up in the room she shared with Dylan, six more outfits just like this one occupied their

Kate Kingsley

very own shelf, each in a different colour, one for every day of the week.

'Here,' Sonia said, straightening up. She handed Georgie a plain black duffel bag. 'This should be everything you need. There's a map in there, too – it shows which rooms and which beds to target. I drew it myself and it's all clearly labelled. Now remember, you plant the stuff in Alice's bed and in Dylan's bed only. Don't get it wrong – or all my work will have been for nothing.'

Georgie nodded. 'I think I can handle it. What about Tally Abbott? I thought you said she was on your hit list, too.'

'Oh, she was,' Sonia snickered. 'But that was before she alienated her entire crew by turning into Jasper von Holstadt's homework whore. Yes, Tally Abbott is doing an excellent job of destroying herself without any help from me. Now go!' She glanced at the clock and started jogging on the spot. 'And good luck. Send me a text when you're done.'

Georgie got halfway out the door. Then she turned back. 'Hey, Sonia?'

'Yes, dear?'

'Our agreement's still the same, isn't it?'

'Agreement, dear?'

'Once I've sabotaged Alice and Dylan for you, you'll sabotage Charlie and Lauren for me?'

Sonia batted her long, mascara-slicked eyelashes. 'Of course I will, sweetie. A deal's a deal, right?'

She waited until Georgie had gone before she uncrossed her fingers behind her back.

Georgie pushed open the front door of Tudor House and listened. The only sound in the hall was her own nervous breathing; most of the rest of the school was at lunch. According to Sonia's map, Alice and Tally's room was on the first floor, the second door on the right. She poked her head inside. Empty. Darting to Alice's bed, Georgie drew back the covers and opened the duffel bag. She chuckled as she emptied the objects on to the sheet – Sonia had really outdone herself with this one. Finally, she placed a piece of typed paper under Alice's pillow, made up the bed again and stood back to admire her handiwork. It all looked undisturbed. No one would ever know.

Dylan and Sonia's room was only a few doors down, and the coast was still clear. Georgie consulted Sonia's map one last time before stuffing it back in the duffel bag. Dylan's bed was the one nearest the door. The one without the purple embroidered coverlet, the plush cushions and the silk-shaded lamp that Sonia had obviously brought from home. Creeping over to Dylan's bed, she drew back the simple sky-blue quilt.

'Hey!'

Shrieking, Georgie leapt backwards. It felt like someone had given her heart an electric shock.

'What the hell do you think you're doing?' Dylan Taylor

was standing in the doorway, her teeth bared like an angry dog.

'I'm . . . I'm looking for something!'

'In *my* bed?'

'I didn't know it was your bed. I thought it was Sonia's bed. She told me—'

'Shut up!' Dylan barked. She took a step closer, shaking with rage. 'How dare you show your face in my room? After what you did to my little sister, I should rip your fucking head off! Maybe I will! I swore I wouldn't lose my temper any more, but this seems like a pretty good reason for one last stand.'

'Wait,' Georgie cried. 'Seriously, I had no idea that was your bed. I'm sorry, honestly. I came to borrow a book from Sonia. She told me it was on her night table. And when I couldn't find it, I thought maybe it had fallen . . . under her duvet.' Georgie could hear how stupid the words sounded. Her only hope was that Dylan Taylor was as dumb as her little sister.

It appeared not. Dylan's mouth was wide open, her face twisted into a sneer.

'What is wrong with this country?' she growled. 'Is every English person an insane, stupid liar? Just get out. Get. Out. Now! And leave my family alone.'

Georgie scampered out of the room and raced down the stairs, so fast that she didn't even notice the piece of paper that fell out of Sonia's bag. OK, so she'd failed to do Dylan's bed – but it wasn't her fault. She'd covered as best she could, and sabotaging Alice should be enough.

Alice Rochester was obviously the primary target – how could it be any other way?

Mrs Hoare's office was in the ground-floor hallway, round the back of the stairs. Georgie straightened her grey school skirt and yellow school blouse, plastered a worried frown across her face and knocked.

'Yes?' Mrs Hoare opened the door, looking annoyed. 'Georgina, my office hours don't start for another half-hour. Teachers need to eat lunch too, you know. We're not at your beck and call.'

'Oh, I'm sorry, Mrs Hoare. But I'm not here about English prep or anything like that. I'm here for another reason. It's urgent,' she whispered. 'And private.'

Mrs Hoare narrowed her eyes. 'If you have a personal problem, you should really speak to your own house-mistress. I'm sure Mrs Gould would be happy to help you.'

'But the thing is, my problem is more of a concern. And it's about a member of the Lower Sixth.' Georgie could tell that Mrs Hoare's interest was piqued. She bit her lip, pressing her advantage. 'Oh dear, maybe I'm sticking my nose in where it doesn't belong. I was just so worried. And ever since my suspension, I've been trying to turn over a new leaf. You know, make St Cecilia's proud.'

'That's very noble, Georgina.' Mrs Hoare folded her arms. 'Now, spit it out. My lasagne is waiting.'

'OK, yes, you're right. It's about – oh gosh, this is just so embarrassing – it's about Alice Rochester.'

Georgie paused. At the mention of Alice's name, Mrs Hoare's nose had visibly wrinkled.

'I think she might be an addict,' Georgie whispered. She opened her eyes until they were as wide as dinner plates. 'A sex addict, Mrs Hoare.'

Chapter 43

Alice's phone buzzed in her pocket, but she ignored it. She was rushing back to Tudor to finish some last-minute French prep before Lunch ended – and besides, it might be Tally. Or Tristan. Or Jasper. Or any one of the other hundreds of people she didn't feel like talking to today.

Then, a few paces away, she saw someone waving.

'Ali!' cried Felicity Foxton. 'Yoohoo! Hello, darling.'

Alice smiled stiffly.

'Can I ask you something? I heard the weirdest gossip about Tally Abbott from the von Holstadts' party, and I wanted to check if it's—'

'Oops, sorry, Flic,' Alice cut in, putting on a regretful voice and pulling out her phone. 'Gotta get this. Catch you later. Hello?' she answered, without looking at the caller's name.

'Hey. It's me. Rando.'

Alice shut her eyes. Great. Out of one minefield and into another. Rando was probably calling to revive that conversation she'd sidetracked about his stupid new girlfriend.

'Are you there?' he asked.

'Yeah. I'm here. Hi.'

'Cool. I was just ringing to check you're OK.'

'OK?' Alice said. 'Of course I'm OK. Why wouldn't I be?'

Rando chuckled. 'Good point, how silly of me to ask – since you sound like you're in such a great mood.'

'Well would you be in a good mood if you were me?' Alice snapped. 'If you'd found out your supposed best friend was involved in some kind of black-market homework ring? Not to mention being chased round small towns by anonymous thugs and disappearing over New Year, leaving no clue as to her whereabouts?'

'Um, no, exactly – that's why I rang. I—'

'I just can't believe Tally's such a liar,' Alice ranted. Now that she'd started talking, she couldn't seem to stop. 'She just does whatever she wants with no regard for anyone else. It's like she's lost all sense of right and wrong. If she ever had one. Sometimes I wonder why I'm friends with her at all!'

Rando paused. 'Are you finished?'

'Yes.'

'OK. Right, here's why you're friends with Tally. Because she's funny, and clever, and spontaneous, and kind, and loyal.'

Alice rolled her eyes. 'OK . . . So you're Tally's biggest fan all of a sudden. That doesn't mean I have to be.'

'Of course not.' Rando sighed. 'Look, Tally's obviously got a lot of problems. I'm the first person to admit that – I went out with her, and I couldn't hack it. The petty stealing, the unpredictable behaviour. But you two have been friends for years. And if she's going through a weird time, maybe now's the moment for you to be caring and accepting – not judgemental and harsh.'

Alice was silent for a moment. 'Excuse me, but did you ring me up just to call me judgemental and harsh? Because if you did, thanks a lot.'

'No.' Rando took a deep breath. 'I rang you because . . . Shit, maybe I shouldn't be bringing this up – after all, it's a bit late now.'

'Bringing what up?'

'Well, think about it. You accuse Tally of lying. You accuse her of being cheating and secretive. But isn't that a better description of you?'

'*Me?*' Alice cried. 'What the hell?'

'No, listen. I'm not trying to be mean. Honestly. I'm just saying – you and I were . . .' Rando lowered his voice, 'we were sleeping together behind Tally's back. And you didn't want to tell her – you insisted we keep it a secret. And now look: you're judging her for keeping her own secrets. Secrets that don't even hurt you – not in the way that yours would have hurt *her.*'

Alice stopped walking. She was in the garden of Tudor House, and suddenly everything – the trees, the grass, the gate – seemed to become very vivid, very sharp in front of her eyes. She blinked. 'So? Why are you saying all this? Why is it any of your business?'

'I don't know. I guess it's not. But I suppose it got me thinking. Maybe, just maybe the reason you were so afraid to come clean about *us* is because of how harshly you judge other people. Maybe you're afraid they'll be just as harsh about you.'

Alice shut her eyes. It was awful to hear it, but she knew it as soon as he'd said it – Rando was right. The thought of ending up like Tally under that portico – scorned and detested and shunned by all her friends – was just too much to bear. But maybe *she'd* been the only one who'd judged Tally like that. When she looked back on the scene at Hurlingham, no one else had reacted as violently as her.

'I'm sorry,' Rando went on. 'I thought maybe this might be helpful. But I probably shouldn't have brought it up again – all that stuff about you and me.'

For a moment, Alice couldn't find any words. Then she swallowed. 'Probably not. We both need to move on I guess. Now that you've got a girlfriend and everything.'

'A girlfriend?'

'Yeah. Tiki's pretty special.'

'Tiki!' Rando exclaimed. 'Do you mean Tiki Hardinge-Smythe?'

'Of course. Unless you're going out with another Tiki as well.'

'Tiki's not my girlfriend, Al. I mean, she used to be. But not any more.'

Suddenly, Alice's heart was hammering. 'What do you mean?'

'Tiki and I went out last year, before I came to Hasted House, but she was awful to me. We had a massive fight and broke up. Now she's decided she wants to get back together. That's why she came to visit me at school last week – she was trying to patch things up. But it's not gonna work.'

'O-oh,' Alice stammered. In a daze, she walked through the door of Tudor. 'I thought, when I saw you two in Hasted, that you guys were going out. I thought—'

'Alice Rochester!' interrupted a voice.

Alice froze.

'Gossiping about boys again, I see.' Mrs Hoare was advancing on her, a strange glint in her eyes.

'Alice?' Rando said. 'Are you there?'

'Alice, hang that up,' Mrs Hoare demanded. 'We have serious issues to discuss.'

'Gotta go,' Alice said. Her head was spinning as she dropped her phone into her pocket. Rando, single? And was it possible – she clutched the cuff of her cashmere coat – was it possible that he still cared? But she had no time to think about this now. For some reason, the Ho had a very nasty look on her face.

Chapter 44

Before Alice knew what was happening, Mrs Hoare was marching her up the stairs of Tudor House.

'Stop dawdling,' the housemistress ordered. 'However slowly you walk, it won't put off the inevitable.'

'The inevitable?' Alice repeated.

'Yes, you heard me. We're going to your room. I need to search a few things.'

'What things?' Alice's mind jumped to the innocent-looking trunk where she and Tally kept their stash of wine. Or the space in the back of the wardrobe where they hid their cigarettes and weed. But how could the Ho have found out about those?

'Perhaps *you* should tell *me* what things,' the Ho snapped. 'I've received some very worrying reports about your . . . habits, young lady.'

'My habits?' Alice was starting to feel like an echo. 'What reports? Who gave you reports?'

Mrs Hoare pursed her lips, as if to stop anyone's name flying out. 'I'm afraid I can't disclose that information. The girl was, naturally, very nervous, and she's entitled to her anonymity. But suffice it to say that she's impartial – she's not even in your year.'

'Huh?' Alice racked her brains. Who in the world – besides Sonia Khan – would want to spread rumours about her? Whatever those rumours were?

The Ho was pushing into her dorm room, making straight for the bed. She yanked back the duvet.

'Wait, what are you doing? There's nothing—' Alice stopped and gasped.

'You call this nothing?' The Ho's beady eyes were almost crazed.

On the white sheet lay four plastic bags, each stuffed to the brim with condoms. Vibrating ones. Flavoured ones. Plain ones. Ribbed ones. Buried among the condoms was a pair of furry handcuffs and – the Ho held it up by her fingertips – a copy of *Playgirl* magazine, plastered with rippling naked men.

Alice's face burned a deep, hot crimson. 'That stuff's not mine!'

'And yet it's in your bed! Is someone else using your bed as a hiding place without you noticing, Alice? Or are you just renting out the space? Because I— What's this?'

Slowly, deliberately, the Ho tugged at a piece of paper that was sticking out under Alice's pillow. As she scanned it, her eyebrows shot so high they almost disappeared into her hairline. 'Oh dear. Oh dear, dear. I hate to say it, but this is the most disturbing thing yet.'

'What is it? Let me see!' Alice took the paper. Her palms

went sweaty. It was a typed list of about thirty Hasted House boys – and every single name had a date, a score out of ten and sometimes a note printed next to it.

TOM HUNTLEIGH. DEC 21. SCORE: 7/10

FREDDIE FRYE. DEC 23. SCORE: 4/10 *Better than I expected!*

JAMIE DARLINGTON, JAN 9, SCORE: 8/10 *Good technique. Hot body!!*

GEORGE DEMETRIOS. JAN 12. SCORE: 2/10 *Tiny penis!*

'Mrs Hoare, I didn't write this, I swear. I promise you, I'd never do something like this!'

'As your housemistress—' the Ho began.

'Ask Tally, ask Jemimah – it isn't me at all!'

'*As your housemistress,*' the Ho repeated, raising her voice, 'I am responsible for your moral and mental well-being. And things like this tell me that you, Alice Rochester, need help. I'll have to insist that you go see the school counsellor. And in the meantime, I'm confiscating this.' She stuffed the *Playgirl* under her arm. When she reached the doorway, she turned round. 'You should be ashamed of yourself, Alice. You must have very low self-esteem to be carrying on like this – a different boy every week. Sometimes two! The most I can say,' she added, eyeing the pile of condoms, 'is that you seem to be taking certain precautions in your . . . activities.'

The Ho swept out. At that moment, Tally appeared, almost knocking the teacher down.

'Oh! Sorry.' Tally giggled.

As soon as they were alone, Alice turned on her. 'Hey! Did you put this in my bed?'

'Put what in your bed?'

'This stuff!' Alice pointed to the handcuffs and condoms. 'Are you trying to get revenge or something? Are you pissed off at me because I haven't been talking to you for the past few days?'

Tally burst out laughing.

'What's so funny?'

'Sorry, babe. Of course I didn't put that in your bed. But whoever did is a fucking genius. That's the funniest thing I've ever seen.'

'Oh yeah? You wouldn't think it was so funny if the Ho thought you were a sex fiend. She's making me go talk to Dr Lisa.'

'Girls!' Before Tally could reply, Dylan rushed in. 'I'm so glad you're both here. I've been waiting for you to show up – so I can show you this.' She held out a crumpled piece of paper, ripped from an exercise book.

Alice took it. 'What the fuck is this?'

'Al,' Tally said, squinting over her shoulder, 'It looks like a map to . . .'

'To my bed!' Alice finished off.

'And mine.' Dylan nodded. 'Freaky, right? And guess where I got it? Georgina Fortescue. She was sneaking around in my room, looking all creepy and underhanded. And when I surprised her, she ran. Leaving this.'

'But not before she left *that*,' Alice grunted, pointing to her mattress.

Dylan's eyes shot open as she took in the mess of condoms and handcuffs.

Tally grimaced. 'But this makes no sense. What would Georgina Fortescue want with you two?'

'Unless . . .' Alice stared harder at the paper. 'Unless it wasn't her idea. Look!' She pointed to the letters of her name. 'This is Sonia's handwriting.'

'Are you sure?' Dylan said.

'I'd know it anywhere. Five years of her leaving me annoying sycophantic love notes – I think I can recognise it.'

'Oh my god,' Tally said. 'Sonia Khan getting Georgie Fortescue to do her dirty work. Does that bitch stop at nothing?'

The three of them stood there, staring at each other. After a moment, Alice bit her lip.

'Hey,' she said to Tally, 'I guess I owe you an apology. I'm sorry I blamed you. That was stupid.'

Tally shrugged. 'It's OK. Must have been quite a shock, the Ho finding all that crap.'

'And I'm . . . I'm sorry I reacted so strongly to the whole homework thing,' Alice went on. She chewed her thumbnail. 'With Jasper. It just caught me by surprise. I guess I feel like you've been shutting me out all term.'

Tally's beautiful sea-grey eyes were suddenly soft and round. 'Oh, sweetie, thank you. It means loads to me to hear you say that. Especially because I know how much you hate apologising.' She sighed. 'Look, I've been thinking. I know it was a bit stupid of me to get involved in that scheme. But I needed the money, and when I mentioned it to Jasper, he just made the whole idea sound so simple. And maybe this is stupid, but it was kind of flattering – knowing that someone would pay me that much money for my work. I mean, I've never thought of myself as clever or anything.'

'Of course you're clever,' Alice said. *Rando thinks so too,* she was about to add. But she stopped herself. She wasn't ready to go there – not yet. Instead, she bit her lip. 'But Tals, there's still something I don't understand.'

'What?'

'Why did you lie about where you were over New Year? That had nothing to do with the whole Jasper thing, right?'

There was a pause. Then Tally shook her head. 'No.'

'So where did you go?'

'I . . . I went to Russia. To see my grandad. And that's the truth, I promise. But babe, do you mind if we just don't talk about it? I was in a bad place. I needed some time alone. And . . . I did things I'm not proud of.'

'But that man in town—' Alice protested.

'That man wasn't dangerous,' Tally interrupted. 'He was just . . . a friend of a friend. Will you trust me? Please?'

Alice was silent. She cast a glance at the small gold pendant round Tally's neck. Then, reluctantly, she nodded.

'OK!' Dylan clapped her hands. 'Ladies, time to change the subject, I think. We're not just going to let Sonia get away with her evil plan, are we?'

'No way!' Tally cried.

Alice grinned. 'No fucking way. It's payback time.'

'Good,' Dylan said. 'So let's hit her where it hurts. What's her weakest spot? The thing that matters to her most?'

'Her incredibly expensive custom-designed nose?' Tally cackled.

'Her Evian collection?' Dylan smirked.

'No,' Alice said. 'I know. Her party.' A scheming smile spread across her face. 'I'm sure if we all put our heads together, we can come up with a special, personalised birthday surprise.'

Chapter 45

Seb and Dylan stepped out of their taxi on the corner of West Street in Soho. The premiere party for *Much Ado About Nothing* was being held at the exclusive Ivy Club, just down the block – but before they could make their way over, they were nearly trampled by a pack of reporters and photographers.

'Wasn't Corey Benson fantastic?' someone trilled.

'Wonderful! And that newcomer, Will Larkin, he was brilliant too.'

'Yes, and so striking! Those eyes – like blue glass.'

'I think we've finally found the new young Brit Pack, everyone. The stage stars of tomorrow.'

Behind them, Seb nudged Dylan in the ribs and grinned.

'Just listen to that praise,' he whispered. 'This is so awesome – can you believe they're talking about our dates?'

'Your date,' Dylan said. 'I don't have a date.' She stopped in the middle of the pavement and swung around. 'Oh shit. I totally shouldn't have come tonight. What am I doing here?'

'You were invited,' Seb said, pointing her back towards the entrance. 'Your name's on the guest list.'

'So? That doesn't mean I belong here. I should have stuck with Alice and Tally. Helped them with their plan for Sonia's party.'

'Right. Where you would have had to bump into Jasper and be totally miserable. Anyway, if you change your mind, you can always come to Sonia's with me. The Paper Bandits are playing at midnight – I'm sure I can sneak you in. You know, friend of the band, and all that.'

'Tempting.' Dylan rolled her eyes. But she started walking again. 'Oh god, is Corey gonna think it's weird that I'm turning up here alone? I told him I had a boyfriend.'

'Well, you did have a boyfriend. And anyway, you're not alone – you're with me.'

'That's sweet of you to say. But you're with Will. And once again I'm the third wheel – and we both know it.'

'Not true!' Seb insisted. 'Will's going to be busy working the room. Anyway, he and I discussed it, and we decided: no coupley stuff or PDA tonight. We both want to keep our private lives secret.'

'Him from the media, and you from your friends.' Dylan snorted. 'I know, I know,' she added, as she saw the look on Seb's face. 'You're not ready to tell them. And I get it, I really do. But at some point you will be – like, when you're at university, or learning t'ai chi in Thailand on your gap year – and then I think your life will be a whole lot easier.'

Seb bit his lip. 'It already is easier, having one person I can talk to about it.'

'Good.' Dylan squeezed his arm as they walked through the Ivy Club's dazzling glass and marble lobby, into a lift that looked like a crystal jewellery box. When the doors slid open again, they were staring into a warmly lit wood-panelled room, packed with people, and fragrant with flowers and perfume.

'Whoa. This is cool,' Dylan said, almost having to shout over the roar of chatter and the clink of cocktail glasses. 'How come hanging out with you means I keep getting to go to all these hidden places?'

'I guess 'cause I'm really hip.' Seb grinned. 'You know membership here is by invitation only?'

'And don't tell me,' Dylan said. 'Your entire family are members.'

Seb chuckled and nodded.

'Why am I not surprised?'

They made their way towards the bar. Halfway there, they were blocked by a crowd of journalists. Dylan stood on tiptoe. Corey Benson was at the centre of it. And so was a gorgeous girl with waist-length chocolate-brown hair, wearing an evening dress that skimmed her perfect figure all the way to the floor. It was Jenna Vance, Corey's love interest in the play.

'Your performance just now in *Much Ado* was so charming, Corey,' a woman reporter was saying, waving a digital recorder in his face. 'I'll bet every female in the audience now has a giant crush on you. I know I do.'

Corey smiled – it was the exact same smile he'd given his rampant fan, Ellie, at Shoreditch House.

Flash! Someone took a picture.

'Well, that's an incredibly flattering suggestion,' Corey said. 'I can't believe I'd be an object of desire for so many fantastic people, though. I'm just a geeky normal guy at heart.'

The media crowd burst into titters and protests.

Dylan hit her forehead against Seb's shoulder. 'Oh god, he's doing it again. His whole humble routine. It's so excruciating!'

Seb laughed. 'Give the guy a break. It can't be easy, keeping your cool while you're mobbed by journalists.'

'Yeah. Whatever.'

'Hey, I think I see Will. Come say hi?'

'Be right there.' For some reason, despite Corey's transparent act, Dylan couldn't tear her eyes away from him. Except to shoot glances at Jenna Vance. Stunning, successful Jenna Vance.

The first reporter, who had recovered herself, was now holding out the recorder again. 'But seriously, Corey, you must know what a babe magnet you are. Is there a special lady in your life? Anyone we should know about?'

'Well, the thing is, I like to keep my private life private. But,' Corey added with a twinkle in his eye, 'let's just say I do have an . . . interest.'

Flash! Another picture.

'Oooh!' the group buzzed. 'An interest.'

'Is she here tonight?' someone called out.

'She might be.'

'Dare I ask if it's the lovely Jenna Vance?'

'You can ask.' Corey grinned, 'but that doesn't mean I'll tell.'

There was more laughter. Dylan bit her lip. Corey Benson's 'interest' so obviously wasn't *her*. How could it be, when girls like Jenna Vance existed, with their perfect teeth and perfect skin and perfect everything? And anyway, why did she even care? It was infuriating, just to be one more admirer in the crowd.

Grabbing a glass of pink champagne, Dylan slipped off to an empty table. She took a handful of crisps from a bowl, looking round the party as she munched them. There were familiar faces everywhere – faces she'd started to recognise from TV in her few months in England – and everyone seemed to know each other. Seb and Will were standing next to each other by the bar, talking to a few of Will's friends from the cast. Dylan sighed. It must be hard for them in public situations like this. Even Will seemed to want to pretend that he and Seb were just friends – and he wasn't even in the closet.

'Hey.'

Dylan looked up. She'd been so absorbed in her thoughts that she hadn't noticed Corey approach.

'Oh, hi,' she said, gathering her handbag.

'No, no, don't get up.' Corey slid into the banquette next to her. 'I've been on my feet all night, it's lovely to take a load off. And to hide away for a minute,' he added with a stagey conspiratorial grin. 'I told my agent I needed the loo. So. You came.'

'Yeah.' Dylan shrugged. 'I did have this birthday party

to go to, but the girl throwing it is a little strange. Actually, what am I saying? She's a complete freak. And Seb wanted a wing-woman here. So, you know, I thought I'd help him out.'

'Aw, wasn't that sweet of you.' Corey chortled. He glanced at Seb, who was laughing in the middle of the group by the bar. 'Yeah, it looks like he desperately needs a wing-woman. Thank goodness you're here.'

Dylan sniffed. 'Did you come over just to make fun of me?'

'Of course. So where's your boyfriend? He didn't want to come?'

'Oh.' Dylan examined the crisp in her hand. 'No.'

'Why not? He isn't the partying kind?'

'Actually, he is. He's just . . . not my boyfriend any more. We broke up.'

'Oh.' Corey's gorgeous hazel eyes flickered for a moment. 'Sorry.'

'Yeah. Me too. Anyway.'

'Are you OK?'

'I'm fine. I mean, I'm the one who ended things. I just don't really want to talk about it.'

'OK, we won't.' Corey swept a hand through his longish brown hair. 'So, aren't you going to ask me how the first night of the play went?'

'I don't have to,' Dylan replied. 'I've been hearing how *marvellous* and *fabulous* it was since I arrived.'

'But still. You could at least care what *I* think. You could at least want to hear it from me.'

'Oh, that is just so typical,' Dylan groaned.

'What is?'

'The whole me, me, me thing. Everyone here is just falling over themselves to talk about you and your performance, how you've got talent *and* looks *and* charm. And then you come find me, and say you want a break from all that – and *still* the only thing you want to talk about is you.' Dylan rolled her eyes. 'Actors.'

'*Actors?* Would you like to tell me what that sweeping generalisation is supposed to mean?'

Dylan stuck her nose in the air. 'It's like I always say – being an actor is basically the same thing as having a personality disorder. You're always pretending to be someone else, and you always need to be the centre of attention.'

'Whereas you, on the other hand, are content to be a shy, retiring wallflower, watching everything from the shadows.' Corey snickered, his eyes crinkling. 'Come on. You know I'm not as bad as you're making out.'

'You are too,' Dylan shot back, trying not to smile.

'Admit it, you like me, even if it's just a little bit.'

'I do not! And anyway, even if I did, it wouldn't matter. You told that journalist you had interests.'

'Correction: I said I had *an* interest. And,' Corey said, leaning closer to Dylan, 'she's right in front of me.'

'Liar.' Dylan shifted away along the leather seat. But her voice was soft.

'It's true. Ever since I met you at Jenna's party, I haven't been able to get you out of my head. I've tried all the usual clichés. Wine, women and song. Eating, drinking and merriment. None of them have worked. The beautiful blonde with the bad temper just won't disappear from my thoughts.'

'Now you really are lying,' Dylan murmured. But her eyes were sparkling, and she was leaning closer and closer towards Corey.

'Does this feel like a lie?' He kissed her. For a moment, Dylan was aware of nothing but Corey's lips, warm and gentle on hers.

The next second, something flashed behind her closed eyes. When she opened them, it seemed like every paparazzo in the place was snapping their photo.

'Oh, no,' Corey said. 'I'm so sorry. You hate this, don't you? I should have just left you alone.'

'No.' Dylan shook her head. 'You shouldn't. Really, you shouldn't.'

'In that case . . .' He leaned in to kiss her again. Then he paused. 'Are you sure about this? If we don't stop now, it could be all over the gossip columns by tomorrow.'

'I'm sure,' Dylan whispered. She kissed him again, and the flashbulbs exploded like fireworks around them.

Chapter 46

'Careful! Don't rip my headdress,' Alice giggled.

'Sorry, it's so dark,' Tally whispered. 'Why don't they have more street lights in this alleyway?'

'Oh no, I'm a bit nervous – do you think this is going to work?'

'Of course it's gonna work, babe. Sonia's going down. OK,' Tally added, 'how do I look?'

Alice burst out laughing. 'Ridiculous.'

Tally was wearing transparent pink pantaloons with a silver bikini top and silver swirls painted across her midriff. Not that Alice herself looked any less absurd. She was wearing a tiny skirt made of gold discs that jangled when she walked, a gold band wrapped round her boobs, and dozens of gold bangles on each arm.

'Right,' Tally said, 'headgear.'

They each put on a small Turkish hat with a veil attached to it. Then, pulling the veils over their faces, they emerged from the dark mews and walked up to the front door of Sonia's house. It was two minutes to midnight.

'Names?' the bouncer said. He was dressed entirely in black leather, which creaked when he moved.

'Melissa and Olivia Wyndham-Rhodes,' Tally trilled, disguising her voice even though she didn't need to.

The bouncer checked his list. 'Go right in, girls.'

'Thank you,' Tally chirped, still in her Wyndham-Rhodes voice. 'That was easy,' she added to Alice, in a whisper.

'I know. Thank goodness the Terrible Twins turn up at least three hours late for everything.'

'You'd have thought Sonia would have slightly better security, though.'

'True.' Alice smirked. 'But the fact that she doesn't will make the rest of our plan so much easier. How long before they show up?'

'About half an hour. I told them half-twelve.'

'Perfect. Just enough time for a few drinks.'

Both girls cackled as they disappeared through the front door.

Neither of them noticed the man lurking in the shadows across the road.

'I literally can't believe Sonia made us wear these turbans,' Seb groaned, catching sight of himself in a giant gilt mirror in the Khans' ballroom.

'And I can't believe how late you got here,' Tristan retorted. 'I thought you weren't gonna show. And how are the Paper Bandits supposed to play without a bassist?'

'All right, all right, I'm here now,' Seb said. 'So keep your turban on.'

Rando and Jasper chuckled and carried on setting up their instruments. The stage where they were about to play had been specially built for tonight. It was swathed in Persian rugs, draped with rich curtains and hung with silk lanterns. And the decorations only got more lavish from there. Glowing crystal balls floated at different heights all over the house, suspended from the ceilings by invisible cords. The living room had been transformed into a giant tent full of magic lanterns, where waiters dressed as genies were flitting about with trays full of cocktails. Giant cinema screens flickered with images of the party on almost every wall. Right now, the screens showed Felicity Foxton and Flossy Norstrup-Fitzwilliam dancing on top of a divan, each downing champagne straight from a bottle. Then they switched to Freddie Frye, who was attempting to tip an entire tray of Turkish delight into his mouth in front of a crowd of Malbury Hall girls. The next moment, the image showed Tom Huntleigh and George Demetrios, who were getting a special lesson from a troupe of belly dancers in the dining room.

Then, suddenly, all over the house, the music stopped. Sonia's face, glittering with make-up, appeared in close-up on every screen.

'Friends, guests, relatives, welcome!' she cried.

The entire party erupted in cheers.

'Oh, how sweet, thank you,' Sonia simpered, clasping her hands to her heart. She was wearing a gauzy white tunic that just skimmed the bottom of her bum, purple sandals that laced all the way up to the knee, and two Egyptian-style arm cuffs. Her hair was fixed into a massive beehive, and on top of it lay a giant jewelled crown.

'I am just so honoured to have you here tonight, helping me celebrate my birthday. I've hand-picked you all especially as my guests, as an acknowledgement of your loyalty, dedication and love over the years.'

Seb nudged Rando. 'Is she completely mental? She's talking like she just won an Oscar.'

'Or crowned herself empress,' Rando snickered.

'That explains the headpiece, I guess.'

'And now,' Sonia said, 'I'd like to introduce one of my favourite bands of the moment. I have a hunch that these boys are going to be very famous one day, and when they are, I'll be able to say: they played for me when I turned seventeen. Ladies and gentlemen, may I present the Paper Bandits!'

Applause went up around the house. Tristan took the mic.

'Thanks, Sonia. And a very happy birthday! Our drummer, Tom Randall-Stubbs, has requested to play the first song. He wrote it. And he'll be singing it alone, since none of us have ever heard it before. So if it's bad, don't blame us.'

There was a laugh. The video screen shot back to Sonia, who looked like she'd just swallowed a rotten egg. Then, realising the camera was on her, she smiled and waved.

Rando took the guitar T handed him, and stood at the mic.

'Thanks, everyone,' he said, ducking his head shyly. His freckled cheeks had gone pink. 'I'm not used to being the front man – that's a job I usually leave to Tristan. But, well, here goes. I call it "Kissing You Already".'

> *How did we get here –*
> *Different ends of the room?*
> *How can love be over*
> *Before it even bloomed?*

The melody was sweet and simple, and Rando's voice was light and clear. He looked around the ballroom as he fingered the chords. There was no sign of Alice. He'd been almost certain she'd turn up – after all, it wasn't like Alice Rochester to give in without a fight.

Then something caught his eye. At the back of the room, a tall, angular, olive-skinned girl was lifting her veil. A familiar mouth came into view. Followed by a familiar nose, and a pair of sparkling brown eyes. A swell of joy ran through Rando as he started the next verse.

> *While we were fighting*
> *Did we miss our last chance?*
> *Let's stop fighting now.*
> *May I have the last dance?*
>
> *I'd rather be kissing you*
> *Than anyone else.*
> *This is the most in love*
> *I've ever felt.*

I'd rather be kissing you.
Your smile of sunbeams.
I'm kissing you already
In my dreams.

I'd rather be kissing you.
Your smile of sunbeams.
I'm kissing you already
In my dreams.

At the back of the ballroom, Alice listened, hardly breathing. Rando's playing stirred something in her – as if the strings of his guitar were somehow bound to the strings of her heart. It was the same tune he'd played for her all those weeks ago in the guitar shop. He'd finished the song. He'd finished it for her.

The whole house remained hushed as the music died. Then, suddenly, a bang echoed through the hall. A young man had burst through the front door and was now standing at the entrance to the ballroom. He was tall, blond and handsome, and he looked about twenty years old.

'Who's that?' hissed Felicity Foxton.

'No idea,' replied Emilia Charles.

'Me neither,' added Flossy Norstrup-Fitzwilliam. 'Never seen him before in my life.'

'Oooh, dishy!' Sonia slurred. During Rando's song, she'd downed three of Penny de Claire's custom 'Palace Nights' cocktails, and was now totally sloshed. She clopped towards the stranger, her face enlarged on the cinema screens all over the house. 'Who are *you*? Are you my birthday pressie?'

'No. Of course I'm not.' The man shrugged her off. 'I'm looking for Natalya Abbott.' His voice was deep but refined, with just a hint of a foreign accent.

'Tally Abbott's not here,' Sonia hiccuped smugly. 'And neither is that hag Alice Rochester. They were both banned. They're not wanted here. They—' The words died on her lips. The man was making a beeline for the back of the room, where a tall, beautiful girl wearing pink pantaloons was drawing her veil away from her face.

'Tally!' Sonia choked.

'Tally?' Alice said. 'Where are you going? Who is this man?'

But Tally was moving forward as if by magnetic force.

'Ivan?' she whispered. 'How did you find me?'

'How could I not find you?' Ivan was running now. He caught Tally in his arms as if she weighed nothing, and she threw herself around his neck.

'Where did you go?' he gasped. 'How could you just leave me like that?'

'I'm sorry,' Tally murmured. 'I'm sorry, I just got . . . scared.'

'Scared? Of me? My necklace,' Ivan said, picking up the gold disc around her neck. 'You're still wearing it.'

'Of course I am. I couldn't bring myself to take it off.'

Alice watched in astonishment as Tally leaned in and

kissed the stranger's lips. Her eyes flitted to Rando, where she saw her own shock reflected on his face. She couldn't stand it any more. She started forward just as Tally slid to the ground.

'Tals! I don't mean to interrupt but . . . who is this guy? Who *are* you?' she added, turning to the stranger.

Tally took his hand. 'Ali, this is Ivan. Don't be angry. I know I've been keeping him a secret all term, but . . . now he's here, and I guess it can't be a secret any more.'

'But *who is he*?'

Tally drew a breath. 'Ivan and I met in Russia, over New Year. I went to stay at my grandfather's manor house, and Ivan had just bought the estate next door. We got to know each other. We fell for each other, actually. But then . . .' Tally turned to Ivan. 'Then you started talking about introducing me to your family. And marriage, and children, and *for ever*. He even gave me this necklace.' She held out her pendant to Alice. 'It says *For ever* on it, in Russian. And I got scared. I mean, we'd only known each other ten days!'

Alice nodded. But in some ways, she could understand how Ivan must have felt. She thought back to what Dylan had said, about her and Rando. *Time doesn't matter, does it? You can be with one person for a year and not feel as much as you do in one week with someone else.*

'So what did you do then?' she said.

'I . . . I ran away.' Tally bit her lip. 'I'm not proud of it. I left in the middle of the night for Moscow and caught the first plane back to London. And then, the next day, I came to see you. I was going to tell you all about it – I'd planned to. But when I got to your house, you seemed so . . . different. Kind of cold. And distant. And I knew then that I couldn't tell you anything. I knew this was a part of my life I wasn't ready to share.'

Ivan squeezed Tally's hand. 'If I was scaring you, you should have said. I'd never want to upset you. I even sent Vladi, my personal bodyguard, round to Hasted. He was supposed to tell you that I still loved you. That it wasn't too late.'

Tally glanced at Alice, and giggled. 'I think he got the tone of the message a bit wrong. But it doesn't matter. You're here now. And I'm glad.'

'Really?'

'Yes. Really. Of course I am.'

Ivan wrapped his arms around Tally. But before they could kiss again, a huge roar arose from the front hall.

'What's that?' Sonia cried. She'd been staring, open-mouthed, at the scene in front of her, but now she seemed shocked back to life.

'Party time!' a voice bellowed from the hall.

'Whoa, look at this place, it's massive!'

'Where's the booze?'

Crash! A marble statue toppled over.

'Where's the food?'

Tally and Alice locked eyes.

'It's half past twelve!' Tally whispered, looking at her watch.

'In that case,' Alice grinned, 'let the fun begin.'

A flood of people burst into the ballroom. They streamed in and kept coming, grabbing bottles, ripping the silk wall hangings, smashing the floating lanterns to the floor.

'Where's the bouncer?' Sonia shrieked. 'Why did he let this rabble in? Why isn't he doing his job?'

'He probably couldn't,' gaped Felicity Foxton. 'There must be at least a hundred of them. Way too many of them to stop.'

'What a useless lump of lard!' Sonia grabbed hold of a dreadlocked boy. 'How did you find out about this party? Who invited you?'

'It was all over Facebook and Twitter,' the boy replied. 'People were posting open invitations. They said there'd be free food and drink from twelve thirty, and rocking tunes all night. Where's the booze? Hey! Let me at that champagne!' Breaking away, he took off after a gang of his friends.

Sonia's eyes bulged. She seized the mic. 'Call the police, everyone! Call the police.'

Tally burst into hysterics, laughing so hard she almost crumpled to the floor. Ivan scooped her up and stroked her hair. He was smiling – an adoring, radiant smile.

At that moment, Alice made her decision. It was now or never, she knew it. She had to make a choice – and she chose to be brave.

Marching on to the stage, she snatched the microphone from Sonia and planted herself in front of the camera. She knew her image was being projected into every one of the Khans' dozens of rooms.

312

'I have an announcement to make.' Alice tapped the microphone. 'Everyone! I have an announcement.'

Most of the people in the ballroom couldn't care less. They were too busy sprawling all over the ottomans, swinging from the drapery, and gobbling baklava and halva and Turkish delight. But that didn't matter. The people who counted turned towards her. Tally, and Tristan, and Rando, and Jasper, and Seb.

'I'm in love,' Alice began. Her voice sounded alien – soaring out there, loud and echoing and beyond her control. Down below, she saw Sonia's eyes narrow. Tally's mouth dropped open as she gripped Ivan's hand.

Alice took a deep breath. 'I'm in love with Tom Randall-Stubbs. I'm in love with him, and I have been for a long time. And . . . and I just thought you should all know.' She faltered.

Tally was gaping at her.

Tristan's eyes were pained, but he was nodding – as if he'd somehow known all along.

'I'm sorry,' Alice went on, quieter now. 'I'm sorry to you, Tally, and to you, Tristan, because I know this must hurt you both. But I really, sincerely hope we can work it out. And most of all, I'm sorry to you, Rando, for not being brave enough to admit this for so long.'

At that moment, someone plugged in the sound system. Music pumped through the house again.

Alice held out her hand to Rando.

'May I have the last dance?'

Her words were swallowed by the racket, but Rando

understood. He approached the stage, his eyes shining. Then his arm was around her waist, and Alice was being pulled against his body. He kissed her. She kissed him back. Their image flickered on every cinema screen in the house, for hundreds of people to see. But Alice didn't mind. She knew that this was the way it should be.